*"A masterfu
urgent contemporary ...
Mahjong group will steal your heart while solving crimes that matter."*

"Richard Osman meets social justice in the Smoky Mountains. Compassionate, clever, and impossible to put down."

"These are the mysteries we need right now—where community fights back, refugees find sanctuary, and ordinary people prove that courage looks like showing up for each other, one Tuesday night at a time."

"Perfect for fans of Richard Osman's Thursday Murder Club and Alexander McCall Smith's No. 1 Ladies' Detective Agency."

WINDS OF DECEIT

Copyright © 2026 by Walter Cook

All rights reserved. No part of this book may be reproduced, stored in a retrieval system, or transmitted in any form or by any means—electronic, mechanical, photocopying, recording, or otherwise—without prior written permission from the publisher, except for brief quotations used in reviews or critical articles.

This is mostly a work of fiction. Names, characters, places, and incidents are products of the author's imagination or are used purposely. Any semblance to actual events, locales, or persons, living or dead, may not be entirely coincidental.

Publisher: Indy Publisher

Printed in the United States of America
First Edition

Dedication

For the neighbors who show up with casseroles and chainsaws after the storm.

For the small business owners who keep Main Street alive with more than commerce—with community.

For the volunteers at farmers' markets, libraries, bookstores, and animal shelters who give their time because a town is only as strong as the people who care for it.

For the real American towns that still say "welcome" to the refugee stepping off the bus with everything they own in a single bag, to the family starting over after loss, to the downtrodden looking for a place to belong—and then prove that welcome with jobs and friendship and a seat at the table.

For Franklin, North Carolina—the real one, with its mountains and its heart, its challenges and its resilience, its past and its future, its old families and its new arrivals who become family.

And for every small town in America where people still know their neighbors' names regardless of where those neighbors came from, still gather to help when help is needed, still believe that community isn't something you find—it's something you build, one Tuesday night, one act of kindness, one choice to stay and fight for home at a time.

This book is for you.

Because every place becomes Franklin when people decide it's worth protecting—and worth sharing.

And every stranger becomes neighbor then family when we choose to show up for each other.

That's the America worth fighting for.

Winds of Deceit

A Mahjong Murder Mystery
Book Two in the Series

Mary Stowell
Walter Cook

Contents

Prologue

Chapter 1

Chapter 2

Chapter 3

Chapter 4

Chapter 5

Chapter 6

Chapter 7

Chapter 8

Chapter 9

Chapter 10

[Chapter 11](#)

Chapter 12

Chapter 13

Chapter 14

Chapter 15

Chapter 16

Chapter 17

Chapter 18

Chapter 19

Chapter 20

Chapter 21

Chapter 22

Chapter 23

Chapter 24

Chapter 25

Chapter 26

Epilogue

Prologue

The sea had not been water that night. It had been a dark, deep grave without bottom.

Bea Tran remembered the screams swallowed by waves, the frantic hands clawing at air, the moment her mother's grip slipped from hers. Her father's face disappeared beneath the black surface, eyes wide, mouth open, then gone. The South China Sea did not care about love or family —it consumed them all the same. Bea did not cry. She stared. She memorized the way drowning looked, the way silence followed when the last gasp was taken. That silence lodged inside her, a parasite that never left. It grew inside her and became her.

The refugee camp was no sanctuary. Camp Galang reeked of sweat, sickness, and despair. Children huddled in corners, their ribs sharp as knives. Nguyen found her there. He promised protection, whispered survival, but his kindness was a mask. He taught her that obedience was the price of food, that her body was currency. Park was worse. His cruelty was blunt, bruising, a reminder that even children could be broken into silence. Bea endured. She learned to fold pain into herself, to paint it later as something beautiful, something others would call art. But beauty was only camouflage. Beneath it, the shadows never lifted.

Forty-five years later, the shadows returned. They had found their way into her refuge. Into her peaceful life, the parasite had crawled out.

The tea was still steaming when Bea found the body. Conrad Fischer lay sprawled across the concrete floor of her studio, his suit twisted, his eyes open and unseeing. The mug slipped from her hands, shattered, tea spreading like seawater across the floor.

The smell rose first. Not just tea—something acrid beneath it, faint but unmistakable, like scorched herbs or bitter roots. Bea inhaled, and for a moment she thought of the plants she had studied, the poisons she knew, the tinctures she had painted into memory. She crouched beside Fischer, her hand hovering near his chest. His skin was cooling, his lips cracked, his face flushed with a purplish hue. She did not touch him, but she lingered there, as if measuring the distance between life and death.

Her breath steadied. She cataloged the scene the

way she cataloged memories before painting.

The north wall was bare. Four paintings from her "Between Waters" series—her parents' death, her escape, her arrival—gone. Stolen. Violated. The body at her feet.

She knew how the police would see it: an immigrant woman, alone, trained in plants and poisons, standing in her studio with a dead man and missing art. The narrative wrote itself.

And she rehearsed it, silently, as she stood there: I was making tea. I came back. He was already on the floor. I don't know what happened. The words formed easily, practiced, as if she had spoken them before.

Her fingers brushed the floor near Fischer's outstretched hand. The tea had pooled there, dark and sticky, mingling with the faint scent of something medicinal. She wondered if anyone else would notice. She wondered if anyone else would understand.

She dialed 911 with steady hands.

"My name is Bea Tran. There's a dead man in my studio."

Her voice did not tremble.

Outside, sirens wailed. Inside, the tea cooled, the body stiffened, the walls gaped with absence. Bea stood in the center of it all, survivor and witness, artist and child of the sea.

And as the red and blue lights strobed through the warehouse windows, one thought flickered in her mind, sharp and undeniable: He deserved it.

Had Bea merely survived again—or had she finally learned to strike back?

Chapter 1

Donnie Carlisle had been retired for eight years, and she still couldn't sleep past six AM. Two hours later, Audrey the poodle knew exactly where they were going the moment Donnie Carlisle turned onto Main Street, and her entire body language shifted from bored tolerance to barely contained excitement.

"Yes, yes, we're going to your bakery," Donnie said, watching Audrey's tail begin its metronome of anticipation. "You're completely spoiled, you know that?"

The Smoky Mountain Dog Bakery occupied a prime storefront on Main Street in Franklin, its cheerful red awning visible from two blocks away. Donnie had bought the business three years ago, right after retiring from Miami-Dade insurance fraud investigation, and had transformed what had been a struggling pet supply shop into what *Southern Living* had called "one of the top ten dog bakeries in America" and what *USA Today* had featured in their "Must-Visit Pet Destinations" list.

Eddie had thought she was insane. "You're retiring from catching criminals to bake cookies for dogs?"

"Dog treats," Donnie had corrected. "Gourmet, all-natural, human-grade dog treats. And yes. It's perfect."

And it had been. Perfectly, surprisingly, absurdly perfect.

The bakery's windows displayed the day's fresh offerings—pupcakes frosted in peanut butter and carob, bone-shaped biscuits studded with blueberries, sweet potato chews cut into perfect strips, bacon-cheddar cookies that smelled so good humans were tempted to try them. Everything made fresh daily, everything using ingredients Donnie wouldn't hesitate to eat herself.

Inside, the space was designed like a hybrid between an artisan bakery and a dog-friendly café. The center of the room featured the Buffet Table —a 12 foot long table of two levels with bowls overflowing with treats so dogs and owners could make their own selection. Along the left side were fancy decorated treats displayed in glass cases like fine pastries, arranged by dietary need and flavor profile.

Grain-free. Limited ingredient. Senior-friendly soft chews. Puppy training treats. Birthday celebration pupcakes. Everything labeled with ingredients and calorie counts because Donnie approached dog nutrition with the same precision she'd once applied to investigating insurance fraud.

The right side of the shop held the "Dog Bar"—comfortable benches and tables, water bowls at multiple heights, a toy basket, and enough space for dogs to socialize while their humans browsed. It had become what the business journals called a "third place"—not home, not work, but somewhere in between. A community gathering spot where Franklin's dog owners met, chatted, shared training tips, and let their pets form friendships, sampling the bakery's wares while the owners enjoyed a mixed drink, beer or cup of coffee.

Tammy the bakery's manager, looked up from where she was arranging a fresh batch of "Chimney Rock Crunchies"—sweet potato and apple treats shaped like the famous rock formation. " Donnie! Audrey! Perfect timing. The salmon training treats just came out of the dehydrator and they're her favorite."

"Don't tell Eddie you're feeding her salmon. He already thinks she eats better than we do."

"She does eat better than you do," Tammy pointed out, reasonable as always. "You had a dry cheddar bagel for breakfast yesterday. Audrey had grain-free chicken and sweet potato kibble with a blueberry antioxidant topper."

"Point taken." Donnie unleashed Audrey, who made a beeline for the buffet table with the dignity of a regular who knew exactly where the good treats lived. "Busy morning?"

"Three birthday party orders, two custom pupcake requests for dogs with allergies, and Mrs. Henderson wants to know if we can make liver-flavored biscuits shaped like cats." Tammy grinned. "Her beagle apparently has a sense of humor."

"I love this town." Donnie surveyed her domain with satisfaction. The bakery smelled like bacon, peanut butter, sweet potato, and the particular clean scent that came from dogs who were well-loved and well-groomed. The treat cases gleamed. The Dog Bar held four dogs currently —two labs, a corgi, and a mixed breed who might have been part shepherd—all socializing peacefully while their owners chatted on the benches.

This was what retirement was supposed to look like. Community. Purpose. The satisfaction of creating something good with your own hands. And dogs. Lots and lots of dogs.

Eddie arrived at noon, carrying a cup of coffee and his laptop to write through the afternoon and be available as an extra hand at the Dog Bar if needed. With a knowing smile, he asks, "Let me guess. You've been here since eight?"

"The bacon-cheddar biscuits don't bake themselves."

"The bacon-cheddar biscuits that you could pay Tammy to bake, since she's the manager and you're supposedly retired." Eddie settled onto a bench in a corner of the Dog Bar, and Audrey immediately abandoned her post overseeing the buffet table to claim her spot at his feet. "But you can't help yourself. You need projects. You need control. You need to know every detail of everything."

"Those are called professional standards."

"Those are called 'Donnie can't actually retire because her brain requires constant stimulation.'" Eddie sipped his coffee, watching the dogs socialize. "I'm not complaining. This place makes you happy. I get some writing done and Audrey's never been more spoiled. Win-win."

"She deserves spoiling. She puts up with you."

"She puts up with both of us. Which is why she gets salmon training treats and organic pupcakes." Eddie scratched Audrey's ears. "How's business?"

"Good. Really good. We had a feature in *Modern Dog* magazine last month. Online orders are up thirty percent. We're shipping treats to customers in twelve states now." Donnie leaned against the counter, watching the bar fill up—it was Saturday morning, prime social hour. "I never thought this would work. A dog bakery in a small mountain town. But Franklin needed a third place for pet owners. Somewhere between home and work. Somewhere to gather."

"You built community," Eddie said simply. "Same thing you did in Miami with your investigation network, but with fewer criminals and more poodles."

"Significantly more poodles."

"And less danger."

Donnie smiled. "Significantly less danger."

The morning passed in the rhythm that had become familiar over three years. Customers came and went. Dogs socialized with other dogs and people who just needed to pet a pup. Treats were purchased, recommendations were made, stories were shared. Mrs. Henderson did indeed order liver biscuits shaped like cats, and her beagle's enthusiasm when picking them up was so comical that Tammy added the design to the regular menu.

By noon, the bakery was full—a dozen dogs, twice as many humans, the air filled with barking and laughter and the smell of fresh-baked treats. This was Franklin at its best. Community gathered around shared love of pets. People who might never otherwise meet becoming friends because their dogs liked to play together.

"You know what's funny?" Eddie said, watching a chocolate lab try to convince a German shepherd to share a tennis ball. "In Miami, you spent thirty years building cases against people who exploited insurance systems. Now you spend your days making dogs happy. Complete opposite."

"Not opposite. Same skill set, different application." Donnie handed a customer a bag of pumpkin digestive biscuits. "Investigation taught me to pay attention to details, to build systems, to create networks of information. I use all of that here. Just with better-smelling outcomes."

"And no one shoots at you."

"That too. Here, everybody is happy about what I do."

Audrey barked—her 'I deserve more treats' bark, which was distinct from her 'there's a squirrel' bark or her 'Eddie's being ridiculous' bark. Donnie had learned to distinguish all of Audrey's vocalizations over the years, the same way she'd learned to read evidence patterns in insurance cases.

"You've already had three salmon treats this morning," Donnie told her.

Audrey's expression suggested this was insufficient and possibly constituted neglect.

"Fine. One more. But that's it." Donnie handed over a salmon training treat, which Audrey accepted with regal dignity before returning to her spot at Eddie's feet.

"You're as bad as I am," Eddie observed.

"Worse. I literally own the bakery. I could give her

infinite treats."

"But you don't, because you're responsible about canine nutrition."

"Exactly." Donnie smiled. "Although sometimes responsibility is overrated and you definitely don't follow an ideal diet."

The afternoon brought more customers. A tour group from Atlanta stopped specifically to visit—they'd read about the bakery in *Southern Living* and wanted to see if it lived up to the hype. A family from Asheville came to pick up a birthday pupcake for their golden retriever's tenth birthday. Three hikers fresh from the Appalachian Trail stopped in with their trail dogs, grateful for a pet-friendly space that welcomed muddy paws.

And through it all, the Dog Bar hummed with canine socialization—dogs learning how to share space, humans learning each other's stories, community building in the way that only happens in third places where everyone is welcome and the atmosphere is warm.

By closing time, Donnie was exhausted in the best way. Her feet hurt. She smelled like bacon and peanut butter. Audrey had eaten at least seven salmon treats despite Donnie's attempt at moderation. And the bakery had made people happy—dozens of people, dozens of dogs, all leaving with treats and smiles and plans to return another day.

"Best retirement ever? " Eddie asked, helping

Donnie lock up.

"It's what I tell you every day because it's true every day. I went from chasing insurance fraudsters in Miami to baking dog treats in the mountains. Just living the dream."

"The very specific dream of a person who loves dogs and needs projects and can't actually retire." Donnie looked at her bakery—the gleaming overflowing buffet table, the comfortable Dog Bar, the cheerful red awning, the spot on Main Street that had become Franklin's gathering place for pet lovers.

Three years ago, this had been a struggling pet supply shop. Now it was a nationally-recognized business, a community hub, a third place where Franklin came together. Not bad for a retirement project.

"Come on," Eddie said, taking her hand. "Let's go home. I'm making smoked salmon flatbread with pickled shallots, feta, dill and capers and you're going to sit down and let me serve you for once."

"Deal. But Audrey gets salmon for dinner too. After consuming that many treats, she needs protein balance."

"Of course she does. Because we're those people now. The people who worry about their poodle's macronutrient ratios."

"We've always been those people," Donnie said. "We just have a business that supports it now."

They walked home through Franklin's

November evening, Audrey trotting between them with the satisfaction of a dog who'd had an excellent day. The mountains rose in the distance, ancient and patient. Main Street was quiet, most shops closed for the evening.

But the Smoky Mountain Dog Bakery's window display still glowed—pupcakes and biscuits and treats arranged like art, visible to anyone passing by. A reminder that Franklin was a place where dog bakeries could thrive, where retirement could mean building something new, where community gathered around shared love of pets.

Tomorrow morning, Donnie would be up at six getting ready to head in to bake bacon-cheddar biscuits.

Because retirement, as it turned out, didn't mean stopping work. It just meant choosing work that made you happy.

And making dogs happy? That was the best work of all. Unless you count catching criminals with your Mah Jong family.

Chapter 2

The next morning she stood in her Franklin kitchen watching the espresso maker hiss and spit, the sound of her old Miami life refusing to die quietly in the North Carolina mountains. November had arrived overnight, turning everything silver with frost and the morning air sharp enough to sting. Through the window, the Smoky Mountains rose in layers of blue and purple and shadow, ancient and patient and completely indifferent to the fact that someone had died in Bea Tran's art studio three hours ago.

Detective Morrison had called at three AM. Donnie had been awake already—the chickens had been making noise, probably a fox prowling too close—so when her phone lit up with the Franklin Police Department's number, she'd answered on the first ring.

"We've got a situation," Morrison had said. No preamble, no apology for the hour. That's how Donnie knew it was bad. "Bea Tran's studio. Body. You need to come."

"Is Bea—"

"She's fine. Physically. But she found him. Collector from Atlanta. Conrad Fischer. And, Donnie..." Morrison had paused, which wasn't like him. "Some of her paintings are missing."

Now, just more than three hours later, Donnie poured Cuban coffee strong enough to strip paint and tried to organize her thoughts the way she'd organized a thousand insurance fraud cases in Miami-Dade: evidence, timeline, suspects, motivation. The coffee was excellent. Her thoughts were chaos.

Bea Tran was one of theirs. Tuesday night mahjong. The group that had somehow become Donnie's found family after thirty years of Miami crime and corruption had taught her that trusting people was mostly how you got disappointed. Bea was quiet, observant to an unsettling degree, and saw things in people that Donnie's professional skepticism usually missed. Bea noticed when Eddie was stressed before Eddie knew it himself. Bea brought tea that somehow always matched the emotional temperature of the room. Bea painted watercolors of the mountains and water and immigration that made Donnie's throat tight with feelings she didn't have names for.

And now Bea had a dead collector in her studio and missing paintings, which meant Bea was about to become a suspect in her own space.

Bless his heart, Morrison was trying. But Donnie knew the pattern: body in Bea's studio, Bea's paintings missing, Bea the last person to see the victim alive. If you followed procedure —and Morrison followed procedure—Bea was suspect number one.

The coffee maker finished its dramatic performance. Donnie poured a second cup and looked out at the chicken coop, where the hens were just starting to stir. Her retirement chickens. Eddie had laughed when she'd announced she was getting chickens three years ago, said it was very "gentleman farmer" of her. She'd told him chickens were low-maintenance and produced eggs, which was more than she could say for most of her insurance fraud witnesses back in Miami.

The truth was simpler and more complicated: the chickens gave her something to protect. Something that depended on her but couldn't disappoint her by lying or stealing or committing fraud. Chickens were honest. They wanted food and safety and a place to sleep. She could provide that. Easy.

People were harder.

Behind her, Eddie's footsteps creaked on the stairs. A moment later he appeared in the kitchen doorway, silver hair wild from sleep, wearing the Old Navy flannel pajama pants she'd bought him for Christmas three years ago and a Florida Gator t-shirt from his restaurant days. After thirty-five years of marriage, she could read his mood from the set of his shoulders. This morning: worried but trying not to show it.

"Coffee's ready," she said. "And before you ask, yes, I'm going to investigate. And yes, I already know what you're going to say."

"Which is?" He poured coffee into his favorite mug—white ceramic with "World's Okayest Husband" in fading black letters. She'd given it to him as a joke on their twentieth anniversary. He'd used it every day since.

"That you support me, that you'll help however you can, and that you think this is excellent material for your next novel."

Eddie smiled, which meant she'd been right. "Bea's one of ours."

"Exactly." Donnie checked her watch: six-fifteen AM. Too early to call Maya, but Maya would be awake anyway—herbalists kept farmer hours. Too early to call Mabs, who was a strict seven AM riser. Definitely too early to call Dodo, who would answer but would be incoherent until at least eight.

The Tuesday night mahjong group had

solved one murder already. Terry Boone's death last spring had pulled them together, tested them, and ultimately proven that six women and one judgmental poodle could be better at investigation than they had any right to be. They'd exposed a corruption network that reached from Franklin to Atlanta, brought down a construction company that had been running insurance fraud and money laundering for fifteen years, and helped the FBI build a RICO case that was still working its way through federal court.

This time would be different, though. This time, one of their own was in the crosshairs.

"What do you need?" Eddie asked, settling into the chair across from her at the kitchen table. The same table where they ate dinner most nights, where Donnie spread out her case files when she was working through a problem, where the mahjong group had played on rainy Tuesdays when the library was being renovated.

Donnie looked out the window at the mountains, beautiful and dangerous and holding Franklin in their ancient embrace. Somewhere out there, someone had killed Conrad Fischer and stolen Bea's paintings. Someone who thought they were clever enough to frame a sixty-five-year-old refugee artist for murder.

Bless their heart. They had no idea what they'd just started.

"Coffee," Donnie said. "Lots of coffee. And then we're going to the studio. Morrison said seven-thirty. That gives us an hour."

"You want me to come with you?"

"You're my civilian consultant. Plus, you notice things about people that I miss." This was true. Eddie had spent forty years running a restaurant in Florida, which meant he'd spent forty years reading customers, defusing conflicts, and understanding human motivation. His novelist brain saw story structure where Donnie saw evidence. They made a good team.

"Fair point." Eddie stood, refilled both their mugs. "What are you thinking happened?"

"Someone killed Conrad Fischer in Bea's studio and stole her paintings. Those are facts. Everything else is speculation." Donnie pulled out her phone, opened a new note. "But if I had to guess? This isn't about Bea personally. She's the patsy. Whoever did this needed a suspect who had motive, means, and opportunity. Bea had all three."

"Motive?"

"Fischer was an art collector. He'd been trying to buy Bea's 'Between Waters' series for months. She kept refusing. That's public knowledge—Maya mentioned it at mahjong in August. So if Fischer turns up dead and the paintings are missing, the obvious conclusion is that Bea killed him and took them back."

"Except Bea would never kill someone."

"We know that. Morrison might even know that. But evidence doesn't care about character."

Eddie was quiet for a moment, thinking. "So who benefits from framing Bea?"

"That's the question." Donnie typed notes: WHY BEA? WHY NOW? WHO BENEFITS? "Someone who wants those paintings but can't risk buying them. Someone who knows Bea well enough to know she'd refuse. Someone who knows about Fischer trying to buy them."

"That's a lot of someone's in a small town."

"Or one someone with good intel." Donnie finished her coffee. "Come on. We're going to be late."

Thirty minutes later, dressed in what Eddie called her "Miami investigator uniform"— black pants, white button-down, black blazer—

Donnie drove them toward downtown Franklin. The sun was just fully up, turning the frost to diamonds on the grass and making the mountains glow like they'd been lit from within. November in Franklin was cold and beautiful and shorter than it had any right to be, compressed between October's leaf-peeping tourism and December's Christmas rush.

The studio was on the south edge of town, in a converted tobacco warehouse that a developer had turned into artist spaces ten years ago. Bea had been there since the beginning, drawn by the north-facing windows and the high ceilings. Donnie had visited twice: once for a group show in the spring, once when Bea needed help moving a particularly large canvas. Both times she'd been struck by how the space felt like Bea herself—quietly organized, surprisingly strong, carrying more weight than seemed possible.

Morrison's cruiser was parked outside, along with the medical examiner's van and two unmarked cars that Donnie recognized as state police. Yellow crime scene tape fluttered in the morning breeze. A small crowd had gathered across the street—early risers, the curious, the ones who'd heard about it on the police scanner. Franklin's gossip network was faster than fiber optic internet.

Morrison met them at the tape. He looked tired—probably hadn't slept at all—but professional. "Donnie. Eddie."

"Detective." Donnie kept her voice neutral. She and Morrison had developed a working relationship during the Terry Boone case, built on mutual respect and the understanding that they both wanted justice, even if they had different ways of getting there. "Thank you for calling me."

"Bea asked for you. And..." He glanced at the crowd, lowered his voice. "I need you to tell me I'm wrong."

"About?"

"About Bea being suspect number one."

So she'd been right about the procedure problem. "Where is she?"

"Inside. Her lawyer showed up an hour ago. David Chen from Asheville."

Good. David Chen was sharp, expensive, and didn't take cases he couldn't win. Someone had called in the big guns fast. "Can I see the scene?"

Morrison nodded, lifted the tape. "Don't touch anything. State boys are touchy about their crime scene."

The warehouse had been divided into eight studios, four on each floor. Bea's was on the ground floor, northwest corner. The door stood open. Inside, Donnie could see the controlled chaos of a professional investigation: the ME photographing the body, state police dusting for prints, someone measuring blood spatter patterns.

And in the corner, on a folding chair that looked like it had been pulled from a closet, sat Bea Tran.

She looked smaller than Donnie remembered. Bea was slight anyway—five-foot-two, maybe a hundred pounds—but grief and shock had a way of shrinking people. Her black hair, usually pulled back in a neat bun, hung loose around her face. She wore the same clothes from yesterday's private showing: dark blue silk shirt, black slacks, jade bracelet that had been her grandmother's. Her hands rested in her lap, very still, but Donnie could see the tremor in her fingers.

Next to her, David Chen stood like a sentinel. He was forty-something, Taiwanese-American, built like someone who'd played football in college and still hit the gym. He saw Donnie and gave a small nod.

"Bea," Donnie said softly.

Bea looked up. Her eyes were dry but haunted. "Donnie."

"I'm here. Maya's coming. Everyone's coming. We're going to figure this out."

"I didn't—" Bea's voice cracked.

"I know you didn't. Everyone knows you didn't." Donnie crouched down so they were eye level. "But I need you to tell me exactly what happened. Everything. Can you do that?"

Bea nodded. "Conrad Fischer contacted me three months ago. He wanted to buy my 'Between Waters' series. All six paintings. He offered..." She paused. "A lot of money."

"How much?"

"Two hundred thousand dollars."

Eddie whistled softly. Donnie shot him a look.

"I said no," Bea continued. "Those paintings are... they're my story. My grandmother's story. Leaving Vietnam. The boat. The camps. Coming here. They're not for sale."

"But he kept asking."

"He was persistent. Called once a week. Came to the studio twice. Yesterday he showed up at five PM, said he had a buyer in Singapore who would pay three hundred thousand. I still said no." Bea's hands trembled harder. "He got angry. Not loud, but... cold. Said I was being stupid, that refugee art was trending, that in five years no one would care. That I should take the money while I could."

"What did you do?"

"I told him to leave. He said he needed to use the bathroom first. I went to the kitchen to make tea—" Bea gestured to the small kitchenette in the back corner. "I was angry. I needed to calm down. When I came back..." Her voice dropped to a whisper. "He was on the floor. Dead. And the paintings were gone."

Donnie looked around the studio. Four empty spaces on the walls where paintings had hung. Not carelessly torn down—the hanging hardware was still in place. Someone had taken them carefully, professionally.

"How long were you in the kitchen?"

"Maybe ten minutes? I put the kettle on, washed some cups, tried to breathe."

"Did you hear anything?"

"No. The kettle was loud. And I was..." Bea trailed off.

"Upset," Donnie finished. "That's normal. That's human." She stood, looked at Morrison, who'd been listening from the doorway. "Ten-minute window. That's not much time."

"No," Morrison agreed. "Which means it was planned. Someone knew Fischer was here."

"Or someone was already here," Eddie said quietly. Everyone turned to look at him. "What? I'm just saying. If I wanted to kill someone and frame someone else, I'd already be in position. Waiting."

Morrison frowned. "The alarm system shows no one else entered. Just Bea and Fischer at four forty-five. No one left except the 911 call at five fifty-two."

"What about the back exit?" Donnie asked.

"Fire door. Alarmed. Didn't go off."

"Windows?"

"All locked from inside."

Donnie looked at the scene again, this time with Eddie's suggestion in mind. A locked room murder. Someone came in with Fischer or was already inside. Killed him while Bea was making tea. Took the paintings. Left without triggering the alarm.

"The bathroom," she said. "Where is it?"

Morrison pointed to a door in the far corner. "Clear. Nothing disturbed."

"Can I look?"

He nodded.

The bathroom was small, clean, barely big enough for a toilet and sink. But the window—Donnie looked up. The window was high, small, the kind that tilted out for ventilation. Open. And below it, a metal stool that usually lived next to Bea's easel.

"Morrison," Donnie called.

He came over, saw what she saw, and swore quietly.

"Someone went out the window," Donnie said. "Small person, or very determined. Used the stool to reach it. Probably had the paintings rolled up—they're watercolors, they'd roll."

"Prints?"

"I'll check." Morrison called over one of the state police techs.

Eddie was looking at the window with interest. "That's what, eighteen inches wide? Twenty?"

"About that." Donnie turned to Bea. "Who knew about this window?"

"Everyone, I suppose. I open it when I'm painting with oils. The ventilation isn't great."

"And who knew Fischer was coming yesterday?"

Bea thought for a moment. "I mentioned it to Maya. At Tuesday mahjong last week. I was annoyed that he kept bothering me."

Donnie's stomach sank. Tuesday mahjong. Which meant Maya knew. Which meant potentially everyone in the group knew. Which meant anyone in the group could have told someone else.

Which meant this was about to get complicated.

"Okay," Donnie said, thinking fast. "Here's what we know. Someone killed Conrad Fischer between five PM and five-fifty PM yesterday. They either came in with him and hid, or they were already here. They went out the bathroom window with the paintings. This was planned. Professional. Which means someone knew Fischer would be here and that Bea would be alone with him."

Morrison was making notes. "And the poison?"

Donnie looked up sharply. "Poison?"

"Preliminary tox screen came back twenty minutes ago. Plant-based alkaloid. Asian variety. Slow-acting but effective. He was dying before he hit the floor."

Bea made a small sound of distress. David Chen put a hand on her shoulder.

"Time of death?" Donnie asked.

"ME says between five-fifteen and five-thirty. So right in your window."

Plant-based poison. Asian variety. In a town where there were exactly two people with serious botanical knowledge: Maya Lin and Bea Tran. And Maya would never—

But someone was trying to make it look like she would.

Or like Bea would.

Donnie looked at Morrison. "Bea didn't do this."

"I know," he said quietly. "But the evidence says she did. And I've got state police breathing down my neck who don't know her and don't care. I need you to prove she didn't. Fast."

"How fast?"

"Seventy-two hours before I have to charge someone."

Three days. Donnie had cracked cases in Miami in less time, but those were insurance fraud cases where the evidence was usually financial and stupid. This was murder. Murder took time.

But Bea didn't have time.

"I'll need access to Fischer's background," Donnie said. "Full financial records. Phone logs. Travel history. Everything."

"I'll send you what I can."

"And I'll need to talk to people without you looking over my shoulder."

Morrison smiled grimly. "I never saw you. You're just a concerned citizen."

"Exactly."

Outside, the sun had fully risen, turning Franklin into a postcard of small-town perfection. Main Street would be opening soon—The Country Kitchen serving breakfast to early birds, Café Rel prepping for lunch service, Maya's apothecary probably already open because Maya never slept either.

And somewhere in this perfect small town, someone had committed murder and tried to frame one of their own.

Donnie pulled out her phone and texted the group chat: EMERGENCY MAHJONG. MY PLACE. 8 AM. BEA NEEDS US.

The responses came fast:
Maya: On my way
Mabs: I'll bring coffee
Dodo: THE CATS KNEW SOMETHING WAS WRONG
Evelyn: What happened?
Frankie: Goddamnit

"Come on," Donnie said to Eddie. "We've got work to do."

They had seventy-two hours to prove Bea innocent. Seventy-two hours to find a killer. Seventy-two hours to solve a locked-room murder that shouldn't be possible.

The mountains watched in silence, beautiful and ancient and impartial. They'd seen this before. They'd see it again. All that mattered was what happened next.

And what happened next was that the Tuesday Night Mahjong Group went to work.

Chapter 3

Maya Lin woke to frost on her bedroom window and Evelyn's arm warm across her waist. November had arrived overnight, turning the herb garden silver and the morning air sharp enough to see your breath indoors until the heat kicked on.

Through the window, the garden looked delicate and temporary—basil already blackened by first frost, rosemary still green but slowed, sage withdrawing into itself, everything moving toward dormancy. Nature's way of protecting itself through winter: pull inward, conserve energy, survive until spring. Maya had learned this from her grandmother, who'd learned it from her grandmother, an unbroken line of Cherokee and Chinese herbalists stretching back further than anyone could remember.

Some knowledge you carried in your bones.

Maya's phone buzzed on the nightstand. Six twenty-three AM. Donnie's name on the screen.

She answered quietly, trying not to wake Evelyn, who'd only fallen asleep around two AM after another nightmare about David. The nightmares came less frequently now—once or twice a week instead of every night—but they still came. Trauma didn't follow a schedule. "Donnie?"

"Bea's in trouble." Donnie's voice was Miami-professional, which meant she was already in investigation mode. No preamble, no gentle lead-in. Just facts. "Dead body in her studio. Some of her paintings missing. Morrison called me three hours ago."

Maya sat up carefully, disentangling herself from Evelyn without waking her. The morning was cold enough that she pulled the quilt up over Evelyn's shoulder, a small gesture of care that had become automatic over the past six months of living together. "Is Bea hurt?"

"Not physically. But she found the body. Atlanta art collector named Conrad Fischer. Private showing last night, just the two of them. She says he was dead when she came back from making tea."

Maya's mind was already racing ahead, connecting patterns the way herbalists connected symptoms to root causes. Tea. Bea made tea the way Maya made tea—as ritual, as medicine, as breathing space when the world pressed too close. And someone had used that ritual, that small moment of self-care, to kill and frame.

"How long was she gone?"

"Ten minutes. Long enough to kill Fischer and steal four paintings."

"The 'Between Waters' series." Not a question. Maya knew those paintings, had watched Bea work on them over two years, adding layers of watercolor like layers of memory. Immigration and identity. Leaving Vietnam as a teenager on a leaking boat. Watching her parents drown. Arriving in America with nothing but survivor's guilt and her grandmother's jade bracelet. Building a life from loss.

Those paintings were Bea's heart rendered in watercolor and rice paper.

"I need you here," Donnie said. "I'm calling emergency mahjong at my place. Eight AM. Morrison's giving us seventy-two hours before he has to make an arrest."

"I'll bring tea," Maya said automatically. Then: "Wait. What does Morrison think happened?"

A pause. "He thinks what the evidence says. Dead man in Bea's studio. Her paintings missing. She was the last person who saw him alive. And Maya..." Donnie's voice dropped lower. "The preliminary tox screen came back. Plant-based poison. Asian variety."

Maya's stomach went cold. "Someone's trying to frame her. Or..." She stopped, the realization hitting hard. "Or frame me."

"That's what I'm thinking. You and Bea are the only two people in Franklin with serious botanical knowledge. Whoever did this knew that."

"I'll make chamomile for Bea. And valerian root. She'll need help sleeping." Maya was already mentally cataloging: chamomile for shock, lavender for anxiety, lemon balm for racing thoughts, ginger for nausea. Bea would need all of them. "Donnie... Bea didn't do this."

"I know. But we're going to have to prove it."

After hanging up, Maya sat in the gray November dawn, watching frost patterns on the window like nature's own watercolor. The garden would survive this cold spell. The perennials had sent their energy underground. The rosemary and sage would endure. Come spring, they'd bloom again.

But first, they had to survive winter.

Behind her, Evelyn stirred. "Maya?"

"I'm here." Maya turned. Evelyn was sitting up, dark hair tangled from sleep, eyes still heavy with the exhaustion that came from nightmares. Six months of living together had taught Maya to read Evelyn's moods from the smallest signs. This morning: worried without knowing why yet.

"Bad news?" Evelyn asked.

"Bea's in trouble. Conrad Fischer—"

"The art collector?" Evelyn was suddenly fully awake, trauma-sharpened instincts kicking in. "The one who's been harassing her about the paintings?"

"He's dead. In her studio. The paintings are missing."

Evelyn pulled the laptop from her nightstand—she kept it there now, ever since the Terry Boone case, ready to research at any hour. David's death had taught her that waiting for morning could mean losing the thread. "When?"

"Last night. Around five PM."

"Plant-based poison, Asian variety, I assume?" Evelyn was already typing, pulling up financial databases and property records with the efficiency of someone who'd spent fifteen years as a forensic accountant for the Georgia Bureau of Investigation.

"How did you—"

"Because that's how I'd frame someone if I wanted it to look local. Use a poison that points to one of two people in town. Make it look personal when it's actually business." Evelyn's fingers flew over the keys. "Conrad Fischer. Let me see what his finances say about him."

Maya got out of bed, pulled on her robe—thick fleece, necessary for November mornings in an old house with drafty windows—and went to make tea. Not for Bea yet. For herself. For Evelyn. For the gathering storm she could feel coming.

The kitchen was cold. She turned on the space heater Eddie had given them last Christmas ("You two need to heat this house properly," he'd scolded, but lovingly) and put the kettle on. While water heated, she gathered herbs from her drying rack: chamomile flowers, dried lavender buds, lemon balm leaves, and a small piece of fresh ginger root.

Her grandmother had taught her that tea was medicine and medicine was tea. That every plant had a purpose. That if you paid attention, the garden would tell you what it needed and what you needed.

This morning, she needed clarity. Focus. The ability to see patterns in chaos.

So: peppermint for mental clarity, rosemary for memory, sage for wisdom. She combined them in her grandmother's old teapot —ceramic, blue and white, carried from China to America in someone's luggage three generations ago—and waited for the water to boil.

Through the window, she could see the Smoky Mountains rising in the November light. Beautiful and terrible and ancient. The Cherokee called them "place of blue smoke" for the way morning mist settled in the valleys. Her mother's people. Her grandmother's people. Mountains that had witnessed everything—Trail of Tears, Civil War, coal mines, tourists, murders—and remained. Impartial. Eternal.

There was always danger lurking over the next ridge in Franklin. This morning, the danger had found one of their own.

"Maya." Evelyn's voice from the bedroom, sharp with discovery. "You need to see this."

Maya brought tea to the bedroom. Evelyn had her laptop balanced on her knees, three windows open, financial records cascading down the screen in the way that looked like chaos to most people but was actually careful organization.

"Conrad Fischer isn't just an art collector," Evelyn said. "He's a dealer. High-end. Specializes in refugee and immigrant art. Vietnamese, Syrian, Afghan, Somali. He's got galleries in Atlanta, Charlotte, and Miami."

"That's not unusual," Maya said slowly. "Refugee art is... valuable. People want to buy stories of survival."

"Right. But look at the money flow." Evelyn turned the laptop. "Fischer's main gallery in Atlanta does maybe two million a year in sales. Legitimate, documented, taxes paid. But these three shell companies here—" she highlighted them "—process another eight million. Moved through offshore accounts. Hidden from IRS. Same pattern as the STX Associates case."

Maya's breath caught. STX Associates. The construction company that had murdered Terry Boone to keep him from testifying. The RICO case that was still working through federal court. The case that had brought Evelyn to Franklin looking for David's killer and had led her to Maya.

"You think Fischer was running the same

kind of operation?"

"I think Fischer was processing money that doesn't want to be traced. Art is perfect for money laundering—subjective value, easy to transport, hard to verify authenticity. You sell a painting for three hundred thousand dollars in cash, who's to say it isn't worth exactly that?"

"But Fischer specialized in refugee art. He approached Bea specifically."

Evelyn nodded slowly. "Which means either he was targeting her for business reasons, or someone is targeting refugee artists systematically. Using their stories, their trauma, to make money."

Maya felt sick. She thought about Bea's paintings. "Between Waters" captured the boat journey from Vietnam—the terror, the hope, the death of Bea's parents, the arrival in America with nothing but survival. They were beautiful and heartbreaking and deeply personal.

And someone wanted to profit from that pain.

"We need to tell Donnie," Maya said.

"Already texted her." Evelyn closed the laptop. "Emergency mahjong at eight. I'm coming."

"You don't have to—"

"Bea's one of ours." Evelyn's voice was firm. She'd lived in Franklin less than a year, but the mahjong group had accepted her after the Terry Boone case. Slowly. Carefully. With the wariness that came from Evelyn's initial deception. But they'd accepted her. Found family wasn't about blood or time. It was about choosing each other when things got hard.

And things were getting hard.

Maya dressed quickly: jeans, turtleneck, the cardigan Bea had given her last Christmas (hand-knitted, sage green, perfect for November). She braided her hair efficiently, the way her grandmother had taught her, keeping it out of the way for work. Some days she wore it down, let it fall past her shoulders. But today was a working day. Today required focus.

She packed her herbalist bag: dried chamomile, valerian root, lemon balm, lavender oil, ginger candies, the emergency tincture she kept for severe shock. Added honey and a small bottle of brandy—sometimes you needed something stronger than tea. Included a notebook and pen. If Bea wanted to talk, Maya would listen. If Bea needed silence, Maya would sit with her. Either way, Maya would be present.

That's what healers did. They bore witness.

"Ready?" Evelyn asked. She'd dressed in her forensic accountant armor: black slacks, gray sweater, the reading glasses she wore for computer work tucked into her pocket. Her hair was pulled back severely. This was Evelyn in professional mode. Evelyn ready to hunt through financial records and find the truth buried in numbers.

"Ready."

They took Maya's ancient Subaru—twenty years old, held together by hope and regular maintenance—through Franklin's waking streets. The town looked peaceful in the early morning light. Main Street shops were just beginning to stir. The Country Kitchen's parking lot already had a few trucks—farmers and early risers getting breakfast before heading to work. Eric's fish market was dark (he only opened Thursday through Saturday, driving to the coast for fresh catch). The library wouldn't open until nine, but Maya would bet money that Mabs was already there, researching.

Donnie and Eddie's house sat on three acres at the edge of town, close enough to walk to Main Street but far enough for chickens and privacy. The house itself was a 1970s ranch that Eddie had slowly renovated over the years, adding a screened porch and updating the kitchen and generally making it comfortable without losing its character.

Donnie's Jeep Wrangler was in the driveway. Eddie's Ford pickup next to it. And as Maya pulled up, she saw Mabs's sensible Honda arriving from the other direction.

Mabs emerged looking like Mabs always looked: neat cardigan, pressed slacks, silver hair cut short and practical, carrying a thermos of what was certainly excellent coffee and probably also a laptop with preliminary research already compiled. Forty-three years as a librarian had taught Mabs that organization was everything.

"Maya. Evelyn." Mabs nodded greeting. "This is bad."

"Very bad," Maya agreed.

"Bea didn't kill anyone."

"We know."

"Then we prove it." Mabs's voice was firm. She'd helped solve Terry Boone's murder with research, organization, and the kind of systematic thinking that came from cataloging information for four decades. She would help solve this too.

Donnie opened the door before they knocked. "Conference room's the living room. Eddie made Cuban pastries. Coffee's hot. Dodo's running late—something about the cats having opinions."

Of course, the cats had opinions. Dodo's three cats—Sherlock, Pancake, and Princess—were consulted on everything from weather predictions to murder investigations. They were surprisingly often correct, which Donnie found deeply irritating and Maya found charming.

The living room had been transformed. Eddie had pushed the coffee table against the wall and set up Donnie's old whiteboard from her Miami days—the one she'd insisted on bringing to Franklin because "you never know when you'll need to solve a crime." On the board, Donnie had already started mapping: CONRAD FISCHER at the center, with spokes leading to BEA, PAINTINGS, STUDIO, and several question marks.

"Sit," Donnie commanded. "We're on the clock."

They sat. Maya pulled out her notebook. Evelyn opened her laptop. Mabs produced a leather binder—of course Mabs had brought a binder—with notes already typed up.

Donnie stood at the whiteboard like she was briefing a team in Miami-Dade's Insurance Investigation Unit. "Here's what we know. Conrad Fischer, fifty-three, art dealer from Atlanta, found dead in Bea's studio at approximately five-fifty PM yesterday. Cause of death: plant-based poison, Asian variety, slow-acting. Time of death: between five-fifteen and five-thirty PM. Bea was in the kitchen making tea from five PM to five-ten PM. When she returned, Fischer was dead and four paintings were missing."

"The 'Between Waters' series," Maya said.

"Right. Four paintings, watercolor on rice paper, approximately three by four feet each. Current estimated value..." Donnie looked at her notes. "Fischer had offered two hundred thousand for the set."

Mabs whistled softly.

"Bea refused," Donnie continued. "Multiple times. Fischer kept pushing. Yesterday was supposed to be a final meeting. He brought the offer up to three hundred thousand. She said no again. According to Bea, he got angry. Cold angry. Said she was being stupid, that refugee art was trending but wouldn't be forever."

"Charming man," Mabs said dryly.

"Dead man," Donnie corrected. "Which brings us to suspects. Morrison's under pressure to charge someone within seventy-two hours. Right now, the evidence points to Bea."

"Evidence?" Evelyn asked.

"Body in her studio. Her paintings missing. She had motive—Fischer was harassing her. She had means—plant-based poison, and she's one of two people in Franklin with botanical knowledge." Donnie glanced at Maya. "The other being Maya."

Everyone looked at Maya. She met their eyes steadily. "I didn't kill Conrad Fischer. And I would never make a poison that would implicate Bea."

"We know that," Donnie said. "But Morrison has to follow the evidence. And right now, the evidence says either Bea or Maya."

"Or someone framing them," Evelyn said. "Someone who knows enough about both of them to make it look convincing."

"Which brings us to suspects." Donnie turned to the whiteboard, started making a list. "Who benefits from Fischer's death and Bea's arrest?"

The room went quiet, thinking.

Finally, Mabs spoke. "Whoever actually wanted those paintings. If Bea's in jail and Fischer's dead, the paintings are available. No one to say where they came from or negotiate price."

"Art theft," Evelyn said. "But more than that. I was researching Fischer's finances this morning. He's running shell companies, offshore accounts, money laundering operation. Same pattern as STX Associates."

Donnie's expression sharpened. "You're saying Fischer was dirty."

"I'm saying Fischer was processing eight million dollars a year that he didn't want the IRS to see. I'm saying he specialized in refugee art for a reason. It's easy to exploit people who are afraid, who don't understand the American legal system, who are desperate to prove their worth."

Maya felt the words like a punch. Bea painting her trauma, trying to prove she deserved to be here. And Fischer seeing profit in that pain.

"So Fischer wasn't just a collector," Donnie said slowly. "He was a predator. Targeting refugee artists. Using their stories to launder money."

"That's my theory," Evelyn said. "And if I'm

right, Fischer had partners. Money laundering is never solo. You need buyers, sellers, transporters, lawyers. A whole network."

"Which means someone in that network might have wanted him dead," Mabs added.

Donnie wrote on the whiteboard: FISCHER'S PARTNERS. "We need names. Financial records. Phone logs. Travel history."

"I can get financial records," Evelyn said. "But it'll take time."

"We don't have time. We have seventy-two hours."

"Then we divide and conquer." Mabs opened her binder. "I'll research Fischer's background—public records, business filings, news articles. Evelyn handles financial forensics. Maya, you work on the poison angle—what exactly was used, where it came from, who had access. Donnie, you coordinate with Morrison and work your sources."

"What about Dodo?" Maya asked.

"Dodo will gossip," Mabs said with the weary affection of someone who'd spent thirty years in book clubs with Dodo. "And somehow her conspiracy theories will turn out to be partially correct, as usual."

The door burst open. Dodo McCray stood in the doorway, slightly out of breath, holding a plate of cookies and radiating dramatic energy. "The cats said this was a setup! They said Bea would never hurt anyone and we need to look at the money! I brought snickerdoodles!"

Donnie pinched the bridge of her nose. "The cats said that?"

"Well, Sherlock did. Pancake was more interested in breakfast. But Princess agrees about the money."

"Of course Princess agrees about the money." Donnie took the cookies. "Come in, Dodo. We're working."

Dodo settled onto the couch, cookies on the table, ready to contribute her particular brand of chaos to the investigation.

And Maya thought: this is my found family. A retired insurance investigator, a forensic accountant, a librarian, a 911 dispatcher with PTSD and three cats, a novelist, and an herbalist. Plus one judgmental poodle who was currently sitting by Eddie's feet, hoping for pastry crumbs.

They'd solved one murder together. They'd solve this one too.

Because Bea was one of theirs. And you didn't abandon family.

"Okay," Donnie said. "Let's go to work."

Chapter 4

By nine AM, Donnie stood at Bea's studio door for the second time that morning, this time with a legitimate reason to be there and Morrison's grudging permission to "ask a few questions."

The crime scene had been released an hour earlier. The state police had taken their photographs, collected their evidence, and departed with promises to "coordinate with local law enforcement." Which meant Morrison was now responsible for solving a murder that everyone assumed had an obvious culprit, except the obvious culprit was a sixty-five-year-old refugee artist who wouldn't hurt a spider.

Bless their hearts, they thought this was simple.

Eddie stood next to her, notebook in hand, playing the role of "concerned community member taking notes." Mabs had gone to the library to start her research. Evelyn was home with three laptops and access to financial databases that were technically legal for her to query as a consultant on the ongoing federal case. Maya had gone to her apothecary to research Asian plant-based poisons and probably also to talk to everyone who came through her door, because Maya's superpower was making people tell her things they didn't mean to share.

Dodo was doing whatever Dodo did, which usually involved gossip and cookies and somehow ended up being surprisingly useful.

Donnie pushed open the door.

The studio looked different in daylight. Less like a crime scene, more like what it actually was—a working artist's space. The north-facing windows let in clear, even light. Canvases in various stages of completion leaned against walls. Paint-stained tables held brushes in jars, palettes covered with plastic wrap, tubes of watercolor and acrylic organized by color in old tackle boxes.

And on the walls, the empty spaces where the "Between Waters" paintings had hung.

Donnie stood in front of the first empty space, looking at the clean rectangle of wall that had been hidden behind art. The hanging hardware was still in place—professional gallery hooks screwed directly into the studs. Whoever had taken the paintings had lifted them carefully, didn't rip them down in haste.

"Professional job," Eddie observed, coming to stand next to her.

"That's what's bothering me." Donnie pulled out her phone, started taking photographs. "This wasn't a crime of passion. This was planned. Executed. Someone knew Fischer would be here, knew Bea would leave him alone for exactly long enough, knew how to get in and out without triggering the alarm."

"Someone who knew Bea's schedule."

"And her habits. And this space." Donnie walked the perimeter, taking in details. The studio was roughly forty by thirty feet, divided into working zones. Painting area near the windows, drying racks along the east wall, storage in the southwest corner, small kitchenette in the back. The bathroom where the killer had escaped was in the far northwest corner, accessible from the main space.

The alarm panel was next to the door. Standard setup. Armed and disarmed with a code. According to Morrison, the system showed Bea and Fischer entering at four forty-five PM. No one else after that. No exits except Bea's 911 call at five fifty-two PM.

Except someone had gone out the bathroom window.

Donnie went to the bathroom, studied it in daylight. Small space, maybe five by seven feet. Toilet, sink, mirror. The window was high—about six feet off the ground—and small. Maybe eighteen inches wide, twenty inches tall. It tilted out on a hinge, currently closed by the state police but clearly recently opened based on the lack of dust around the frame.

Below the window, the metal stool from Bea's easel. Someone had used it to reach the window, climbed through, dropped to the ground outside with four rolled watercolor paintings.

Donnie went outside, circled the building to the bathroom's exterior. The window opened onto a narrow alley between the studio building and the warehouse next door—maybe four feet wide, not visible from the street. Perfect for an unseen exit.

Below the window, crushed grass. A few scuff marks in the dirt. The state police had photographed everything, but Donnie took her own pictures anyway. Sometimes you saw things in your own photographs that you missed in someone else's.

"Anything?" Eddie asked from the alley entrance.

"Someone landed here. Small person, or at least light enough not to leave deep impressions." Donnie crouched down, studying the disturbed earth. "And they were careful. No dropped evidence, no obvious shoe prints."

"So what do we know about our killer?"

Donnie stood, dusted off her hands. "Small enough to fit through that window or desperate enough not to care about the squeeze. Strong enough to lift themselves up and through. Organized enough to plan this. Cold enough to poison someone and walk away."

"That's not many people."

"No." Donnie looked at the mountains, visible between the buildings, blue and impassive in the November sun. "But it's someone in Franklin, or someone who knows Franklin well enough to plan this. This wasn't random. This was personal."

They went back inside. Donnie stood where Conrad Fischer had died—the ME had marked the spot with tape before leaving, a surprisingly thoughtful gesture—and tried to think like an investigator instead of a friend protecting one of her own.

Conrad Fischer. Fifty-three. Art dealer. Wealthy. Connected. Dead on the floor of a refugee artist's studio while she was making tea.

The poison was the key. Plant-based, Asian variety, slow-acting. That meant someone with botanical knowledge, access to rare plants, and enough cold calculation to poison someone and then calmly steal paintings while they died.

Maya would never. Donnie knew that with the certainty of someone who'd spent thirty years reading people for a living. Maya healed. She didn't hurt.

But someone wanted it to look like Maya. Or like Bea.

Which meant someone knew them both well enough to frame them convincingly.

"The paintings," Donnie said suddenly. "Why those four specifically?"

Eddie consulted his notes. "Bea said Fischer wanted the whole 'Between Waters' series. Six paintings total. Four are missing. Two are still here."

"Where?"

Eddie pointed to the storage area. Two large flat portfolios leaned against the wall, the kind designed for transporting unframed works.

Donnie crossed the studio, opened the first portfolio carefully. Inside, protected by acid-free paper, was a watercolor that made her throat tight. A boat on dark water. People crowded together. Two figures in the water, reaching up. The style was spare, economical, every brushstroke carrying weight.

This was Bea's parents drowning.

Donnie closed the portfolio carefully. Opened the second. Another watercolor. A young girl standing on a beach, everything she owned in a plastic bag, looking at a distant shore.

This was Bea arriving in America.

"These two stayed," Donnie said. "Why?"

Eddie came over, looked at the paintings.

His novelist brain was working—she could see it in the way his eyes moved, connecting story beats. "These are the most personal. The most painful. Fischer wanted the series, but maybe the killer only wanted the marketable ones."

"The ones that tell a story that sells."

"Right. Escape, journey, arrival, survival—those are the romanticized parts. But dead parents and arriving with nothing? Those are too real. Too uncomfortable for wealthy collectors who want inspiration without actually thinking about what refugees survive."

Donnie looked at her husband and thought, not for the first time, that marrying him had been the smartest thing she'd ever done. "So our killer is practical. Wants profit, not the whole story."

"Or wants specific paintings for a specific buyer."

"Which means this is business, not personal. Fischer was targeted because he had access to Bea's paintings. Bea was framed because she's a convenient suspect. The paintings were the real goal."

Donnie pulled out her phone, texted Evelyn: NEED TO KNOW IF FISCHER HAD SPECIFIC BUYERS FOR BEA'S WORK.

INTERNATIONAL COLLECTORS. FOLLOW THE MONEY.

The response came immediately: ALREADY ON IT. WILL HAVE SOMETHING BY NOON.

"Let's talk to the neighbors," Donnie said. "Someone in this building saw something. They always do."

The tobacco warehouse had been divided into eight artist studios, four on each floor. Donnie and Eddie made the rounds systematically, knocking on doors, introducing themselves, asking careful questions that sounded like concern but were actually investigation.

Studio 1: Ceramicist named Robert, sixty-something, working on a series of vases. He'd been here until four PM yesterday, left before Fischer arrived. Noticed nothing unusual. Hadn't heard about the murder until this morning. Was appropriately shocked.

Studio 2: Empty. The artist had moved out last month, space not yet rented.

Studio 3: Photographer named Sarah, late thirties, specializing in mountain landscapes. She'd been out of town yesterday, returning this morning to crime scene tape and gossip.

She knew Bea casually—they'd had coffee a few times, talked about art and Franklin and the complicated relationship between making beauty and making rent. Sarah said Bea had mentioned Fischer bothering her about paintings, had seemed annoyed but not frightened.

"Did she mention anyone else asking about the paintings?" Donnie asked.

Sarah thought for a moment. "There was someone. She didn't give a name, but... three weeks ago? Four? We were having coffee and she got a phone call. Stepped outside to take it. When she came back, she looked upset. Said it was another collector interested in the same paintings Fischer wanted. Said she was tired of her trauma being for sale. Tired of those bringing that trauma back."

Donnie wrote this down. Another collector. "Did she say anything else about them?"

"Just that they were persistent. And that they knew too much about her story—about the boat, her parents, the camps. She said it felt invasive. She said they lived it."

Another collector who knew Bea's story in detail. That was interesting.

Studios 5-7 upstairs were also empty when Donnie knocked. Working artists, probably out at day jobs or running errands. She'd have to come back.

But Studio 8, directly above Bea's, had someone home. The door opened to reveal a woman in her seventies, Southeast Asian, wearing an apron covered in paint splatters. Her gray hair was pulled back in a practical bun. She looked at Donnie with sharp, assessing eyes.

"You are investigating," she said. Not a question. Slight accent, Vietnamese maybe.

"I'm a friend of Bea's," Donnie said carefully. "I'm trying to understand what happened."

"Bea did not kill that man."

"I know."

The woman studied Donnie for a long moment, then stepped back. "Come in."

The studio was similar to Bea's in layout but completely different in aesthetic. Where Bea's space was serene and organized, this was controlled chaos. Paintings everywhere—abstract acrylics in bold colors, mixed media pieces incorporating fabric and paper, sculptural installations made from found objects. The work was striking, aggressive, unapologetic.

"I'm Lin Anh," the woman said. "I paint above Bea."

"Donnie Carlisle. This is my husband, Eddie."

"I know who you are. Bea speaks of you. The Tuesday night mahjong group. The ones who solved the murder last spring." Lin gestured to chairs. "Sit. I will tell you what I know."

They sat. Lin poured tea from a pot that had been steeping—oolong, by the smell—and settled into her own chair with the ease of someone who'd been expecting this conversation.

"Yesterday, five o'clock, I was here painting. I heard voices below. Bea's voice and a man's voice. The man was angry."

"Could you hear what they were saying?"

"Some. He wanted her paintings. She said no. He said she was being foolish, that refugee art wouldn't be valuable forever. She told him to leave." Lin sipped her tea. "Then I heard footsteps. Bea's footsteps going to the kitchen. She walks lightly. Then I heard... different footsteps. Heavier. A man, but not the same man."

Donnie leaned forward. "There was someone else there?"

"Yes. I heard the man—Fischer, you said his name was?—I heard him go to the bathroom. Then I heard other footsteps. Quick. Purposeful. Moving through the studio."

"Did you see who it was?"

"No. But I heard them." Lin set down her tea cup with precision. "And I heard them leave. Through the bathroom, I think. The window."

"What time was this?"

"Maybe five-ten? Five-fifteen? I was focused on my painting. But it wasn't long after Fischer went to the bathroom."

So someone else had been there. Had waited until Fischer was isolated, until Bea was making tea, until the moment was perfect. Had killed Fischer—probably the poison was already working by then, if it was slow-acting—and had stolen the paintings and escaped through the window. All while Lin painted upstairs and Bea made tea in the back.

"Why didn't you tell the police?" Donnie asked.

Lin's expression was complicated. "I told

them I heard voices. They asked if I saw anyone. I said no. They wrote it down and left." She paused. "I am Vietnamese. I am seventy-three. When police ask, 'Did you see?' and I say no, they stop listening. They think: old woman, immigrant, probably confused."

Donnie felt a familiar anger rise in her chest. The same anger she'd felt a thousand times in Miami when witnesses were dismissed because of age or accent or the color of their skin. "I'm listening."

"I know." Lin refilled their tea cups. "That is why I am telling you. The police think Bea did this. But Bea did not do this. Someone else was there. Someone who knew her schedule, knew the studio, knew when to strike."

"Someone small enough to fit through that window."

"Or determined enough." Lin smiled slightly. "You think I am too old to fit through a window. But I grew up in Vietnam during war. I escaped in a boat smaller than your car. I have climbed through spaces you would not believe. Size is not always the constraint. Will is."

Point taken. "Do you know of anyone who would want to hurt Bea?"

"Hurt Bea? No. Bea is..." Lin searched for

words. "Bea is good. She helps other artists. She shares supplies. She talks to the young ones who are afraid they are not good enough. She brings soup when you are sick. She remembers your grandmother's death anniversary and lights incense." Lin's voice was fierce. "Bea survived the boat. She survived the camps. She survived America. And now someone tries to take even her art from her? No. This is not acceptable."

"Do you know Conrad Fischer?"

"I know of him. Art dealer. He contacted me two years ago about my work. I told him no. I do not trust dealers who specialize in refugee stories. They want to profit from our pain. I paint my pain for myself, not for wealthy white people who want to feel good about diversity."

Donnie liked Lin Nguyen more with every sentence. "Did Fischer persist after you said no?"

"A few calls. I stopped answering. He found easier targets."

"Like Bea."

"Like Bea. But Bea's work is different from mine. More... gentle. More palatable to collectors who want inspiration without discomfort. My work makes people uncomfortable. That is the point."

Eddie had been quietly taking notes. Now he spoke. "Did Bea mention anyone else interested in her paintings? Besides Fischer?"

Lin nodded. "There was another man. Asian. Professional. He came to visit Bea about a month ago. I saw him leaving as I was arriving. Expensive suit. Expensive car. He looked... familiar. Like I had seen him before but could not place where."

"Did you mention this to Bea?"

"I asked her about him. She said he was another collector. She looked disturbed. I did not push."

Another Asian collector. Expensive. Familiar to Lin but she couldn't place him. And Bea had been disturbed by his visit.

"Could you describe him?"

Lin thought for a moment. "Fifties. Well-dressed. Vietnamese, I think, or maybe Chinese-American. Hard to tell. Short hair. Confident. The kind of confidence that comes from money and power."

Donnie wrote this down. An Asian collector with money and power, interested in Bea's paintings, making her uncomfortable. That was someone to find.

"If I showed you photographs, could you identify him?"

"Perhaps. If I saw his face clearly, I might remember where I know him from."

"Thank you." Donnie stood. "This has been incredibly helpful. If you remember anything else—"

"I will tell you. Not the police. You." Lin stood as well. "Find who did this to Bea. She deserves justice. We all deserve justice."

Walking back to the truck, Eddie was quiet. Donnie knew that silence. It meant his brain was working, connecting narrative threads, seeing story structure in the chaos of real life.

"Someone else was there," he finally said. "Someone who knew the perfect moment to strike. That takes planning. Observation. Patience."

"Professional hit," Donnie agreed. "But why frame Bea? If you wanted Fischer dead, just kill him. Why complicate it with stolen paintings and a refugee artist taking the fall?"

"Because the paintings were always the goal. Fischer was just in the way. And Bea... Bea's the perfect patsy. Refugee, traumatized, has motive, has botanical knowledge through her friendship with Maya. She fits the profile so well that no one looks further."

Donnie's phone buzzed. Text from Evelyn: FOUND SOMETHING. COME TO MAYA'S. BRING EVERYONE.

She showed Eddie the message. He read it and smiled grimly. "Time to compare notes."

"Time to find a killer," Donnie corrected.

They had sixty hours left before Morrison had to make an arrest. Sixty hours to prove Bea innocent, find the real killer, and figure out who was systematically exploiting refugee artists in Franklin, North Carolina.

The mountains watched as they drove away, ancient and patient. They'd seen this story before—murder, greed, justice. They'd see how it ended this time.

Donnie just hoped the ending was the right one.

Chapter 5

Mabel Carter had been a librarian for forty-three years, and she knew that information was power. Not the dramatic, movie-version power of secret documents and classified files. The real power: knowing where to look, how to organize what you found, and which questions to ask next.

She sat at her usual desk in the Franklin Public Library's research room—technically she'd retired six months ago, but the current librarians still let her use the space whenever she needed it—with three laptops open, two legal pads covered in notes, and a thermos of coffee strong enough to strip varnish.

Conrad Fischer wasn't going to stay a mystery for long.

The library didn't open to the public for another hour, but Mabs had her own key. Forty-three years of service earned you certain privileges, including the ability to show up at seven AM and commandeer the research room when a friend needed help.

Bea needed help.

Mabs opened the first laptop—her personal one, connected to her own accounts—and started with the basics. Conrad Fischer, Atlanta, art dealer. Google search. Sort by date to get the most recent information.

The first results were news articles from

this morning: "Atlanta Art Dealer Found Dead in Franklin, NC" and "Murder Investigation at Local Studio." Mabs skimmed them. Basic facts, no speculation, quotes from Morrison about "ongoing investigation." Nothing useful yet.

She moved backward in time. Last month, Atlanta Journal-Constitution had run a profile: "Conrad Fischer: Champion of Refugee Art." Mabs read it carefully, taking notes.

Fischer, fifty-three. Born in Charlotte. BA in Art History from UGA, MFA from SCAD. Opened his first gallery in Atlanta in 2005, specializing in contemporary Southern artists. Shifted focus to refugee and immigrant art in 2015 after, quote, "witnessing the Syrian refugee crisis and wanting to amplify marginalized voices."

Mabs made a note: WHY 2015? WHAT CHANGED?

The profile included photographs of Fischer's galleries—three locations, all upscale. Atlanta's gallery was in Buckhead, Charlotte's in South End, Miami's in Wynwood. Premium locations. High overhead. The kind of spaces that required serious money to maintain.

The article quoted Fischer extensively. He talked about "ethical collecting," about "paying fair prices to refugee artists," about "using art to build bridges across cultures."

It all sounded lovely. It all made Mabs's librarian instincts itch.

She'd read enough fundraising pitches and grant applications to recognize performative language when she saw it. Fischer talked about ethics and fair prices, but the article didn't include any actual numbers. Didn't quote any artists he'd worked with. Didn't provide any concrete evidence of this ethical practice beyond his own assertions.

Suspicious.

Mabs switched to the second laptop—the library's computer, which had access to newspaper archives and professional databases—and started digging deeper. Business filings. Articles of incorporation. Tax records.

Conrad Fischer Fine Arts, LLC. Registered in Georgia in 2005. Annual revenue... Mabs squinted at the numbers. Two million dollars last year. Not bad for a gallery, but not spectacular either. Certainly not enough to maintain three premium locations in three expensive cities.

Unless there was money coming from somewhere else.

She pulled up property records. The Atlanta gallery space: leased. The Charlotte space: leased. The Miami space: owned. Purchased in 2017 for $800,000 cash.

Cash. For a gallery owner whose business showed two million in annual revenue.

Mabs wrote: WHERE DID THE CASH COME FROM?

She checked Fischer's other assets. House in Atlanta suburbs: $450,000, purchased 2010. Car registration: BMW 7 Series, 2022. Boat: 30-foot cabin cruiser, docked at Lake Lanier, purchased 2020.

The math wasn't adding up. Fischer's visible income didn't match his lifestyle and assets.

Which meant invisible income.

The third laptop was connected to... well, technically Mabs wasn't supposed to have access to this database anymore, but her old colleague at the Georgia Bureau of Investigation had never removed her credentials, and Mabs believed that information that existed to serve the public good should be accessible to people who would use it for public good.

It was a gray area. Mabs was comfortable

with gray areas.

She logged into the GBI database and searched for Conrad Fischer.

Two results.

The first was a complaint filed in 2018 by an Afghan artist named Rashid Ahmadi. Allegations of contract fraud—Fischer had allegedly agreed to sell Ahmadi's paintings for $5,000 each, sold them for $15,000 each, and only paid Ahmadi the original $5,000. Ahmadi claimed Fischer had pocketed the difference. The complaint was dismissed after Ahmadi withdrew it. Note in the file: "Complainant stated he did not wish to pursue further. Possible immigration concerns."

Immigration concerns. Which meant Ahmadi had been afraid that complaining would jeopardize his status in the US.

Predator, Mabs thought coldly. Fischer had targeted someone vulnerable and counted on their fear to avoid consequences.

The second result was from 2020. An FBI inquiry into Fischer's finances, flagged as part of a larger investigation into art-based money laundering. The inquiry had gone nowhere—insufficient evidence to proceed. But the flag remained in the system.

So the FBI suspected Fischer of money laundering. They just hadn't been able to prove it.

Mabs sat back, thinking. Fischer had money from somewhere that wasn't his gallery's official revenue. He targeted refugee artists, possibly exploiting them. The FBI suspected money laundering but couldn't make it stick.

And now he was dead in Bea's studio with her paintings missing.

This wasn't about Bea personally. This was business.

Her phone buzzed. Text from Dodo: THE CATS SAID I SHOULD BRING SNICKERDOODLES TO THE LIBRARY. ARE YOU THERE?

Mabs smiled despite herself. Twenty years of book club had taught her that Dodo's chaos usually contained useful information if you paid attention. She texted back: RESEARCH ROOM. DOOR'S OPEN.

Five minutes later, Dodo burst in carrying a plate of cookies and radiating dramatic energy. She wore a flowing purple caftan, multiple necklaces, and the expression of someone who had just solved all the world's problems.

"Mabel, Sherlock told me something very

important." Dodo set down the cookies and settled into a chair with the confidence of someone who knew she was about to be vindicated.

"What did Sherlock tell you?" Mabs took a cookie. They were excellent—Dodo might believe her cats were psychic, but she also made the best snickerdoodles in Western North Carolina.

"That we should look at who benefits from Bea being suspected of murder."

Mabs blinked. "That's... actually a very good point."

"Sherlock is a very intelligent cat. Pancake is pretty but not brilliant. Princess has opinions about everything." Dodo helped herself to a cookie. "So I've been thinking: if Bea didn't kill Conrad Fischer—"

"She didn't."

"—then someone wanted it to look like she did. Which means someone benefits from her being arrested."

"Who benefits?"

Dodo pulled out her phone, which had a cover featuring cats wearing crowns, and scrolled through notes. "I made a list. First:

whoever stole the paintings. They're valuable, and with Fischer dead and Bea in jail, there's no one to say where they came from."

"True."

"Second: anyone who wanted Fischer dead but didn't want to be a suspect themselves. Framing Bea gives them cover."

"Also true."

"Third: anyone who wants to silence Bea specifically. Those paintings tell her story. Maybe someone doesn't want that story told."

Mabs put down her cookie. "Dodo, that's brilliant."

"The cats are brilliant. I'm just their translator." Dodo preened slightly. "But also, I was thinking about the poison. Morrison told his niece, who told Linda at The Country Kitchen, who told me that it was Asian plant-based poison. Slow-acting."

"Linda from The Country Kitchen is a gossip," Mabs said automatically.

"Linda from The Country Kitchen knows everything that happens in Franklin within four hours of it happening. She's a resource." Dodo consulted her phone again. "So. Asian poison. That points to someone with botanical knowledge, which means Maya or Bea. But it could also be someone framing them specifically. Like the killer knew exactly what kind of poison would implicate the right people."

"Suggesting the killer knows both Maya and Bea well enough to frame them convincingly."

"Right. So I made another list." Dodo produced a handwritten sheet covered in purple ink and cat hair. "People who know both Maya and Bea well enough to frame them."

The list was surprisingly comprehensive:
- Anyone from Tuesday night mahjong (eliminated because family)
- Maya's customers at the apothecary (too many to investigate)
- Bea's fellow artists at the studio (possible)
- Anyone who's attended Bea's art shows (public, many people)
- Someone from Bea's past (Vietnam? refugee camps? early days in America?)

"I think it's someone from Bea's past," Dodo said. "Because this feels personal. Not just business. Personal."

Mabs looked at her friend—conspiracy theorist, cat enthusiast, retired 911 dispatcher who'd spent thirty years managing crisis calls and developed PTSD that manifested as elaborate theories about how everything was connected.

Sometimes Dodo's theories were completely wrong. But sometimes, buried in the chaos, there was truth.

"Personal how?" Mabs asked.

"The paintings they stole. The four they took are about the journey, the escape, the survival. The two they left are about her parents dying and arriving with nothing. If you wanted to profit, you'd take all six. But they only took the ones that tell a marketable story." Dodo's voice was surprisingly clear, no drama for once. "That's calculated. That's someone who knows refugee art sells better when it's inspiring instead of devastating. That's someone in the art world."

Mabs added to her notes: KILLER = ART WORLD INSIDER. KNOWS WHAT SELLS.

"And," Dodo continued, "if they know Bea well enough to frame her, they probably know she'd refuse to sell those paintings. So they had to steal them and remove Fischer at the same time. Two birds, one stone. Murder and art theft in one convenient frame-job."

"With Bea as the fall guy."

"Exactly." Dodo ate another cookie. "The cats think we should look at Fischer's business partners. And I think the cats are right."

Mabs turned to her computer and started a new search: Conrad Fischer's business partners, gallery associates, anyone else in his network.

What she found was interesting.

Fischer's galleries were officially owned by Conrad Fischer Fine Arts, LLC. But the LLC had three partners: Conrad Fischer (60%), Minh Nguyen (30%), and Lotus Holdings LLC (10%).

Minh Nguyen. Vietnamese name. Thirty percent ownership.

Mabs searched for Minh Nguyen. Found a website for Nguyen Fine Arts International. Galleries in Atlanta, Houston, San Francisco, Los Angeles. Specializing in—of course—Asian and refugee art.

Minh Nguyen's website included a biography. Born in Vietnam, came to America as a young man, built a gallery empire over thirty years. "Dedicated to amplifying Vietnamese voices through art." Photographs showed an elegant man in his fifties, well-dressed, confident.

And familiar. Mabs had seen that face

somewhere before.

She clicked through to Nguyen's gallery websites. The Los Angeles location had hosted an exhibition last year: "Between Worlds: Vietnamese-American Artists." The exhibition catalog included photographs.

One photograph showed Nguyen at the opening, standing next to an artist. And in the background, slightly out of focus but clearly visible, was Bea Tran.

Mabs enlarged the photo. Yes. Definitely Bea. She'd been at Nguyen's gallery in Los Angeles.

When? The exhibition was in March. Eight months ago.

Had Bea known Nguyen? Or had this been a chance attendance at an exhibition featuring Vietnamese-American artists?

Mabs texted Donnie: FOUND FISCHER'S BUSINESS PARTNER. MINH NGUYEN. VIETNAMESE ART DEALER. 30% OWNERSHIP. BEA WAS AT HIS LA GALLERY LAST MARCH. NEED TO KNOW IF SHE KNOWS HIM.

Response came immediately: GOOD WORK. WILL ASK BEA. KEEP DIGGING.

"We found something," Mabs told Dodo.

"The cats knew we would." Dodo looked smug. "What's next?"

"Next, we find out everything about Minh Nguyen. Where he is, what he does, who he knows, and whether he had any reason to kill his business partner and frame Bea Tran."

Mabs's fingers flew over the keyboard, searching databases, cross-referencing information, building a picture of a man who owned galleries across America and specialized in the exact kind of art that had been stolen from Bea's studio.

An hour later, she had a comprehensive file:

Minh Nguyen, fifty-four. Born in Saigon, 1970. Came to America in 1978—boat person, like Bea. Settled in California. Built gallery business starting in the 1990s. Now owned four galleries, all successful. Net worth estimated at $15 million.

Property records showed he owned a house in Santa Monica ($2.3 million), a condo in Atlanta ($600,000), and a vacation home in Vietnam ($400,000). He traveled frequently—TSA records showed multiple international trips per year, mostly to Vietnam, Singapore, and

Hong Kong.

No criminal record. No complaints filed. No red flags.

Except.

Mabs found a mention in an art world newsletter from 2019. A Vietnamese artist named Tran Bao had accused Nguyen of selling his paintings without permission and keeping the proceeds. The accusation was quickly retracted, with Tran Bao issuing a statement that it had been a "misunderstanding."

Another artist. Another accusation. Another retraction.

The pattern was there if you looked for it.

And Minh Nguyen had been business partners with Conrad Fischer, who was now dead.

Mabs picked up her phone and called Donnie.

"Tell me you found something," Donnie answered.

"Minh Nguyen. Fischer's business partner. Owns galleries, specializes in refugee art, particularly Vietnamese. Clean record publicly, but there are accusations that keep getting retracted. Artists claiming exploitation, then recanting."

"Intimidation?"

"Or immigration pressure. Most of these artists are refugees or immigrants. They're vulnerable."

"So Nguyen and Fischer were partners in a gallery business that may have been systematically exploiting refugee artists."

"That's what it looks like. And Donnie? Nguyen travels to Vietnam frequently. According to his social media, he was there last month."

"Doing what?"

"According to his posts: sourcing new artists, supporting the Vietnamese art community. But I'm thinking maybe also: acquiring art that can't be traced, bringing it to America, selling it as refugee stories."

"Art trafficking."

"Maybe. And if Fischer and Nguyen were partners but Fischer was getting too greedy or too careless—"

"Nguyen eliminates the liability and frames someone convenient."

"Exactly." Mabs looked at her notes, at the careful research that had turned a random art dealer into a possible murderer. "Do we know where Nguyen is now?"

"Let me find out. Good work, Mabs."

After hanging up, Mabs sat back and looked at her three laptops, her legal pads, her organized chaos of research. Forty-three years as a librarian had taught her that stories had patterns. That information, properly organized, revealed truth. That if you asked the right questions and looked in the right places, you could solve almost any mystery.

Dodo was feeding cookies to an invisible audience—possibly her cats spiritually, possibly just herself. "We did good work today."

"We did," Mabs agreed.

"Can I tell you something?" Dodo's voice was quieter now, less performative.

"Always."

"The reason I'm good at this—at seeing patterns, at connecting things—is because I spent thirty years on 911 calls hearing people in the worst moments of their lives. And I started seeing patterns there too. The way abusers talk. The way victims sound. The way witnesses remember things differently but the truth is always somewhere in the middle."

Mabs reached across the desk and took Dodo's hand. "I know."

"And then I retired and I needed the patterns to still make sense, so I started seeing them everywhere. In the news. In my neighbors. In my cats." Dodo laughed, but it was a sad sound. "My therapist says it's how I process trauma. By making everything a conspiracy, I make it controllable."

"The world is scary when bad things are random," Mabs said gently. "It's less scary when there's a pattern, even if the pattern is conspiracy."

"Exactly." Dodo squeezed her hand. "But this? This really is a conspiracy. Someone really did systematically plan to kill Fischer and frame Bea. So for once, I'm not being paranoid."

"For once, you're exactly right."

"The cats will be so pleased."

They sat together in the library's research room, two retirement-age women with cats and coffee and laptops, solving a murder that the police thought was simple but they knew was complex.

Found family came in many forms. Tuesday night mahjong. Cookies and conspiracy theories. Research and friendship and the knowledge that when one of your own was in trouble, you showed up with skills and cookies and refused to stop until justice was done.

Bea hadn't killed anyone. They all knew it.

Now they just had to prove it.

And maybe, in the process, expose a systematic exploitation of refugee artists that had been hiding in plain sight for years.

Mabs looked at her comprehensive notes on Minh Nguyen and thought: You made a mistake. You thought Bea was alone. You thought she was vulnerable.

But Bea had a mahjong group. And a mahjong group was a force of nature when properly motivated.

"Let's go to Donnie's," Mabs said. "It's time to share what we found."

"Should I bring more cookies?"

"Always bring more cookies."

They gathered their materials—laptops, notes, cookies—and headed out into Franklin's November morning, ready to take the next step in proving Bea innocent and bringing down a murderer.

The mountains watched in their ancient silence, knowing that truth always surfaced eventually. The only question was whether it surfaced in time.

Chapter 6

Evelyn Cho had spent fifteen years as a forensic accountant for the Georgia Bureau of Investigation, and she knew that money always told the truth. People lied. Documents could be forged. Witnesses forgot or misremembered or deliberately obscured. But money—money moved in patterns, left trails, revealed motivations with mathematical precision.

She sat in Maya's apothecary back room, surrounded by the scent of dried lavender and chamomile, with three laptops running simultaneous searches and her old GBI credentials giving her access to databases that technically she shouldn't use anymore but nobody had bothered to revoke.

Conrad Fischer's finances were speaking volumes.

Maya came in with tea—green tea with ginger, the kind Evelyn drank when she needed to think clearly—and set it down without a word. Six months of living together had taught Maya when Evelyn needed conversation and when she needed silence. This was a silence moment.

"Thank you," Evelyn said anyway, reaching for the cup without looking away from her screen.

"Find something?"

"Everything." Evelyn pulled up a spreadsheet showing Fischer's financial network. "Fischer wasn't just an art dealer. He was running a full-scale money laundering operation disguised as refugee art sales."

Maya pulled up a chair. "Show me."

Evelyn turned the laptop. "Here's Fischer's main gallery—Conrad Fischer Fine Arts in Atlanta. Official revenue: two million dollars annually. Documented sales, taxes paid, everything legitimate. But look at these three shell companies." She highlighted them. "Eclipse Holdings, Lotus Trading, Pacific Arts LLC. They're registered in Delaware, operated by Fischer, and they process eight million dollars annually in cash transactions."

"Cash?"

"Cash. Art purchases from 'private collectors,' sales to 'international buyers,' all documented just enough to avoid immediate scrutiny but not enough to actually trace."

Evelyn pulled up another screen. "And it gets better. These shell companies share bank accounts with Minh Nguyen's galleries."

"The business partner Mabs found."

"Right. Nguyen owns thirty percent of Fischer's business. But he also owns his own gallery network—Nguyen Fine Arts International. Four galleries across the US, all specializing in Asian and refugee art." Evelyn's fingers flew across the keyboard. "And Nguyen's network processes another twelve million annually through similar shell companies."

Maya was quiet for a moment, thinking. "So Fischer and Nguyen were partners in both the legitimate galleries and the money laundering operation."

"Exactly. And the refugee art angle is perfect for it. Art values are subjective—who's to say whether a painting is worth five thousand or fifty thousand? You buy a painting from a desperate refugee artist for cheap, document it as a much higher purchase price, then 'sell' it to a shell company for an inflated price. The money gets cleaned, the refugee artist gets paid a fraction, and you pocket the difference."

"That's..." Maya's voice was tight with anger. "That's exploiting trauma for profit."

"That's exactly what it is." Evelyn pulled up another document. "And it's systematic. Look at this list—refugee artists Fischer and Nguyen have worked with over the past ten years. Vietnamese, Syrian, Afghan, Somali, Cambodian. All documented, all 'ethically sourced,' all sold for amounts that don't quite match the payments to artists."

The list was long. Dozens of names. Dozens of artists whose stories had been bought cheap and sold expensive.

And fourth from the top: Bea Tran.

Evelyn stared at the name. "Bea sold to Fischer before?"

"She must have. Early on, before she understood what he was doing." Maya leaned closer. "When did she work with him?"

"2018. Three paintings. Documented purchase price: twenty thousand each. Actual payment to Bea..." Evelyn clicked through to the wire transfer records. "Five thousand each."

"He stole forty-five thousand dollars from her."

"And she probably didn't realize it. If he told her paintings were worth five thousand and that's what she got paid, how would she know he was selling them for four times that?"

Maya stood up, paced to the window. Outside, Franklin was going about its Tuesday morning business—people walking to The Country Kitchen for breakfast, shops opening on Main Street, the mountains standing witness to everything. "This is why she wouldn't sell him the 'Between Waters' series. She learned."

"She learned he was a predator." Evelyn pulled up more records. "And she wasn't the only one. Look at this pattern—artists sell to Fischer once or twice, then stop. Either they figure out what he's doing, or they get scared off."

"But Fischer kept pushing Bea."

"Because the 'Between Waters' paintings are valuable. Really valuable. Those aren't small watercolors—they're four-by-six-foot pieces, masterfully executed, telling a compelling refugee story. Conservative estimate? They're worth three hundred thousand as a set. But Fischer could have sold them internationally for twice that."

"So he kept harassing her."

"And when she wouldn't sell, someone killed him and took them anyway." Evelyn sat back, thinking. "But here's what doesn't make sense. If Nguyen and Fischer were partners, and the money laundering operation was working, why kill Fischer? They were making millions together."

"Unless they weren't partners anymore," Maya said slowly. "Or unless one of them wanted a bigger share."

Evelyn pulled up the partnership documents. Conrad Fischer Fine Arts LLC. Fischer: sixty percent ownership. Nguyen: thirty percent. Lotus Holdings LLC: ten percent.

"What's Lotus Holdings?" Maya asked.

"That's what I'm trying to figure out." Evelyn searched business registries, corporate filings, tax documents. Lotus Holdings LLC was registered in Delaware in 2015, same year Fischer shifted his focus to refugee art. Officers: listed as "various." Address: a mail forwarding service in Wilmington.

Classic shell company setup. Designed to hide ownership.

"Whoever owns Lotus Holdings owns ten percent of Fischer's business," Evelyn said. "And they're carefully hidden."

"Can you find them?"

"Maybe. If I follow the money backwards."

Evelyn pulled up banking records, started tracing deposits and withdrawals from Lotus Holdings' accounts. The company received quarterly payments from Fischer's gallery—profit distributions. And those payments were immediately transferred to...

Evelyn stopped.

"What?" Maya asked.

"The payments go to a bank in Singapore." Evelyn clicked through screens, following the trail. "From Singapore to Hong Kong. From Hong Kong to..." She paused, not believing what she was seeing. "To Pyongyang."

"North Korea?"

"North Korea." Evelyn sat back, mind racing. "Fischer and Nguyen were laundering money through refugee art, and some of that money was going to North Korea. That's not just money laundering. That's sanctions evasion. That's federal."

"That's why David died," Maya said quietly.

Evelyn looked at her. Maya stood by the window, backlit by November sun, and Evelyn could see in her expression the understanding that was dawning.

"David found this," Maya continued. "When he was prosecuting STX Associates. He found the art trafficking connection. And someone killed him to stop him from exposing it."

Evelyn's hands were shaking. She put them flat on the desk to steady them. For six months she'd been living with the knowledge that David had been murdered. For six months she'd been tracking the conspiracy that killed him. And now, finally, she understood the full scope.

"STX Associates was construction company laundering money," Evelyn said. "But they were connected to a larger network. Fischer and Nguyen were part of that network. Using art instead of construction, but the same principle—take dirty money, clean it through transactions, send it where it needs to go."

"And when David got too close, they killed him."

"And made it look like an accident. Car forced off a mountain road." Evelyn's voice was steady but her hands were still shaking. "Just like they killed Fischer and tried to make it look like Bea did it."

Maya crossed the room, pulled a chair next

to Evelyn's, took her hands. "We're going to stop them. We're going to get justice for David and for Bea and for every refugee artist they exploited."

"How?"

"Same way we always do. We gather evidence, we work together, and we refuse to stop until the truth comes out." Maya squeezed her hands. "You have the financial evidence. Mabs has the research. I have the community connections. Donnie has investigation expertise. We put it together and we take them down."

Evelyn nodded, steadying herself. David's death had broken her. Healing had been slow, painful, incomplete. But she'd survived. She'd built a new life in Franklin, found Maya, joined the Tuesday night mahjong group, learned that found family was real and powerful and worth fighting for.

And now she'd found the people who killed David.

"I need to call AUSA Walsh," Evelyn said. "The prosecutor from the STX case. This is federal. FBI needs to be involved."

"Do it. But Donnie needs to know first. If FBI comes in, Morrison loses jurisdiction and Bea might get caught in the middle."

Evelyn checked her watch. Ten-thirty AM. Donnie had said noon for the emergency mahjong session. But this couldn't wait.

She texted Donnie: URGENT. FOUND NORTH KOREA CONNECTION. FISCHER = SANCTIONS EVASION. DAVID'S DEATH CONNECTED. NEED TO TALK NOW.

Response came in thirty seconds: MAYA'S APOTHECARY. 10 MINUTES.

Evelyn looked at the screens full of financial data—the evidence of systematic exploitation, money laundering, international conspiracy. It was all there. Everything they needed to prove Bea innocent and bring down the people who'd killed David.

But she also knew that exposing this would have consequences. FBI would take over. Federal prosecutors would want to control the narrative. And Bea, innocent Bea who'd just wanted to paint her story in peace, would be caught in the machinery of federal investigation.

"We need to protect Bea," Evelyn said.

"We will." Maya stood, went to her herb cabinet, started pulling down jars. "I'm making protection bundles. Herbs for clarity and strength. We'll need both."

"That's not scientific."

"Neither is hope. We're doing it anyway." Maya smiled, and Evelyn felt something settle in her chest. Hope. Love. The determination that came from choosing someone every day despite how hard it was.

They'd been through so much together. Evelyn's deception during the Terry Boone case, Maya's broken trust, the slow rebuilding. The nightmares about David. The therapy. The deliberate choice to keep trying, keep choosing each other, keep building something real.

And now this. Another murder. Another conspiracy. But this time they weren't alone. They had the mahjong group. They had each other.

The door chimed. Donnie and Eddie came in, moving fast. Donnie took one look at Evelyn's face and knew. "How bad?"

"International money laundering ring using refugee art to evade North Korean sanctions. Fischer and Nguyen were partners. David found the connection when he was prosecuting STX. They killed him."

Donnie pulled out a chair, sat down. Eddie stood behind her, hand on her shoulder. "Show me everything."

Evelyn walked them through it. The shell companies. The inflated art sales. The Singapore and Hong Kong banks. The Pyongyang connection. The pattern of exploitation. David's case file from 2023 showing he'd been investigating art trafficking in his last weeks.

Donnie listened in silence, her Miami investigator brain processing everything, connecting dots, seeing patterns. When Evelyn finished, Donnie sat back and said one word: "Goddamnit."

"Yeah."

"This is federal. This is FBI, Treasury, State Department. This is way above Morrison's jurisdiction."

"I know."

"And if we bring in federal, Bea gets caught in it. Witness protection maybe. Definitely relocated. Her life here in Franklin is over."

"I know that too."

Donnie rubbed her face. "But if we don't bring in federal, Fischer's killer stays free and the conspiracy continues. More artists get exploited. More money goes to North Korea. More people die."

It was the fundamental problem. Justice for Bea versus justice for everyone. Personal versus systemic. The choice that wasn't really a choice.

"We have to tell," Eddie said quietly. "Bea would want us to tell. She wouldn't want other artists exploited to protect her."

"Bea might not have a choice about what she wants," Donnie countered. "Federal witnesses don't get to choose their own lives. They get protection and relocation and anonymity. Bea came to Franklin to build a life. We'd be taking that from her."

"Someone already took it from her," Maya said. "The moment they killed Fischer in her studio, her life here changed. We can't pretend it didn't."

Evelyn understood both sides. She'd spent years as a federal witness consultant, helping accountants and informants navigate the justice system. She knew what happened when you testified against international conspiracies. She knew the cost.

But she also knew that silence had costs too.

"Here's what we do," Evelyn said. "We tell Bea everything. We give her the choice. If she wants to testify, we support her. If she wants to walk away, we find another path to justice."

"There isn't another path," Donnie said. "Without Bea's testimony about Fischer harassing her, without her art as evidence, the case falls apart."

"Then we build a case that doesn't depend on her. We focus on Fischer and Nguyen's money laundering. On the shell companies. On the North Korea connection. We make it about the conspiracy, not about Bea."

"Can you do that?"

"I don't know. But I have to try." Evelyn looked at her hands, steady now, ready for work. "David died trying to expose this. I'm not letting that be for nothing."

Donnie stood. "Okay. Here's the plan. We bring Bea here. We tell her everything. We let her decide. Then we call AUSA Walsh and Morrison together, coordinate how this gets handled. We protect Bea as much as we can while still pursuing justice."

"And if Bea wants out?" Maya asked.

"Then we find another way." Donnie's voice was firm. "Bea is one of ours. We don't sacrifice our own for the greater good. We find a way to protect her AND bring down the conspiracy."

"That might not be possible."

"Then we make it possible. That's what we do." Donnie pulled out her phone. "I'm calling David Chen, Bea's lawyer. He needs to be in the room for this conversation."

While Donnie made calls, Evelyn looked at her screens full of evidence. The shell companies. The money trails. The pattern of exploitation that stretched across years and continents. She thought about David, idealistic prosecutor who'd died trying to protect people from corruption. She thought about Bea, refugee artist who'd survived Vietnam only to be targeted in America. She thought about all the artists whose names appeared on that list, whose trauma had been commodified and sold.

And she thought about justice. The messy, complicated, imperfect kind that required sacrifice and compromise and hoping you made the right choices.

"We're doing the right thing," Maya said, reading her thoughts the way she always did.

"Are we? We're about to destroy Bea's life to pursue justice for people we've never met."

"We're giving Bea the choice. That's all we can do."

"What if she chooses wrong?"

"There is no wrong choice. There's just her choice." Maya took Evelyn's hand again. "We support her either way. That's what found family means."

Found family. Tuesday night mahjong. The group that had somehow become the most important people in Evelyn's life, more than her remaining relatives in Atlanta, more than her old GBI colleagues, more than anyone except Maya and David's memory.

They'd found each other through murder and investigation and the slow building of trust. They'd proven that family wasn't about blood or time or even complete honesty. Family was about showing up. About choosing each other when things got hard. About refusing to let the people you loved face darkness alone.

Donnie finished her calls. "David Chen is coming. Morrison is coming. Bea will be here in twenty minutes. We brief her, then we brief law enforcement, then we figure out next steps."

"Should we wait for the emergency mahjong session?" Eddie asked.

"No time. This is too urgent." Donnie checked her watch. "But text the group. Mabs, Dodo, Frankie, Liz. Tell them noon at my place. We're going to need everyone."

While Eddie texted, Maya prepared the space. She lit candles—not for mysticism but for comfort, the ritual of creating sacred space. She arranged chairs. She made more tea. She did what healers did: created an environment where truth could be told and received.

And Evelyn organized her evidence. Printed key documents. Created a presentation that would explain the conspiracy clearly. Prepared to reveal everything she'd found, knowing it would change lives, hoping it would bring justice.

The door chimed again. Morrison came in first, looking harried. Then David Chen, Bea's lawyer, professional and alert. And finally Bea herself, small and quiet, carrying the weight of suspicion that she didn't deserve.

They all sat. Maya poured tea. Evelyn opened her laptop.

"Bea," Donnie said. "We found out why Fischer was killed. And we need to tell you everything. Then you get to decide what happens next."

Bea looked at each of them—Donnie, Evelyn, Maya, Eddie, Morrison, her lawyer. The mahjong group and the officials and the people who wanted to protect her. She nodded once.

"Tell me."

So Evelyn did.

She told Bea about the money laundering. About the exploitation of refugee artists. About the North Korea connection. About David's death. About the conspiracy that had been hiding in plain sight for years, using trauma and survival stories to clean dirty money and evade sanctions.

She told Bea that she'd been targeted. Not randomly. Not personally. But systematically, because her story was valuable and her vulnerability was exploitable and someone had decided that her 'Between Waters' paintings were worth murder and frame-up.

And she told Bea that bringing down the conspiracy would require testimony. Would require publicity. Would require sacrifice.

When she finished, the room was silent except for the sound of Maya's candles burning and the distant noise of Franklin going about its day.

Finally, Bea spoke.

"They stole my parents' deaths," she said quietly. "They took the worst thing that ever happened to me and tried to profit from it. And when I wouldn't let them, they tried to destroy me."

"Yes," Evelyn said.

"And David died trying to stop them."

"Yes."

Bea looked at Morrison. "If I testify, what happens to me?"

Morrison glanced at David Chen, who nodded permission to be honest. "Federal case. FBI takes jurisdiction. You'd be a key witness. Probably witness protection, at least during trial. Relocation after, if they think you're at risk. New identity maybe. Definitely not Franklin."

"So I lose everything again." Bea's voice was steady but her hands trembled. "I lose this life I built. This home. This community. My studio. My work. Everything."

"We don't know that for sure," David Chen said. "I'll fight for alternatives. But Morrison's being realistic. Federal witnesses often do relocate."

"And if I don't testify?"

Morrison looked uncomfortable. "The case against whoever killed Fischer gets weaker. Maybe the money laundering charges stick without you, but the murder case needs your testimony. Without it, they might walk."

Bea was quiet for a long time. Outside, a customer came into the apothecary. Maya went to help them, giving Bea space to think. When Maya returned, Bea had made her decision.

"I'll testify," she said. "Not for me. For all the other artists they exploited. For David. For anyone else they might target." She looked at each of them. "I didn't survive Vietnam to let predators win in America."

Evelyn felt her throat tighten. Bea, small and quiet and so much stronger than anyone realized, choosing justice over safety.

"We'll protect you," Donnie said. "Whatever it takes."

"I know you will. That's what family does." Bea smiled slightly. "And you are family. Tuesday night mahjong is family. Franklin is family. Even if I have to leave, I'll take that with me."

Morrison stood. "I need to make calls. FBI needs to be read in immediately. AUSA Walsh needs to know. This is going to move fast."

"One thing first," Evelyn said. "We need to find Minh Nguyen. He's the key. He knew Bea's story. He had access to the studio. He had motive to kill Fischer if they were fighting over money. He benefits from Bea being silenced."

"Where is Nguyen now?" Morrison asked.

"That's what we need to find out." Evelyn pulled up her phone. "Last known location was Los Angeles. But if he knows we're investigating, he could run."

"I'll put out a BOLO," Morrison said. "Be On the Lookout. If he tries to leave the country, we'll know."

After Morrison left, the group sat together in Maya's apothecary back room, processing what they'd just set in motion. Federal investigation. International conspiracy. The end of Bea's life in Franklin and the beginning of something else.

"I'm scared," Bea said quietly.

"Me too," Maya said.

"Me three," Evelyn added.

"All of us," Donnie confirmed. "But we're scared together. And that makes it bearable."

They sat in the scent of lavender and chamomile, in the warmth of Maya's carefully created space, and they prepared for what came next. Investigation. Testimony. Justice. Change.

The mountains outside watched through the window, ancient and patient. They'd seen this before—people making hard choices, facing consequences, choosing courage over comfort.

And they'd see how this story ended. Whether justice would win. Whether the conspiracy would fall. Whether Bea would survive this second uprooting.

For now, all they could do was move forward together. Found family facing federal conspiracy. Tuesday night mahjong against international money laundering.

It was ridiculous. It was impossible. It was exactly what they were going to do anyway.

Because that's what family did. They showed up. They chose each other. They fought for justice even when it cost everything.

And they refused to let the darkness win.

Chapter 7

The emergency Tuesday night mahjong session began at noon on a Wednesday, which told you everything about how serious this was.

Donnie stood in her living room watching the group arrive. Maya and Evelyn together, holding hands like they needed the physical connection. Mabs with her laptop and binder, organized as always. Dodo with cookies and dramatic energy. Frankie pulling up last, parking his truck with military precision and walking to the door with that slight limp from a workplace accident years ago.

Eddie had already set up the mahjong table—the portable one they kept for occasions when the library wasn't available. He'd pushed aside the coffee table, arranged chairs, and was now in the kitchen making Cuban sandwiches because "people think better when they're fed."

Audrey the poodle sat by the door in judgment position, her tuxedo markings perfectly groomed, her expression suggesting that whatever chaos the humans were about to discuss, she'd already assessed it and found them all wanting.

"Everyone's here," Donnie said when

Frankie walked in. "Let's work."

They settled around the table. Maya unpacked tea supplies. Mabs opened her laptop. Evelyn had her financial documents ready. Dodo produced cookies and an expression that suggested the cats had given her significant intel.

And in the center of the table, waiting, was the mahjong set. White tiles with green characters, organized in their wooden case. The game they played every Tuesday. The ritual that had somehow become the foundation of their found family.

"We're not actually playing," Mabs said.

"No," Donnie agreed. "But we're thinking better with the tiles here."

It was true. Something about having the mahjong set visible, ready, grounded them. Reminded them why they were doing this. Tuesday night mahjong wasn't just a game. It was community. It was choosing each other. It was the deliberate creation of family from friendship.

And family protected their own.

"Okay," Donnie began. "Here's where we are. Conrad Fischer is dead. Bea is framed. The real killer is almost certainly Minh Nguyen,

Fischer's business partner. And the whole thing is part of an international money laundering and sanctions evasion conspiracy."

"Jesus," Frankie muttered.

"It gets worse. David Cho's death is connected. Evelyn's husband. He was prosecuting STX Associates, found the art trafficking connection, got killed for it."

Everyone looked at Evelyn, whose face was controlled but whose hands were clasped tight on the table. Maya put an arm around her.

"So we're not just solving Bea's case," Donnie continued. "We're exposing a conspiracy that reaches from Franklin to North Korea. And we have..." She checked her watch. "Fifty-six hours before Morrison has to charge someone. Right now, that someone is either Bea or Maya, because the poison points to botanical knowledge."

"Which is why the killer chose that poison," Maya said quietly. "Frame one of us, investigators focus there, real killer escapes."

"Exactly. So we need to prove Nguyen did it, find the missing paintings, and build a case strong enough that FBI can prosecute. All in fifty-six hours." Donnie looked around the table. "Who wants to start?"

Mabs raised her hand like she was still in library school. "I researched Nguyen. He's Vietnamese, came to America as a boat person in 1978, same as Bea. Built a gallery empire over thirty years. Worth about fifteen million dollars. Owns properties in California, Atlanta, and Vietnam. No criminal record, but there are complaints from artists that keep getting retracted."

"Intimidation," Frankie said. "Classic. Threaten witnesses, they recant."

"Or immigration pressure," Evelyn added. "Most of these artists are refugees. Vulnerable. Nguyen could threaten their status, their families, their ability to stay in America. They'd withdraw complaints to protect themselves."

"So Nguyen has a pattern of exploiting refugee artists," Donnie said, writing on her whiteboard. "What else?"

"He travels to Vietnam frequently," Mabs continued. "According to his social media, he's 'sourcing new artists' and 'supporting Vietnamese art community.' But I'm thinking it's more like: finding vulnerable artists, bringing their work to America, selling it for profit."

"Art trafficking," Evelyn confirmed. "We found evidence that Fischer and Nguyen were buying art from refugee artists for low prices, documenting higher purchase prices for money laundering purposes, then selling internationally for even higher prices. They were making money on three ends: exploiting artists, laundering dirty money, and evading sanctions."

Dodo raised her hand. "The cats said we should follow the paintings. Where are the four stolen ones now?"

"Unknown," Donnie said. "But good question. Nguyen killed Fischer and took them. Where would he put them?"

"Storage facility," Frankie suggested. "Climate controlled. Professional. He couldn't take them to his galleries—too obvious."

"Or he already sold them," Maya said. "If he had a buyer waiting, he could have transported them immediately."

"Transported how?" Mabs asked. "They're four-by-six feet. Hard to hide."

"Roll them," Evelyn said. "Watercolors on rice paper can be rolled carefully. Put them in a tube, ship them anywhere. FedEx, DHL, private courier."

Donnie wrote on the board: WHERE ARE PAINTINGS? STORAGE? SHIPPED? BUYER

WAITING?

"We need to find them," she said. "They're evidence. And they're Bea's work. She deserves to have them back."

"Morrison put out a BOLO on Nguyen," Evelyn said. "Be On the Lookout. If he tries to leave the country, we'll know."

"But he's smart," Donnie countered. "He's not going to try to flee obviously. He'll stay put, act normal, and let Bea take the fall. Unless we force his hand."

"How do we force his hand?" Frankie asked.

Donnie thought for a moment. In Miami, when she'd worked insurance fraud, the best way to catch a suspect was to make them think they'd gotten away with it. Let them relax. Let them make a mistake. Then catch them in it.

"We leak that Bea's going to be charged," Donnie said slowly. "Let Nguyen think he won. Then we watch what he does next."

"That's risky," Mabs said. "What if he runs?"

"Then we catch him running. Morrison has eyes on airports, borders. But I don't think

Nguyen will run. I think he'll try to sell the paintings. He killed Fischer and framed Bea to get those paintings. He's not going to abandon them now."

"So we set up a sting," Frankie said, military-strategic thinking kicking in. "Leak that Bea's being charged. Watch Nguyen. When he moves the paintings, we're there."

"With FBI backup," Evelyn added. "This is federal now. We coordinate with AUSA Walsh."

Dodo was eating a cookie thoughtfully. "The cats said something about Bea's past. About boat people. About who helped and who didn't."

Everyone looked at her. Dodo's conspiracy theories were usually twenty percent accurate and eighty percent wild speculation. But that twenty percent was often crucial.

"What do you mean?" Maya asked gently.

"Well, when Bea escaped Vietnam, there were boat people who helped each other and boat people who betrayed each other for advantage. Right? That's how it works in crisis. Some people stay human. Some people don't." Dodo pulled out her phone, scrolled through notes. "So I was thinking: what if Nguyen knew Bea from the boat? Or from the camps? What if they have shared history?"

Silence around the table.

"That would explain why he targeted her specifically," Maya said slowly. "Not just business. Personal. He knew her story intimately because he lived it."

"Or near it," Mabs added. "Same timeframe, same route, same camps possibly. Even if they weren't on the same boat, they might have crossed paths."

Donnie felt pieces clicking into place. "If Nguyen knew Bea from back then, he'd know her trauma triggers. He'd know exactly how to exploit her. And he'd know she'd never trust him, which is why he used Fischer as the front man."

"And when Fischer became a liability—too greedy, too careless, too willing to push Bea too hard—Nguyen eliminated him."

"Business and personal," Eddie said from the kitchen doorway, where he'd been listening. "The best villains always have mixed motives. Pure evil is boring. But someone who survived trauma and decided to exploit other survivors? That's complex. That's interesting. That's human and terrible at the same time."

"This isn't a novel," Frankie said.

"Everything's a novel if you're paying

attention." Eddie brought out sandwiches. "But Donnie's right. If Nguyen and Bea have shared history, that's the key. That's what we need to find."

"Bea would know," Maya said. "If she saw Nguyen's photo, she'd recognize him from the boats or camps."

"Then we show her photos," Donnie decided. "Mabs, can you pull up everything on Nguyen? Photos from his website, social media, gallery events. Print them. We take them to Bea and see if she recognizes him. See if she admits it."

"On it." Mabs's fingers flew over her keyboard.

While Mabs worked, the group ate Eddie's sandwiches—Cuban-style, with roast pork and ham and Swiss cheese and pickles, pressed until crispy. Comfort food. Fuel for difficult work.

Audrey positioned herself strategically near Eddie's feet, hoping for dropped crumbs and maintaining her judgmental expression. The poodle had impeccable timing for appearing whenever food was involved.

"I've been thinking about the poison," Maya said. "Morrison said it was Asian plant-based, slow-acting. That's not many options.

Probably something from the aconite family or similar alkaloids."

"Can you source it?" Donnie asked.

"Maybe. There are specialty importers, botanical supply companies, traditional medicine suppliers. It's not common, but it's available if you know where to look." Maya pulled out her phone. "I'll contact my network. Someone will know who sells this."

"And if we can trace the purchase to Nguyen, that's evidence," Evelyn said.

Frankie had been quiet, thinking. Now he spoke. "The window exit. We know someone went out the bathroom window. I want to examine it more closely. Size restrictions, physical requirements. If we can prove Nguyen fits the profile, that helps."

"Good," Donnie said. "Frankie, you check the window. Maya, you trace the poison. Evelyn, you keep digging into finances—any connection between Nguyen and North Korea directly. Mabs, you research Nguyen's Vietnam history—when he came over, which camp, any records. Dodo, you..." Donnie paused. "You do whatever it is you do that somehow always turns out to be useful."

"The cats and I will investigate the astral plane," Dodo said seriously. "And also

I'll bake more cookies and talk to everyone at The Country Kitchen because Linda knows everything."

"Perfect. Everyone reports back at..." Donnie checked her watch. "Six PM. Let's meet up at The Slanted Window. We regroup, share intel, plan next steps."

"What about Bea?" Maya asked.

"Bea's with her lawyer and Morrison, making official statements for the federal case. She's safe. And she's made her choice—she's testifying. Our job is to make sure there's someone to testify against."

The group dispersed to their assigned tasks. But before they left, Maya did something that had become tradition. She built the walls for mahjong—stacking tiles two high, creating the square that defined the game space.

"For luck," she said.

"For focus," Mabs corrected.

"For family," Evelyn added.

They stood around the table, looking at the tile walls. The ritual that held them together. The game that had become more than a game.

"Fifty-six hours," Donnie said. "We can do

this."

"We've done harder," Maya agreed.

"We solved Terry Boone's murder in less time," Mabs pointed out.

"And we had less evidence then," Evelyn said.

"Plus the cats are on our side," Dodo added. "That's significant cosmic support."

Frankie just grunted, which was his way of saying agreement without actually committing to optimism.

They left in ones and twos, each to their task. Eddie started cleaning up, Audrey supervising from her position of judgment. And Donnie stood at her whiteboard, looking at the web of connections they'd built.

Conrad Fischer: murdered. Minh Nguyen: suspect. Bea Tran: framed. Four paintings: missing. International conspiracy: exposed. David Cho: finally getting justice.

Fifty-six hours to solve it all.

Donnie had spent thirty years as an insurance fraud investigator in Miami-Dade. She'd cracked cases that seemed impossible. She'd followed evidence through mazes of deception. She'd caught liars and frauds and criminals who thought they were untouchable.

This was no different. Just higher stakes.

And this time, she wasn't alone. She had a mahjong group. A found family. People who showed up when things got hard and refused to leave until justice was done.

Bless their hearts if they thought she was scary in Miami. They hadn't seen her with a mahjong group backing her up.

"You're smiling," Eddie said from the kitchen.

"I'm thinking about how badly Nguyen miscalculated."

"Because?"

"Because he thought Bea was alone. Vulnerable. Easy to frame. He didn't count on Bea having six women, one novelist, and a judgmental poodle who refuse to let injustice stand."

"Seven women," Eddie corrected. "Don't forget Liz."

"Eight if we count Norma. And Eric will help because Eric helps everyone." Donnie's smile widened. "Nguyen has no idea what's coming for him."

"Good," Eddie said. "Let's keep it that way."

Donnie took a photo of her whiteboard, sent it to Morrison with a message: WORKING ALL ANGLES. WILL UPDATE AT 6PM. TELL FBI WE'RE COORDINATING.

Morrison's response: FBI WANTS TO MEET. TOMORROW 9AM. BRING EVERYTHING.

Tomorrow. Less than twenty-four hours. They'd have to work fast.

But that's what they did. Tuesday night mahjong didn't quit. Didn't give up. Didn't let the darkness win.

Donnie looked out her kitchen window at the November afternoon. The chickens were scratching in their run, happy and safe and completely unaware that their owner was about to take down an international money laundering conspiracy.

The mountains rose beyond, blue and purple in the slanting light. Beautiful. Ancient. Patient.

They'd witnessed everything that mattered in these mountains: love, death, justice, injustice, survival. They'd seen people at their best and worst. And they'd keep witnessing long after everyone currently alive was gone.

But for now, in this moment, they were witnessing a mahjong group choosing courage over fear. Justice over convenience. Family over everything.

Fifty-six hours and counting.

Time to work.

Chapter 8

Donnie called Rosa Delgado at three PM, which was midnight in Kabul, but Rosa answered on the second ring because Rosa never slept properly anyway.

"Donnie Carlisle. It's been four months. You forget about your old partner?" Rosa's voice came through clear, that Miami accent that Donnie had missed without realizing it.

"I've been busy."

"Busy with murder, I heard. Franklin, North Carolina got more exciting than Miami?" Rosa laughed. "Tell me everything."

Donnie walked out to the back porch—their sacred space, the two Adirondack chairs where she and Eddie spent evenings with bourbon and conversation—and settled in. The November air was cold enough to see her breath, but she needed the privacy and the mountains as witness.

"Conrad Fischer. You know him?"

Pause. "Art dealer. Atlanta. Bad reputation in certain circles. What about him?"

"He's dead. Murdered in my friend's studio. The friend is being framed. And when I started digging, I found you were right—Fischer was dirty. Money laundering through refugee art sales, sanctions evasion, North Korea connection. The whole thing."

Another pause, longer. "You sure you want to be in this, Donnie? This is federal. This is dangerous."

"My friend needs help. And it connects to something bigger—a prosecutor named David Cho who was killed last year investigating similar patterns. His widow is one of mine now. This is personal."

"Everything's personal for you. That's why you were a good investigator and why you retired before it killed you." But Rosa's voice had shifted to business mode. "What do you need?"

"Everything you know about Fischer. Everything about his partner, Minh Nguyen. Everything about Vietnamese art trafficking. And I need it in forty-eight hours."

"That's ambitious even for you."

"Rosa. Please."

"Okay, okay. Let me make some calls. I still have contacts at FBI, ICE, State Department. Give me two hours."

Donnie hung up and sat in the cold November afternoon, looking at the mountains and thinking about her old life. Twenty years partnering with Rosa Delgado in Miami-Dade's Special Investigation Unit. Twenty years of insurance fraud cases that turned into organized crime investigations. Twenty years of building cases against people who thought they were smarter than two Cuban-American women with badges and determination.

They'd been good. Really good. Closed

cases that other teams gave up on. Took down schemes that seemed impossible to crack. Built reputations as the SIU team you didn't want investigating you.

And then Donnie had retired. Moved to Franklin. Started a dog bakery. Thought she was done with investigation. Rosa had gone to big time investigating fraud and bond defaults by government contractors working in war zones in the Middle East.

Turns out you're never done with investigation when investigation is who you are.

Her phone rang. Not Rosa—too soon. Morrison.

"Donnie. We have a problem."

"What kind of problem?"

"Nguyen's on the move. TSA flagged him at LAX thirty minutes ago. He's booked on a flight to Singapore in two hours."

Donnie stood up fast. "Singapore? That's one step from Vietnam. He's running."

"FBI knows. They're coordinating with LAX security to delay him. But Donnie, if he gets on that plane, we lose him. Singapore doesn't have extradition for financial crimes. We'd have to prove murder to get him back, and our murder case is circumstantial right now."

"What do you need?"

"Evidence. Anything. The paintings, the poison source, a witness who saw him in Franklin. Anything that ties him directly to Fischer's death."

"You have forty-eight hours."

"Nguyen has two hours." Morrison's voice was tight. "FBI is holding the plane, claiming mechanical issues, but that only buys us ninety minutes maximum. After that, either we arrest him or we let him go."

Ninety minutes. Donnie's investigator brain went into overdrive. What could they prove in ninety minutes?

"The paintings," she said. "If Nguyen has them, he's transporting them somehow. He wouldn't leave them behind if he's fleeing. Check his luggage."

"On it. But Donnie, even if we find paintings, how do we prove they're Bea's? He could claim he bought them legitimately."

"They have her signature. And Bea can identify them—the brushstrokes, the specific colors, the rice paper she uses. She'd know her own work."

"Get me photos. Fast. I'll have FBI search his bags."

Donnie ran inside, texted Maya: NEED BEA NOW. PHOTOS OF HER PAINTINGS. NGUYEN FLEEING TO SINGAPORE. 90 MINUTES.

Response in seconds: ON IT. CALLING BEA.

Then Donnie called Frankie. "The window exit. What did you find?"

Frankie's voice was distracted, like he was measuring something. "Window's eighteen by twenty inches. Bathroom is on first floor, six feet off ground. Someone who went through that window had to be small—under 150 pounds probably—and physically fit. No way a big person makes it. And they'd need upper body strength to pull themselves up and through."

"Nguyen?"

"Let me check." Sound of typing. "Nguyen's website has his bio. Five-foot-eight, approximately 155 pounds based on photos. Athletic build. Could fit through that window if he was determined."

"How determined?"

"Pretty determined. It wouldn't be comfortable. But possible."

"Possible is enough. Write it up. Send it to Morrison. We need everything."

Next, Evelyn. "Financial ties between Nguyen and North Korea. What do you have?"

"Nothing direct. But I found travel records—Nguyen goes to Singapore and Hong Kong frequently, and those are common transit points for North Korea trade. And his shell companies do business with companies that have North Korean ties. It's all circumstantial but it's there."

"Send everything to Morrison. Anything that connects Nguyen to illegal activity. We have ninety minutes to stop him from fleeing the country."

Mabs was next. "Vietnam records. Tell me you found something."

"I found the camps." Mabs's voice had that librarian precision that meant she'd hit gold. "Nguyen was in the same refugee camp as Bea. Camp Galang, Indonesia, 1978-1979. They overlapped by six months."

"So he knew her."

"Maybe. The camp had thousands of

people. But they were there at the same time, same age range, both Vietnamese boat people. It's possible they crossed paths."

"More than possible. It's probable. Bea would remember. Send this to Morrison. We need to establish prior connection."

Donnie hung up and texted the group: NGUYEN FLEEING. 90 MINUTES TO STOP HIM. SEND ALL EVIDENCE TO MORRISON NOW.

Her phone rang. Rosa.

"Two hours, I said. I'm giving you thirty minutes." Rosa's voice was all business. "Conrad Fischer. Known to FBI since 2016 for suspected art-based money laundering. Multiple investigations, never enough to prosecute. Partner with Minh Nguyen since 2015. Together they've moved approximately thirty million dollars through shell companies over nine years."

"North Korea connection?"

"Circumstantial but strong. Fischer and Nguyen both travel to Singapore and Hong Kong frequently. Their shell companies do business with known North Korean fronts. Treasury Department has been watching them for sanctions evasion but can't prove direct contact."

"What about Nguyen specifically?"

"Minh Nguyen, fifty-four, Vietnamese refugee, came to US in 1978 as a refugee. Built gallery business starting in early '90s. Very successful, very connected. Also very careful. No criminal record, no complaints that stuck, no red flags except financial patterns that look like laundering."

"He's exploiting refugee artists."

"Of course he is. That's the perfect crime. Refugees are vulnerable, often desperate, don't understand American legal system. You buy their art cheap, document higher prices, sell expensive, pocket the difference. And you get the added benefit of looking ethical because you're 'amplifying marginalized voices.'"

Donnie felt sick. "Any complaints from artists?"

"Four in the past ten years. All withdrawn. One artist—Rashid Ahmadi, Afghan—recanted after his immigration status was suddenly threatened. Pattern suggests intimidation."

"So Nguyen threatens deportation if artists complain."

"That's the theory. But proving it requires artists willing to testify, and they're too scared."

"What if I had one willing to testify?"

"Then you'd have a case. But Donnie..." Rosa's voice changed. "Be careful. If Nguyen's running, he's desperate. Desperate people are dangerous."

"He killed someone and framed my friend. I'm past careful."

"I know. That's what worries me. Don't be a hero. You're retired. You have a husband and chickens and a dog bakery. Let FBI handle this."

"FBI had nine years to handle it. They didn't. Now it's personal."

Rosa sighed. "You never change. Okay. I'm sending you everything I have. Financial records, travel patterns, known associates, complaint history. Use it to nail him."

"Thank you."

"Don't thank me yet. Thank me when you're safe and Nguyen's in federal custody." Rosa paused. "And Donnie? Visit sometime. Miami misses you."

"Franklin's home now and Afghanistan doesn't meet my idea of a great vacation spot."

"Yeah. I figured." Rosa's voice was warm. "But you were a hell of a partner. Best twenty years of my career."

"Same, Rosa. Same."

After hanging up, Donnie sat for a moment feeling the weight of nostalgia. Miami had been good. Rosa had been family. The work had mattered. But she'd burned out. The constant grind of fraud and lies and corruption had worn her down until she couldn't sleep, couldn't eat, couldn't separate work from life.

Franklin had saved her. Eddie had saved her. The decision to retire and start a bakery and just be herself had saved her.

But apparently retirement didn't mean stopping investigation. It just meant investigating for family instead of for salary.

And family was worth more.

Her phone buzzed. Message from Maya: BEA IDENTIFIED PAINTINGS FROM NGUYEN'S SOCIAL MEDIA. HE POSTED PHOTO THREE WEEKS AGO WITH PAINTINGS IN BACKGROUND. "ACQUIRING NEW PIECES." BEA SAYS DEFINITELY HERS. SENDING TO MORRISON.

Then Evelyn: FOUND WIRE TRANSFER TO NGUYEN FROM A SINGAPORE ACCOUNT YESTERDAY. $300,000. SAME AMOUNT

FISCHER OFFERED BEA. NGUYEN WAS BEING PAID BY BUYER.

Then Mabs: BEA CONFIRMS SHE KNEW NGUYEN FROM CAMP. HE WAS "KIND" TO YOUNG GIRLS. HELPED THEM WITH FOOD AND WATER. SHE TRUSTED HIM. THEN SHE GOT QUIET. THAT'S HOW HE KNEW HER STORY.

Pieces falling into place. Nguyen had known Bea from the refugee camps. Had gained her trust. Had learned her story intimately—the boat, her parents drowning, the survival guilt. He'd waited forty-five years, built a gallery empire, and then targeted her specifically because he knew exactly what art to steal and exactly how to exploit her trauma.

Predator. Cold. Calculating. Patient.

Donnie called Morrison. "Tell me you got him."

"FBI searched his bags. Found four rolled canvases in a tube labeled 'prints for Singapore gallery.' Bea's signature on all four. Nguyen claimed he bought them legally but can't produce receipts. They're holding him."

"Charge him."

"With what? Possession of stolen art gets him detained but not arrested. We need murder charges."

"You have opportunity—he knew Bea, knew the studio, knew her schedule. You have means—he's physically capable of the window exit, he has connections to get poison. You have motive—he wanted the paintings, he needed to eliminate Fischer, and he needed Bea silenced."

"It's still circumstantial."

"Then make it not circumstantial. Put Bea in a room with Nguyen. See if he confesses."

"That's dangerous."

"That's necessary." Donnie stood, paced. "Nguyen thinks he's won. He thinks Bea's going to be charged and he's going to escape. Use that. Let him think Bea's broken, desperate, willing to deal. See if he slips."

Morrison was quiet. "You want me to use Bea as bait."

"I want you to give Bea the chance to face her predator and get justice. She's strong enough."

"Let me talk to FBI. And Bea. And her lawyer. This is above my pay grade."

"Call me back in twenty minutes."

Donnie hung up and looked at the mountains, beautiful and impassive in the afternoon light. Cold November afternoon, sun slanting through bare trees, the smell of woodsmoke from somewhere nearby.

This was home now. These mountains. This town. These people. This life she'd built with Eddie and Audrey and chickens and a bakery that sold treats for dogs.

And the Tuesday night mahjong group that had somehow become the most important thing in her life.

They'd solved Terry Boone's murder. They were going to solve Conrad Fischer's murder. And they were going to expose a conspiracy that had been hiding for years.

Because that's what family did. Showed up. Fought. Refused to quit until justice was done.

Her phone rang. Morrison.

"FBI agreed. Bea agreed. Nguyen's in interrogation room B at LAX federal facility. We're setting up video feed. You can watch from my office."

"I'm there in ten minutes."

Donnie grabbed her truck keys, yelled to Eddie that she was leaving, and drove to Franklin PD faster than was strictly legal. The whole mahjong group was probably converging on Morrison's office right now. They wouldn't miss this.

Forty-five years Nguyen had been free. Forty-five years he'd been exploiting refugees, laundering money, profiting from trauma.

And now, in an interrogation room at LAX, a sixty-five-year-old artist who'd survived a boat escape was going to take him down.

Bless his heart. Nguyen had no idea what was coming.

Chapter 9

Bea Tran sat in the federal interrogation room in front of a bank of monitors and thought about water.

The boat. The South China Sea. Her mother's hand slipping from hers as the wave hit. Her father disappearing below the surface, weighted down by the small bag of valuables he'd insisted on carrying. The water dark and endless and swallowing everything that mattered.

She'd been fifteen years old. She'd survived. And for forty-five years, she'd carried the guilt of that survival like a stone in her pocket.

Why am I alive when they died?

The question never left. Not when she arrived in America with nothing but her grandmother's jade bracelet. Not when she learned English and went to art school and built a life from loss. Not when she painted the "Between Waters" series, trying to make sense of survival through watercolor and rice paper.

The question was always there. Why me?

And now, sitting viewing Minh Nguyen in a federal interrogation room, Bea finally understood the answer.

I survived so I could be here. Right now. Facing him.

Nguyen looked older than she remembered from Camp Galang. Then he'd been young—twenty-three, maybe—confident, helpful to the young girls, always knowing how to get extra food or water or space away from the crowds. She'd trusted him. Everyone had trusted him. At first.

Now he was looking well-dressed in expensive clothes. Professional. Successful. The kind of refugee success story that politicians liked to point to as proof that the American dream worked.

Except his success was built on the suffering of others. On exploitation. On taking trauma and turning it into profit.

"Bea." Nguyen smiled like they were old friends meeting for coffee. "I didn't expect to see you here."

She didn't smile back. In the other monitors she could see Morrison and the FBI were watching. The Tuesday night mahjong group was watching from Franklin. Her lawyer sat next to her. And Maya was there somewhere —Maya who'd made her special tea this morning, who'd driven her to this office, who'd held her hand until the last possible moment.

You're not alone, Maya had said. We're with you. All of us.

Found family. The thing she'd built in

Franklin after forty-five years of being careful, being quiet, being grateful just to exist.

"You remember me," Bea said. It wasn't a question.

"Of course. Camp Galang. You were the quiet girl who painted on whatever paper she could find. Always drawing the water, the boats. Processing your trauma." Nguyen's English was perfect, American accent with just a trace of Vietnamese. "I admired that. Art as healing."

"Is that why you targeted me? Is that why you used me? Because you knew my trauma intimately?"

Nguyen's smile flickered. "I don't know what you mean."

"Yes, you do." Bea kept her voice steady, the way she'd learned to keep her hands steady when painting. Control. Precision. "You knew me from the camp. You knew my story—my parents drowning, the guilt, the survival. You used me to get to others. You traded me for information, money and favors. You waited forty-five years, came after me again and hid behind Conrad Fischer to pressure me into selling my paintings. When I refused, you killed him and stole them anyway."

"That's an interesting story. You have

evidence?"

"You have my paintings in your luggage. Four watercolors from the 'Between Waters' series. You can't produce receipts because you didn't buy them. You stole them."

"I acquired them through a third party. Perfectly legal."

"Conrad Fischer?"

"Perhaps, perhaps others."

Bea watched him. She'd spent sixty-five years reading people—learning to see the truth in body language, in the small gestures people made when words lied. It came from survival. From needing to know who to trust on a boat full of desperate people, in camps full of predators, in America full of people who saw refugees as problems instead of people.

Nguyen was lying. But he was good at it. Practiced. Professional.

"Why?" Bea asked. "You survived the same thing I survived. You know what we lost. Why would you exploit other refugees?"

"Exploit?" Nguyen laughed. "I gave refugees a platform. I sold their art to wealthy Americans who wanted to support refugee voices. I made them money."

"You made yourself money. You bought art cheap, sold it expensive, kept the difference. And when artists complained, you threatened their immigration status."

"That's slander."

"That's truth. Rashid Ahmadi. Tran Bao. Four others. All complained. All recanted after you threatened them." Bea leaned forward. "And me. You couldn't threaten me—I'm a citizen, I have a lawyer, I have community. So you eliminated your partner and framed me instead."

Nguyen's expression finally changed. The professional mask slipped slightly, revealing calculation underneath. "You can't prove any of this."

"Actually, we can." Bea pulled out her phone—her lawyer had coached her on this, Morrison had approved it—and showed him a photograph. "This is you at Camp Galang, 1978. I found it in the camp archives. You're standing next to the water distribution station."

Nguyen looked at the photograph. Bea watched his face carefully.

"You helped distribute water," she continued. "You knew who needed it most. Who was desperate. You learned who to manipulate." She showed another photograph. "And here you are in the same camp, talking to a group of young girls. Including me. I'm fifteen, sitting on the ground in front of you, looking up like you're someone important."

"This proves nothing."

"It proves you knew me. It proves you had access to my story. It proves forty-five years ago you positioned yourself to gain trust so you could exploit it later." Bea set down her phone. "You're very patient. I'll give you that. But that patience made you predictable. Now I'm going to tell them what you did to me."

"You're grasping, why would they believe you over me?" Nguyen said. But his hands had clenched slightly. Small tell.

"The poison," Bea said. "Plant-based, Asian variety. Designed to implicate me or Maya, the two people in Franklin with botanical knowledge. But you had to acquire that poison somewhere. And Maya traced it to a specialty importer in Asheville. They have records of a purchase three weeks ago. Paid in cash. Security camera footage shows you."

Nguyen's jaw tightened.

"The window," Bea continued. "Bathroom

exit, eighteen by twenty inches. You fit through it. Barely. FBI found cotton fibers on the window frame that match your shirt. The shirt you were wearing when they detained you."

"Circumstantial."

"The paintings in your luggage have my signature. My specific watercolor technique. Rice paper I special order from Vietnam. Bea pulled out another photograph—one of her paintings, clearly showing her signature and distinctive style. "You can't reproduce that. You can't claim you bought these legally without receipts. And the FBI already ran the purchase history—no record of sale anywhere."

Nguyen sat back. Bea could see him calculating, trying to find an exit, trying to figure out if he could still lie his way clear.

"And Conrad Fischer's murder," Bea said quietly. "You were his business partner. You knew about the money laundering. When he got too greedy or too careless with the Bea Tran acquisition, you eliminated him. Poisoned him. Stole my paintings. Framed me. All in one neat package."

"Why would I kill my business partner?"

"Because he was a liability. Because he was pushing me too hard and I was about to expose you both. Because you could eliminate him, take the paintings, and frame me for murder all at once. Three problems solved."

Nguyen was silent for a long moment. Outside the interrogation room, Bea could hear muffled movement—FBI agents, Morrison, probably her lawyer preparing more evidence.

"You can't prove it," Nguyen finally said.

"We don't have to. You're already caught with stolen art. That's federal. That's jail time. The FBI is building the murder case now. They have forty-five years of your exploitation patterns. They have financial records. They have artist complaints. They have my testimony."

"Your testimony of what? That I knew you from a refugee camp forty-five years ago? That proves nothing."

"It proves motive. It proves you knew exactly how to target me. It proves you're not just a art dealer who made a mistake. You're a predator who spent forty-five years positioning yourself to exploit refugees systematically."

Bea stood. She was done. She'd said what she needed to say. Faced the man who'd tried to destroy her. Looked him in the eye and refused to disappear.

"You made a mistake," she said. "You thought I was alone. Vulnerable. Easy to break. You didn't count on me having family. Found family. People who refuse to let predators win."

"Family?" Nguyen's voice was dismissive. "You have a mahjong group."

"I have six women and one excellent poodle who will burn down the world to protect their own. You never stood a chance."

Bea walked to the door. Her lawyer followed. Behind them, Nguyen sat at the table, his professional mask finally cracking, showing the predator underneath.

In the observation room, Morrison was waiting. So was David Chen. And on video call from Franklin, the whole Tuesday night mahjong group.

"You did perfect," Donnie said from the screen.

"He confessed nothing," Bea pointed out.

"He didn't have to. You rattled him. He confirmed his connection to you. He couldn't explain the paintings. And when FBI searched his storage unit in Los Angeles twenty minutes ago, they found financial records linking him to the North Korea sanctions evasion. He's done."

Bea felt something settle in her chest. Justice. Not the clean kind from movies. The complicated, messy kind where you had to sacrifice and testify and probably relocate. But justice nonetheless.

"What happens now?" she asked.

Morrison spoke. "FBI files formal charges. You'll need to testify at trial. Federal prosecutors will want full cooperation. And Bea..." He paused. "You'll probably need witness protection. At least during trial. Maybe after."

"So I lose Franklin."

"Maybe temporarily. Maybe permanently. We don't know yet."

Bea looked at the screen, at her mahjong group watching from Donnie's living room. Maya, Evelyn, Mabs, Dodo, Frankie. Her found family. The people who'd solved a murder to protect her. Who'd exposed an international conspiracy to get her justice.

"I already lost everything once," Bea said quietly. "Vietnam. My parents. My first life. I survived that. I'll survive this."

"You won't survive it alone," Maya said from the screen. "Wherever you go, we're still family. We still play Tuesday night mahjong. We just figure out how to do it long-distance."

"The cats agree," Dodo added. "Family doesn't end at geographic boundaries."

"I'll visit wherever you are," Mabs said. "I've got vacation time."

"Same," Frankie grunted.

"We'll make it work," Evelyn said. "Family makes it work."

Bea felt tears prick her eyes. She'd spent forty-five years asking why she survived. Why she was alive when her parents died. Why she deserved to exist when so many others didn't.

And now, finally, she understood.

She survived so she could testify. So she could expose predators like Nguyen. So she could protect other refugee artists from exploitation. So she could be part of a found family that chose each other despite everything.

She survived for this moment. For this choice. For justice.

"Okay," Bea said. "I'll testify. I'll do whatever it takes. And when it's over, I'll paint again. Wherever I am. Whatever name I have. I'll paint."

"That's the spirit," Donnie said. "Now get on a plane and come home. We're having emergency mahjong tonight. Tiles are already set up."

Bea smiled. Home. Franklin. Tuesday night mahjong. The life she'd built. The family she'd chosen.

She might lose it. Probably would lose it. But she'd survive that too.

Because survival was what she did. Had done for forty-five years. Would keep doing for forty-five more if necessary.

And this time, she wouldn't survive alone.

This time, she had family.

Chapter 10

The Slanted Window Tasting Room was warm with November evening and the sound of Norma Hendrix's flute weaving through conversation like smoke through still air.

Donnie Carlisle sat at the corner table with most of the Tuesday night mahjong group, watching the relief and tension compete on everyone's faces. They'd come here directly from the phone call—from Morrison's report that FBI had arrested Minh Nguyen at LAX, that Bea had identified him and confronted him, that he was being transported to federal detention. Victory, yes. But incomplete. Ambiguous. The kind that left you celebrating while looking over your shoulder.

Dion brought a bottle of wine to their table, setting glasses carefully. "On the house," he said. "For catching another killer. You're making my place famous."

"We prefer to think of it as community hub," Maya said, accepting her glass of Rosé Saignée—the sangiovese rosé from Dion's own Senamore Vineyard & Farms, bold and refreshing, grown and vinted here in Macon County. The only vineyard and winery making local wines in Franklin. The wine seemed to reflect the light, pink and clear, with the color of the sunset and the taste of the mountains.

Eric Hendrix's guitar joined his wife's flute in an old Appalachian tune, something about mountains, memory and the long road home. The music filled the tasting room's warm space a retired 1950's filling station, the venue that had been converted to feature the family's wines. The name, Slanted Window came from the 1878 family farmhouse where Dion's family had discovered the distinctive slanted window on their second floor porch, previously covered over with siding, revealing a beautiful view of the sky and vineyard beyond.

Norma caught Donnie's eye from the stage area, flute pausing mid-phrase, raising her eyebrows in question. Celebrating or consoling? Donnie nodded toward celebration with a slight smile and a nod of her head. Play. Let Franklin have this moment of victory, however incomplete.

Dion returned with their charcuterie board—the Traditional: prosciutto, genoa salami, manchego, whole grain dijon, valencia almonds, all arranged beautifully with seasonal fruit, house-made pickled vegetables, and multi-seed crackers. The board was a work of art, ingredients sourced carefully, everything speaking to quality and local pride.

"So what happened?" Eric asked during the break between songs, settling at their table with his own wine. Norma joined him, flute still in hand, her silver hair catching the warm lighting.

"International art trafficking conspiracy," Evelyn said, spreading whole grain dijon on a cracker with precise movements. "Money laundering. Sanctions evasion. And two murders, Conrad Fischer and my husband David."

Norma's expression shifted to sympathy. "Oh, Evelyn. I'm so sorry."

"Don't be. We caught him. He'll never hurt anyone again." Evelyn raised her glass, "To justice. Slow. Imperfect. But justice nonetheless."

They toasted.

Morrison, still in his detective uniform, dark blue sport coat with a tartan plaid tie reached for another piece of salami. "FBI's processing Nguyen now. He'll be arraigned Monday. Federal RICO charges—racketeering, money laundering, conspiracy, two counts of murder. They've got him cold."

"But?" Frankie asked because there was always a 'but' in their investigations. He nursed his wine. After his wife had died, there had been times when that was not the case.

"But the paintings didn't stay in his luggage after they arrested him," Morrison admitted. "Four paintings, worth potentially half a million dollars, and now they're gone. Not with Nguyen. Not in FBI possession. The FBI had them and lost them."

The table went quiet. The celebration dimmed slightly, reality intruding.

"So where are they?" Mabs asked, ever

practical. She'd been taking notes between bites of Manchego, documentation never stopped, even during celebration.

"That's the question." Morrison took a long drink. "Nguyen claims he doesn't know. Says the FBI is setting him up."

"Because there's someone else," Donnie said slowly, the pieces coming together. "Someone else is working and traveling with Nguyen. Someone who stepped in and reclaimed them when the opportunity presented itself. Someone who's still out there."

Evelyn pulled out her laptop, she'd brought it even to celebration, because financial forensics didn't stop for wine and charcuterie. "I've been reviewing Nguyen's financial records. There are payments. Monthly. Fifteen thousand dollars to a shell company. Seven years of payments. That's over a million dollars to someone."

"For what?" Maya asked, selecting a slice of prosciutto.

"For this. For muscle. For someone who handles the dangerous work while Nguyen keeps his hands clean." Evelyn's fingers flew across the keyboard. "Nguyen ran the business side—galleries, buyers, money laundering. But someone else did the dirty work. The threats. The violence. Maybe the actual killing."

"So we caught Nguyen but not his partner," Frankie said flatly. "We got the mastermind but the killer's still free."

"We don't know that for certain," Morrison cautioned. "Could be Nguyen acting alone. Could be the paintings were moved after the arrest and they just haven't found them again, yet."

"Do you believe that?" Donnie asked, spreading cheese on a cracker.

Morrison was quiet for a long pause then, "No. The evidence doesn't support solo operation. The bathroom window escape at Bea's studio—that required someone on site while Nguyen was probably elsewhere. Someone athletic enough to climb through an eighteen-inch window. Someone who knew how to handle stolen art. Someone professional."

"Desperate now," Frankie added. "If there is a partner, and Nguyen's arrested, he's alone. No protection. No network. Possibly watching us right now."

Maya's hand tightened on her wine glass. Donnie immediately covered it with her own. "Bea's still with FBI. They're keeping her in protective custody until she testifies. No one's getting to her."

"But we're here," Dodo pointed out, gesturing to the table. "All of us. Together. Publicly celebrating. If there is someone watching, we just advertised that we're the ones who caught Nguyen."

The table went silent. Norma and Eric exchanged glances from the stage, picking up on the sudden tension.

Eddie, who'd been listening with his novelist's attention to subtext and foreshadowing, spoke up while swirling his wine absentmindedly, "You know what bothers me? The timing. Fischer was killed November 1st. That's ten days ago. Ten days for Nguyen's partner—if he exists—to move the paintings, to cover tracks, to disappear. But the paintings were still here in the states. Not sold. Not transported out of country. But now…just... gone."

"Which means what?" Mabs asked, trying the smoked trout.

"Which means either the partner was still around when Nguyen was arrested, then someone messed up and his partner waited for the right moment to grab them back. Or the FBI misplaced them. It wouldn't be the first time. Either way, there's unfinished business. And unfinished business is dangerous."

Dion approached with wine refills and the offer of desserts—the menu listed chocolate torte, key lime pie, warm Italian almond cake. "You folks want something sweet? On the house for the heroes."

"Not heroes," Maya said quietly. "Just community doing what community does."

"Should we leave you to discuss this privately?" Norma asked, flute lowered, concern evident.

"No," Maya said firmly. "Stay. Play. Franklin needs to hear music tonight. We all need to remember that life is more than investigation and danger." She looked around the table. "Yes, there might be a partner. Yes, the paintings are still missing. Yes, there are more questions than answers. But tonight, we celebrate. We caught a predator. We exposed a conspiracy. Bea survived her confrontation with the man who exploited her for forty-five years. That's worth celebrating."

Donnie raised her glass higher "To incomplete victories. Better than complete defeats."

"To questions that still need answers," Evelyn added.

"To the cats' wisdom in uncertain times," Dodo contributed, because even in crisis, the cats apparently had opinions.

They toasted again. The glasses glowed warmly in the tasting room's light, outside, November darkness settled over Franklin, cold and clear. The mountains held everything in their ancient embrace—the celebration, the uncertainty, the ambiguity, the hope.

Norma and Eric returned to their instruments. The music started again—something livelier this time, more celebratory. A few other patrons joined in clapping.

But Donnie caught Morrison's eye across the table. Saw the same thought reflected there. This wasn't over. Someone had killed Fischer with professional efficiency. Someone had stolen four valuable paintings and made them disappear from federal custody. Someone had been receiving fifteen thousand dollars a month from Nguyen for seven years.

And that someone was still out there. Watching, maybe. Planning, certainly. Waiting for whatever came next.

Tomorrow they'd worry about finding him. Tomorrow they'd review the evidence, coordinate with FBI, develop theories about

Nguyen's mysterious partner.

Tonight, they'd let Franklin have its partial victory. Let Norma and Eric play. Let wine flow. Tthe rosé and the red and the sweet pyment, all from the only vineyard in Macon County, all carrying the taste of these mountains. Let the charcuterie be shared, the local ingredients celebrated, the music fill the spaces where anxiety tried to creep in.

Tonight, they'd celebrate surviving another investigation. Another conspiracy. Another brush with darkness.

And if the victory felt incomplete? If the sense of unfinished business lingered despite the arrest? If they couldn't quite relax into celebration because somewhere in the November darkness, a killer was still free?

Well. That was Tuesday night mahjong. Solving one mystery only to discover deeper questions. Catching one predator only to realize the network ran deeper than they'd thought.

The slanted window on the second floor of Dion's restored 1878 farmhouse—the one that gave this place its name, the one that offered a beautiful view of sky and vineyard—that window had been covered over for years before being discovered. Hidden for decades. Forgotten by all. Then revealed.

Sometimes perspective required discovering what had been hidden all along.

Outside, somewhere, a killer was planning his next move.

Inside The Slanted Window, the Tuesday night mahjong group was fortifying themselves with food, wine, and community strength.

Whatever came next, they'd face it together.

That was the promise. That was the power.

That was home.

Even when victory was ambiguous, even when the fight wasn't finished, even when questions outnumbered answers.

Especially then.

Chapter 11

The FBI arrived in Franklin three days after Nguyen's arrest, and they arrived like an occupying force.

Donnie stood in Morrison's conference room watching Special Agent Katherine Parker set up her laptop, her briefcase, and her jurisdiction with the efficiency of someone who'd done this a hundred times. Parker was forty-something, Black dressed in the federal uniform of dark suit and sensible shoes. Her partner, Special Agent James Rodriguez, was younger, Hispanic, and had the look of someone who'd rather be anywhere else.

"Thank you for your cooperation," Parker said, which everyone in the room knew meant "thank you for getting out of our way."

Morrison sat at the head of the table, his expression carefully neutral. David Chen, Bea's lawyer, sat next to Bea, who had accompanied the FBI agents. The Tuesday night mahjong group occupied the remaining chairs—Donnie, Maya, Evelyn, Mabs, with Dodo and Frankie standing in the back because there weren't enough seats.

"Let's establish parameters," Parker began. "Minh Nguyen is in federal custody in Los Angeles, charged with art theft, money laundering, and sanctions evasion. We're building the murder case for Conrad Fischer, but that takes time. We need witness testimony, forensic evidence, and a timeline that puts Nguyen in Franklin on the night of Fischer's death."

"We can provide that," Donnie said.

Parker looked at her. "You're the retired insurance investigator."

"I'm the person who solved this case while you were filing paperwork."

Parker's expression didn't change. "Ms. Carlisle, I appreciate your... enthusiasm. But this is a federal investigation now. We have protocols, procedures, chain of custody requirements. Your amateur investigation, while admirable, isn't admissible in court."

"My amateur investigation caught Nguyen before he fled to Singapore."

"And we're grateful. But from this point forward, we handle it. We'll need statements from all of you, we'll be working particularly Ms. Tran. After that, you step back and let us work."

Donnie felt her Miami investigator instincts flare. She'd spent thirty years dealing with federal agents who swooped in at the end of investigations, took credit, and acted like the local work didn't matter. She'd hated it then. She hated it now.

"Agent Parker," Evelyn said quietly. "I'm Evelyn Cho. Forensic accountant. I consulted on the STX Associates case that AUSA Walsh is prosecuting. I found the financial evidence linking Fischer and Nguyen to North Korean sanctions evasion."

Parker's expression shifted slightly. "You're David Cho's widow."

"Yes."

"I'm sorry for your loss. David was a good

prosecutor."

"David was murdered because he found the art trafficking connection. This case is personal for me. And I'm not stepping back."

Parker and Rodriguez exchanged glances. Finally, Parker nodded. "AUSA Walsh speaks highly of you. You can continue as consultant on the financial aspects. But only in coordination with our team."

"Agreed."

Parker turned to Bea. "Ms. Tran. You're our key witness. We need your full cooperation. That means complete testimony about your interactions with Fischer and Nguyen. It means identifying the stolen paintings. And it means..." She paused. "It may mean witness protection."

Bea's voice was steady. "I understand."

"Witness protection means relocation. New identity. No contact with people from your previous life. It's not temporary. If we determine you're at risk, it's permanent."

The room went silent. No contact with people from your previous life meant no Tuesday night mahjong. No Maya bringing tea. No Mabs researching. No Dodo's cookies. No found family.

"How at risk is she?" Maya asked.

"Nguyen has connections. International art trafficking network. Money laundering associates. North Korean operatives, possibly. If he views Ms. Tran as the reason his empire is falling apart, she's a target."

"So I have to disappear," Bea said. "Again."

Parker's expression softened slightly. "I know this is hard. But it's safer."

"Safer isn't the same as living." Bea looked at the mahjong group, at the people who'd risked everything to protect her. "I already lost everything once. I survived. I built a new life. And now I have to give it up again because a predator decided I was easy prey."

"Yes," Parker said simply. "I'm sorry. But that's the reality."

Donnie watched Bea's face and saw something she recognized from thirty years of witnessing victim impact. The moment when someone realizes the crime doesn't end with the arrest. That justice has costs. That even winning means losing something.

"Can we minimize the disruption?" David Chen asked. "Trial prep without full relocation? Protection in place rather than witness protection?"

"Maybe. Depends on threat assessment. We're evaluating Nguyen's network now. If it's limited to him and Fischer, in-place protection might work. If it's bigger..." Parker trailed off.

"It's bigger," Evelyn said. "I found evidence of at least twelve shell companies, operations in five countries, connections to North Korean sanctions evasion. This isn't two guys running a scam. This is organized."

"Which is why we need time." Parker pulled

up documents on her laptop. "We're building a RICO case. Racketeer Influenced and Corrupt Organizations. It's the only way to take down the whole network. But RICO takes months, sometimes years."

"Bea doesn't have years to live in limbo," Maya said.

"Then Bea cooperates, testifies, and we get convictions as fast as possible." Parker's voice was firm but not unkind. "I know this isn't fair. Crime isn't fair. But this is how justice works."

Morrison had been quiet, watching the federal agents assert control. Now he spoke. "What do you need from us? Specifically."

"Full statements from everyone involved in the investigation. Timeline of events. Chain of custody for any evidence collected. Access to Ms. Tran's studio, her financial records, her communication with Fischer. And we'll need to depose the mahjong group about your involvement."

"Depose?" Dodo asked. "Like in legal shows?"

"Exactly like in legal shows. You're witnesses. Some of you handled evidence, conducted interviews, pursued leads. Defense attorneys will question all of it. You need to be prepared."

Frankie crossed his arms. "We solved the damn case."

"You did. And defense will argue you contaminated evidence, conducted illegal searches, and coerced statements. They'll try to get everything you found thrown out." Parker looked around the table. "That's why from now on, everything goes through proper channels. No more amateur investigation."

Donnie felt Eddie's hand on her shoulder—he'd been standing behind her chair, quiet observer as always. The touch said: pick your battles. This isn't the one.

He was right. The FBI was here. Federal jurisdiction was established. Fighting it would just waste energy.

"Understood," Donnie said. "We'll provide full cooperation. But Agent Parker? We're not amateurs. We're citizens who care about justice. And we're not going anywhere."

Parker almost smiled. "I wouldn't expect you to. Just... coordinate with us. Please."

After the meeting, the mahjong group gathered in Morrison's parking lot. Late morning sun, November cold, mountains watching in their impassive way.

"Well," Mabs said. "That was patronizing."

"Federal agents are always patronizing," Evelyn said. "It's in the training manual."

"What do we do?" Maya asked. "They basically told us to stop investigating."

"They told us to stop investigating alone," Donnie corrected. "They didn't say we couldn't assist. Evelyn's consulting on finances. We can all be consultants."

"Consultants on what?" Frankie asked.

"Community knowledge. Witness coordination. Local intelligence." Donnie pulled out her phone. "And we can investigate things that aren't officially part of the FBI case. Background. Context. The stuff federal agents don't care about but that matters."

"Like what?" Dodo asked.

"Like Bea's story. Her art. The other refugee artists Nguyen targeted. The human cost of this conspiracy." Donnie looked at Bea. "The FBI sees you as a witness. We see you as family. They're building a case. We're protecting a person."

Bea's eyes were bright with unshed tears. "Thank you."

"No thanks necessary. That's what family does." Donnie checked her watch. "Okay. Here's the plan. Maya and Evelyn, you're with me. We're going to Bea's studio. FBI will process it as a crime scene, but before they do, we're documenting everything. Every painting, every sketch, every piece of Bea's work. We're creating a record."

"Why?" Maya asked.

"Because Bea might lose this studio. Might have to relocate. Might never come back. And I'll be damned if the only record of her art is federal evidence photos." Donnie turned to Mabs. "You research other refugee artists Nguyen worked with. Find them. Document their stories. Build a victim impact narrative."

"The FBI won't care about that," Mabs pointed

out.

"The FBI won't. But juries do. And public opinion does. And when this goes to trial, we want the world to know what Nguyen destroyed." Donnie looked at Frankie and Dodo. "You two work the community angle. Talk to people. Find out if anyone saw Nguyen in Franklin. Get timeline confirmation. Build the local case."

"FBI said not to interfere," Frankie said.

"We're not interfering. We're assisting. There's a difference." Donnie's smile was sharp. "FBI has protocols. We have community. Let's use it."

They dispersed to their assignments. Donnie, Maya, and Evelyn drove to Bea's studio in Maya's ancient Subaru, heater rattling, mountains scrolling past.

"You know the FBI is going to be pissed," Evelyn said.

"Let them be pissed. We're not breaking laws. We're documenting art."

"You're skirting protocols."

"I spent thirty years following protocols. Now I'm retired. I can skirt whatever I want." Donnie looked out the window at Franklin passing by —Main Street with its small businesses, The Country Kitchen with its gossip network, the library where they had played Tuesday mahjong, the mountains holding everything in their ancient embrace.

This was home. Bea's home. The life she'd built after surviving Vietnam.

And the FBI was about to take it away in the name of protection.

Donnie understood the necessity. Understood witness protection saved lives. Understood that sometimes justice required sacrifice.

But she also understood that Bea had already sacrificed enough. Had already lost her parents, her country, her first life. Had already survived the unsurvivable.

And if there was any way-any way at all-to let Bea keep this life she'd built, Donnie was going to find it.

The studio was quiet when they arrived. Morrison had released the crime scene yesterday, and Bea had been too traumatized to return. The space sat empty, waiting, holding the memory of violence.

Maya unlocked the door with Bea's keys. They stepped inside.

The studio looked different in daylight. Less ominous than the crime scene Donnie had investigated days ago. Just an artist's workspace, paint-stained tables, brushes in jars, canvases in various stages of completion.

And on the walls, the empty spaces where the "Between Waters" paintings had hung.

"Let's document everything," Donnie said, pulling out her camera. "Every painting, every sketch, every piece of work. We're creating a complete archive."

Maya started with the portfolios. Carefully

opening each one, photographing the contents, making notes. Evelyn set up a spreadsheet on her laptop, cataloging pieces by size, medium, date if known.

Donnie worked the walls, photographing the paintings still hanging. Watercolors mostly, all featuring water in some form. Rivers. Oceans. Rain. Mist. Bea's obsession with water made sense. It was what had taken her parents and what had carried her to America. The thing that destroyed and saved simultaneously.

"This one," Maya said softly. She stood in front of a large watercolor—maybe five by four feet—that showed a girl standing on a beach, looking at a distant shore. The technique was spare, economical, every brushstroke carrying weight.

"That's her," Donnie said. "Arriving in America. That's Bea."

"Look at the detail." Maya pointed to the girl's hands, clasped in front of her, holding a small jade bracelet. "That's her grandmother's bracelet. The one she wore on the boat."

"She's painting her own history."

"She's processing trauma the only way she knows how. Through art."

They worked in silence for an hour, documenting everything. The finished paintings. The works in progress. The sketches pinned to a corkboard. The tubes of paint organized by color. The brushes worn from use.

This was Bea's life. Her work. Her healing

rendered in watercolor and rice paper.
And someone had tried to steal it, profit from it, destroy it.

"I'm angry," Maya said suddenly. "I'm so angry I can barely see straight."

"Good," Donnie said. "Use it."

"Use it how?"

"Use it to fight. To protect Bea. To make sure Nguyen and everyone like him pays for attacking refugees." Donnie took another photograph. "Anger is fuel. Burn it for justice."

Evelyn looked up from her laptop. "I found something."

"What?"

"Bea's financial records. I've been reviewing them with her permission. She sold paintings to Fischer five years ago—2019. Three pieces for fifteen thousand total. But I cross-referenced with Fischer's gallery sales records from the financial investigation. Those same three paintings sold for ninety thousand."

"He stole seventy-five thousand from her."

"And she probably never knew. If he told her paintings were worth five thousand each and that's what she was paid, how would she know he was selling them for thirty thousand?"

Maya's hands clenched. "That's why she wouldn't sell him the 'Between Waters' series. She must have figured it out. Realized he was exploiting her."

"So when she refused," Donnie continued,

"Nguyen decided to just take them. Kill Fischer, frame Bea, steal the paintings. All the profit, none of the negotiation."

They finished documenting around one PM. Donnie's camera was full of photographs. Evelyn's spreadsheet was comprehensive. Maya had notes on every piece, contextualizing Bea's artistic journey.

"What now?" Maya asked.

"Now we make sure Bea's story gets told. Not as evidence. As art. As survival. As the thing Nguyen tried to destroy but couldn't." Donnie looked around the studio one last time. "And we figure out how to keep Bea in Franklin."

"The FBI said witness protection might be necessary."

"The FBI said might. Not definitely. Which means there's room to negotiate." Donnie's mind was already working. "If we can prove Nguyen's network is limited, that the threat is containable, maybe Bea can stay. With protection, sure. But here. Home."

"That's optimistic," Evelyn said.

"That's necessary. Because Bea's already lost too much. I'm not letting her lose Franklin without a fight."

They locked up the studio and drove back to town. Main Street was busy with lunch crowd—The Country Kitchen packed, Café REL serving early diners, people going about their usual business with no idea that their community had just been caught in an international conspiracy.

Donnie's phone rang. Morrison.

"FBI wants to interview the mahjong group tomorrow. Nine AM at the station. Everyone who was involved in the investigation."

"We'll be there."

"And Donnie? Agent Parker asked me to tell you that documenting Bea's studio was 'helpful but not necessary.'"

"I'm sure she did."

"She also said if you keep investigating, she'll charge you with obstruction."

"She also said that, I bet. Tell her I'm not investigating. I'm assisting. There's a difference."

Morrison laughed. "You're going to drive the FBI crazy."

"Good. They can use some chaos in their protocols."

After hanging up, Donnie looked at Maya and Evelyn. "Tomorrow we talk to FBI. Tonight we regroup with the mahjong group. My place and we plan how to keep Bea safe, keep her in Franklin, and make sure Nguyen never hurts anyone again."

"That's ambitious," Maya said.

"That's Tuesday night mahjong any night," Donnie corrected. "We do impossible things regularly. This is just another Mahjong day. I'll see you later."

Maya and Evelyn continued down Main Street,

strolling the shop's windows.

"There you go," Maya said, squeezing Evelyn's hand. "Liz's theory proven once again." On the chalkboard beside the door of the Novel Escape Bookstore, the owner Liz had written in her distinctive script: *My toxic trait is that I think a bad day can be cured with a quick trip to the bookstore.*

Evelyn smiled despite the exhaustion of another day spent investigating murder and those that preyed on the most helpless.

"She's not wrong," Evelyn admitted.

The bookstore smelled of paper and coffee and the particular scent that only comes from hundreds of books gathered in one warm space. A Novel Escape occupied a storefront on Main Street, its windows displaying staff picks and local author features, its shelves packed with exactly the kind of careful curation that made independent bookstores essential.

Liz looked up from the counter where she'd been unpacking a shipment. "There are my favorite investigators! I was wondering when you two would show up. You've got that 'we need books to survive this week' look."

"Is it that obvious?" Maya asked, already gravitating toward the mystery section—her comfort zone, the place she always started.

"Honey, I've been running this bookstore long enough to recognize every variation of book emergency. You two are definitely in the 'therapeutic browsing' category." Liz came around the counter, wiping her hands on her jeans. "How's the federal case going? I've been following it in the paper. You caught that art trafficker?"

"We did," Evelyn said. "but the case keeps looking bigger. More victims. More documentation. More everything."

"Which is why you need books," Liz concluded. "Sarah's in back organizing the book club space. We've got your regular table set up—I figured you'd stop by before the next meeting."

Maya felt Evelyn's hand tighten in hers—the same hand she'd first touched in this exact bookstore fourteen months ago, the moment that had changed everything.

They'd both reached for the same book. A mystery novel, naturally. Maya's hand had landed on top of Evelyn's on the spine, and the shock—actual electrical shock, static or chemistry or fate—had made them both pull back, startled.

"Sorry," they'd said simultaneously.

And then Evelyn had smiled. That devastating smile that Maya now knew meant Evelyn was calculating probabilities, assessing possibilities, deciding whether to take a risk.

"You take it," Evelyn had said. "I can order my own copy."

"Or," Maya had countered, heart pounding with

the kind of bravery that only happened in bookstores, "we could both read it and discuss it. At the book club, maybe?"

Evelyn's smile had widened. "I'd like that."

The book had been a thriller about an FBI agent investigating art fraud. They'd laughed about the coincidence later—after book club, after coffee, after the first tentative admission that maybe this was more than literary discussion.

Now, fourteen months later, they navigated A Novel Escape like home. Maya headed to mysteries while Evelyn checked new releases in nonfiction. They'd developed a system: browse separately for twenty minutes, then reconvene with their finds, compare selections, read back cover copy aloud to each other.

It was ritual. Like Tuesday night mahjong. Like Maya's morning tea preparation. Like all the small ceremonies that built a life together.

Sarah emerged from the back room, arms full of books for display. "Maya! Evelyn! Please tell me you're coming to book club. We're discussing that new refugee memoir and I need someone who actually understands the legal complexities."

"We'll be there," Maya promised. "Wouldn't miss it."

"Even with the everything going on?"

"Especially with that." Evelyn corrected. "Book club is sanity maintenance. Drug of choice. Required, not optional."

Sarah grinned. "That's what I like to hear. Oh, and Liz ordered that botanical mystery you requested, Maya. The one about the herbalist who solves murders using plant knowledge? Seems relevant to your interests."

"Too relevant," Evelyn muttered. "She's going to get ideas."

"I already have ideas," Maya said primly. "The book just validates them."

They browsed in comfortable silence, the kind that only came after months of learning each other's rhythms. Maya pulled three mysteries, one botanical reference guide, and a poetry collection. Evelyn gathered two historical nonfiction works about refugee resettlement, a memoir, and—surprisingly—a romance novel.

They met at their usual spot, the armchairs in the corner that the staff had started calling "Maya and Evelyn's reading nook."

"Romance?" Maya asked, eyebrow raised at Evelyn's selection.

"David used to say I needed more lightness in my reading diet. He'd be pleased to know I'm finally taking his advice." Evelyn's voice was steady, but Maya saw the grief underneath—still present, always present, but integrated now rather than overwhelming.

Maya took Evelyn's hand again. Here, in this bookstore, they'd first touched. Here, they'd had their first real conversation together. Not required, polite or social, but real. Here, Evelyn had first mentioned David without crying. Here, they'd realized that maybe grief and new love could coexist.

"Show me what you found," Evelyn said, setting her stack on the side table.

Maya handed over the botanical mystery. "It's set in Appalachia. Called "Sanctuary" by a local author, Walter Cook. Local herbalist gets framed for murder using plant-based poison. Sound familiar?"

"Art imitating life imitating art." Evelyn flipped through the pages. "Although our version has better character development. Donnie's more interesting than most fictional detectives and who can even imagine a character like, Dodo."

"Don't tell Donnie that. Her ego's already dangerous."

They compared the rest of their selections, reading passages aloud to each other, debating whether the historical nonfiction would be too dry, agreeing that Maya's poetry collection was probably pretentious but in a good way as it was written by a local writer, Ron Rash's daughter.

Liz approached with two mugs of coffee—they'd become such regulars that she knew their orders without asking. "On the house. Consider it payment for making my bookstore a romantic landmark."

"Romantic landmark?" Evelyn asked.

"Honey, you two met here. Had your first date at book club. Come here every week to browse and hold hands and look at each other like romance novel protagonists. You're excellent for business. People see happy couples in bookstores and think, 'I want that.' Then they buy more books."

"We're a marketing strategy?" Maya asked solemnly.

"You're a love story," Liz corrected with a grin. "Which happens to also be good marketing. Win-win."

They took their coffee to the armchairs, surrounded by books and the quiet sounds of other customers browsing. Through the front window, Main Street was visible—Franklin going about its business, mountains rising in the distance, the whole town wrapped in the particular peace that comes just before the holidays.

"I love this place," Evelyn said quietly. "Not just the bookstore. Franklin. The mountains. Tuesday night mahjong. But especially this bookstore."

"Because of the books?"

"Because this is where I found you. Where we found each other." Evelyn looked at Maya, and there was that smile again—the one that meant risk and possibility and choice. "I was so broken when I moved here. David's death. The guilt. The grief. I thought I'd never feel anything again except loss and hate."

"And then?"

"And then you reached for the same book I did.

And when our hands touched, I felt something. Electric. Alive. And I thought, 'Oh. Maybe I'm not completely broken after all.'"

Maya's throat tightened. "I felt it too. That shock. I thought it was static electricity from the carpet."

"It was. But it was also more than that." Evelyn took Maya's hand, threaded their fingers together. "It was possibility. Permission to start feeling again. To risk caring about someone new while still loving the person I lost."

"David would have liked this place?" Maya questioned. "The bookstore. The careful curation. Liz's chalk wisdom."

"He would have loved you," Evelyn corrected. "Your kindness. Your herbalism. Your tendency to solve murders using plant knowledge and community networks. He'd have thought you were perfect for me."

"Am I? Perfect for you?"

"You're real. That's better than perfect." Evelyn squeezed Maya's hand. "You're patient with my grief. You understand that loving you doesn't mean stopping loving him. You make tea appear exactly when I need it. You believe in justice and community and showing up for people even when it's hard. You're everything I didn't know I needed."

Maya kissed her. Right there in the bookstore, surrounded by mysteries and memoirs and the quiet presence of Liz pretending not to watch from behind the counter.

When they pulled apart, Evelyn was smiling. "Now we're definitely a romance novel."

"Good," Maya said. "I like our story."

They sat in the armchairs for another hour, reading passages aloud to each other, drinking coffee that Liz kept refilling, existing in the particular intimacy that bookstores created. Around them, other customers browsed. Sarah organized the book club space. Liz unpacked shipments and made recommendations and wrote new wisdom on the chalkboard.

And Maya and Evelyn held hands in their reading nook, in the bookstore where they'd first touched, where they'd first risked, where they'd first understood that maybe love didn't end when someone died—it just made room for new love alongside the old.

"We should buy these books," Evelyn said eventually.

"We should," Maya agreed. "And come back next week to browse for more."

"And the week after that."

"And the week after that. For as long as Liz keeps writing wisdom on her chalkboard and stocking mysteries and letting us occupy her armchairs."

"So forever, basically."

"Forever sounds about right, besides, without us Liz will lose her marketing edge and have to lay off staff."

They brought their selections to the counter. Liz

rang them up with the efficiency of someone who'd processed hundreds of book purchases but still treated each transaction like it mattered.

"Book club next Thursday at seven," Liz reminded them. "We're discussing the refugee memoir. I expect thoughtful commentary from you two, given your current investigation."

"We'll be there," Maya promised.

"With bells on," Evelyn added.

"Just bring yourselves. And maybe convince Donnie to join. That woman needs more fiction in her life. All that investigation work is making her too serious."

"Donnie? Serious?" Maya laughed. "You haven't seen her during happy hour with Eddie's chickens."

"Fair point. But still. Invite her. The more the merrier."

They left A Novel Escape carrying their bag of books, stepping out into oncoming winter cold that bit through coats but felt clean and sharp. The mountains rose in the distance, ancient and patient. Main Street stretched in both directions, familiar and home.

"Thank you," Evelyn said, tucking herself against Maya's side as they walked.

"For what?"

"For dragging me to the bookstore when I was drowning in case documentation. For knowing that books cure bad days. For being patient while I figure out how to love again."

"Liz's toxic trait is thinking bookstores cure everything," Maya said. "Mine is thinking tea cures everything. Yours is thinking you need to thank me for loving you."

"That's not a toxic trait."

"It's not a trait that needs fixing, anyway." Maya kissed Evelyn's temple. "Come on. Let's go home. I'll make tea. You can start your romance novel. We'll pretend the federal case doesn't exist for a few hours."

"Can't pretend it doesn't exist. Too much documentation left."

"Then I'll make tea while you work. And read you passages from the botanical mystery. And remind you that even in the middle of international trafficking investigations, there's still room for books and love and the occasional trip to A Novel Escape."

"Liz would approve."

"Liz definitely approves. She told us we're a marketing strategy."

They walked home through Franklin's streets, carrying books and each other and the memory of a first touch that had shocked them both into possibility.

Behind them, A Novel Escape glowed warm in the gathering dusk. Inside, Liz was already updating her chalkboard wisdom for tomorrow's customers.

The best stories, she wrote, *are the ones that start in bookstores and never really end.*

Maya and Evelyn would have agreed.

But they were too busy living their story to notice.

Donnie headed toward her house, where the group would gather tonight. Emergency mahjong session. Strategy planning. Community coordination.

The mountains watched her drive by, ancient and patient. They'd seen this before—people fighting for justice, for family, for the right to live without fear.

And they'd see how this story ended. Whether the FBI would protect Bea or uproot her. Whether Nguyen would go to prison or slip through legal loopholes. Whether justice would win or just claim another casualty.

For now, all Donnie could do was fight. Use every skill from thirty years of investigation. Use the mahjong group's combined expertise. Use the community's support.

And refuse to let the darkness win.

That's what family did. They fought. Together. Until justice was done or they'd exhausted every option.

And the Tuesday night mahjong group had plenty of options left.

Chapter 12

Maya Lin spent Friday afternoon talking to every business owner on Main Street who'd ever interacted with Bea Tran, and what she learned confirmed her worst fears.

Nobody had seen Minh Nguyen in Franklin.

She sat in The Country Kitchen at three PM—late enough that the lunch rush was over, early enough that Linda would have time to talk—and reviewed her notes. Eric at the fish market: never seen Nguyen. Liz at the bookstore: never seen Nguyen. The manager at Gracious Plates: never seen Nguyen. Even Dodo's extensive gossip network had no sightings.

Which meant either Nguyen was incredibly careful, or he'd had help.

"More coffee, hon?" Linda appeared with the pot, already pouring before Maya could answer. Linda was sixty-something, had worked at The

Country Kitchen for thirty years, and knew every piece of gossip in Franklin within four hours of it happening. If Nguyen had been in town, Linda would know.

"Linda, did you ever see an Asian man, fifties, expensive clothes, around the time of Conrad Fischer's murder? Maybe at one of the nicer restaurants?"

Linda's eyes sharpened with interest. "This about Bea?"

"Yes."

"That poor woman. First that art dealer harasses her, then she finds him dead, then the FBI comes sniffing around like she did something wrong." Linda refilled her own coffee cup and sat down uninvited. "I didn't see anyone like that. But..."

"But?"

"There was someone else asking about Bea. Week before Fischer died. Young guy, Asian, maybe thirty. Professional-looking. Came in for breakfast, asked me if I knew Bea Tran, said he was an art collector interested in her work."

Maya pulled out her phone. "Can you describe him more specifically?"

"Tall—maybe six feet. Slim build. Korean or Chinese, I think, though I'm not great at telling the difference. Expensive watch. Good suit. Polite but... cold. You know the type. Smiled with his mouth but not his eyes."

"Did he give a name?"

"Said his name was James Park. Paid cash, left a

good tip, asked me where Bea's studio was. I told him—the tobacco warehouse on the south side." Linda looked guilty. "Should I not have?"

"You didn't know. Did he say anything else about Bea or why he was interested?"

"Just that he collected Vietnamese art. Said he'd heard Bea was talented and wanted to see her work. Seemed like a normal collector thing."

Maya wrote this down. James Park. Thirty. Professional. Asking about Bea a week before Fischer's murder. That wasn't coincidence.

"Linda, this is important. Did you see where he went after breakfast?"

"Toward the south side. Probably to Bea's studio like he said." Linda leaned closer. "Maya, is Bea in trouble? Real trouble?"

"She's in federal witness protection kind of trouble. The man who was killed was part of an international art trafficking conspiracy. They think Bea might be targeted."

Linda's expression hardened. "In Franklin? Someone wants to hurt Bea Tran in my town?"

"Possibly."

"Well, that's not acceptable." Linda stood up with the determination of someone who'd worked service industry for three decades and wasn't afraid of anything. "I'll put the word out. Every server, every cook, every business owner. We'll watch for strangers asking about Bea. And if this James Park comes back, I'll call Morrison immediately."

"Thank you."

"Bea's one of ours. Franklin protects its own." Linda headed back to the kitchen, already pulling out her phone to start the gossip network.

Maya finished her coffee and headed to her next stop: The Slanted Window Tasting Room. The upscale farm-to-table restaurant had been mentioned in Donnie's investigation—Fischer had been seen there with someone. Maybe James Park. Maybe someone else.

The Slanted Window wouldn't open for dinner until five, but Maya knew the chef started prep around three. She knocked on the back door.

Dion, the owner, opened the door, smiled, and asked, "Maya. Everything okay?"

"I need to ask about Conrad Fischer. He dined here in October, right?"

Marcus frowned. "The art dealer who got murdered? Yeah, he came in twice. Why?"

"Was he alone?"

"First time, yes. Second time, he was with another man. Asian guy, professional, expensive taste—ordered the ninety-dollar wine pairing without blinking."

Maya showed Marcus her phone. "Did the man look like this?" She'd pulled up a photo of Minh Nguyen from his gallery website.

Marcus studied it. "No. This guy's older. The man with Fischer was younger. Thirty maybe. Tall. Different build."

"What was his name?"

"I don't know. They didn't introduce themselves formally. But I remember the conversation—I was doing my rounds, checking on tables, and I overheard them talking about Vietnamese art. The younger guy was saying something about 'acquiring the right pieces before the market shifts.'"

"Did you hear anything else?"

"They mentioned Bea Tran by name. The younger guy said 'the Tran paintings are essential' and Fischer said 'she's being difficult.' Then they noticed me listening and changed the subject."

Maya's stomach tightened. Two men discussing Bea's paintings two weeks before Fischer's murder. Planning. Coordinating.

"Marcus, this is important. When was this exactly?"

Marcus pulled out his phone, checked his reservation system. "October 18th. Tuesday night. Seven PM reservation under the name, James Park."

Two weeks before the murder. And it had been a Tuesday—mahjong night. Which meant Bea was at the library, publicly visible, predictably occupied. Anyone watching would know her schedule.

"Did you see where they went after dinner?"

"No. But they were talking about meeting 'later at the site.' I assumed they meant an art gallery or studio."

The site. Bea's studio, probably. Where one of them—or both—would return on November 1st to kill Fischer and frame Bea.

Maya thanked Marcus and headed back to her car. She had a name now: James Park. Thirty, professional, expensive taste, discussing Bea's paintings with Fischer two weeks before the murder. Possibly the actual killer while Nguyen provided planning and resources.

She called Donnie.

"I found someone," Maya said. "James Park. Thirty. Asian. Professional. He was asking about Bea a week before the murder and dining with Fischer two weeks before. I think he's the killer."

"James Park?" Donnie was typing—Maya could hear keys clicking. "Don't know. But I'm thinking James Park might be Nguyen's operative. The one who actually killed Fischer while Nguyen was in Los Angeles establishing alibi."

"That would explain how Nguyen was at LAX trying to flee but could also be the killer. He wasn't. He had help." Donnie's voice shifted to investigator mode. "We need to find this James Park. Photo, background, connections to Nguyen."

"I'm going to Bea's studio. See if the other artists remember him."

"I'll research. Meet you there in thirty."

Maya drove to the tobacco warehouse, her herbalist brain connecting symptoms to root causes. Nguyen was the architect. Park was the operative. Fischer was the mark. And Bea was the patsy. A conspiracy with multiple moving parts, each person playing their role.

At the studio, Lin Aah, the artist who painted above Bea, was working. Maya could see lights on in the upstairs window. She knocked.

Lin opened the door, paint-spattered and alert. "Maya. Come to document more?"

"Come to ask about another man. Asian, thirty, professional. Did you see anyone like that around here in October?"

Lin's expression changed. "Yes. He came here twice. Said he was an art collector. Wanted to see Bea's studio. I told him she wasn't home, but he could come back during open studio hours."

"Did he give a name?"

"James. James something. Park maybe? I didn't write it down."

"Did you see what he did after you turned him away?"

"He walked around the building. Looking at windows, I think. Checking access points." Lin's voice hardened. "I should have known. I should have called police."

"You couldn't have known. He was professional. Careful." Maya pulled out her notebook. "Can you describe him in detail? Every feature you remember."

Lin did, and Maya wrote it all down. Tall. Slim. Korean-looking. Expensive clothes. Cold eyes. No distinguishing marks. Professional haircut. The kind of person who blended into upscale spaces but vanished from memory afterward.

A professional.

"Lin, this is important. Did you see him the night of Fischer's murder?"

"No. But I heard someone. Remember? I told the police. Fischer and Bea, then footsteps going to the bathroom, then different footsteps moving quickly."

"Could the different footsteps have been this man? Park?"

Lin thought for a long moment. "Maybe. The footsteps were quick. Confident. Someone who knew where they were going."

After leaving Lin's studio, Maya sat in her car and made a list:

JAMES PARK (aka?)
- Age: ~30
- Build: 6', slim
- Features: Asian (Korean?), professional
- Clothing: Expensive, professional
- First sighting: Week before murder (Country Kitchen, asking about Bea)
- Second sighting: Two weeks before murder (Slanted Window with Fischer)
- Third sighting: October (Studio, checking access points)
- Possible: Night of murder (Lin heard different footsteps)

This was the killer. Maya was certain. Nguyen planned it, Park executed it. And together they'd tried to frame Bea for a murder they'd committed.

She called Morrison. "I have a suspect. James Park. Thirty. I have witness descriptions, timeline, connections to Fischer and Nguyen."

"Bring everything to my office. FBI needs to hear this."

Twenty minutes later, Maya sat in Morrison's conference room with Agent Parker and Agent Rodriguez.

"Tell me everything," Agent Parker said.

Maya did. Linda's sighting. Marcus's testimony about the dinner. Lin's description of the man checking access points. The timeline that put James Park in Franklin multiple times before the murder.

Agent Parker made notes. "We'll look into it. But Maya, without a photo or full name, this is just a description."

"Then find him. Nguyen must have records. Phone calls. Travel arrangements. Payments. Track the connection."

"We are tracking it. But it takes time."

"Bea doesn't have time. She's in protective custody, separated from her community, waiting to see if she has to disappear permanently." Maya's voice was sharp. "Find James Park. Prove he killed Fischer. Then maybe Bea can come home."

After the meeting, Maya drove to Donnie's house, where an emergency mahjong session was scheduled for six PM. Everyone was gathering —Donnie, Evelyn, Mabs, Dodo, Frankie, Eddie. They needed to coordinate, share information, plan next steps.

The mountains stood witness as always, blue-purple in the late afternoon light. Beautiful and impassive and holding Franklin in their ancient embrace.

Somewhere out there, James Park was free. Possibly still in Franklin. Possibly watching. Possibly planning his next move.

And somewhere in federal protection, Bea was waiting. Hoping. Trusting that her found family would solve this.

Maya pulled into Donnie's driveway and looked at the house—warm lights in windows, smoke from the chimney, the comfort of home and community.

This was what Bea stood to lose. This warmth. This belonging. This carefully built life after trauma.

And Maya would be damned if she let that happen without a fight.

She grabbed her herb bag and headed inside, ready to work.

Tuesday night mahjong wasn't just a game. It was resistance. It was community. It was choosing each other over fear.

And tonight, they'd choose Bea. Again. As many times as necessary until justice was done and she could come home.

Chapter 13

The Macon County Farmers Market opened at nine AM on Saturday mornings, but Dodo arrived at eight-thirty because the cats needed time to properly assess the tactical situation.

"Reconnaissance complete," Dodo announced to no one in particular, watching Sherlock, Pancake, and Princess fan out across the vendor stalls like a furry SWAT team. "The goat cheese lady is back. The honey vendor brought samples. Mrs. Henderson has those lavender sachets that Princess likes to knock off tables. Everything is optimal for Cat Sak sales."

Donnie, who'd driven Dodo and the feline sales force to the market, watched Sherlock disappear under the fresh produce tent. "Should I ask how cats conduct reconnaissance?"

"Probably not. The answers involve more chaos theory than you're comfortable with before coffee."

"Fair point."

Dodo's booth was strategically positioned between the baked goods vendor and the handmade crafts lady, maximizing foot traffic while providing the cats easy access to the entire market. Her display table held approximately thirty Cat Saks—hand-knitted sleeping bags and carriers in colors ranging from "Tuna Surprise" (gray with orange accents) to "Midnight Zoomies" (black with reflective yarn) to "The Sunset Special" (orange, pink, and purple in combinations that shouldn't work but somehow did).

Each Cat Sak was a masterpiece of feline engineering. Sleeping bags that cats could burrow into, emerging only when they wanted treats or attention. Carriers with peek-a-boo windows and cozy fleece lining. Combination sleeping bag-carriers that transformed with strategically placed zippers and Velcro. Dodo had been knitting them for three years, ever since realizing that cats required specialized equipment and regular stores sold nothing remotely adequate.

"The cats say you're going to have a good day," Dodo told the baked goods vendor, a woman named Sarah who'd learned to just accept that Dodo translated feline prophecies.

"The cats told you this?"

"Pancake knocked over your sample tray twice

during setup. That's the sign for 'abundant sales and possible romance.'"

"Romance?"

"Or indigestion. The cats are sometimes unclear on emotional distinctions." Dodo arranged a particularly flamboyant Cat Sak—"The Drama Queen," neon green with gold sequins—in prominent display position. "But probably romance. Unless you ate something questionable for breakfast."

Sarah wisely decided not to pursue this conversation further.

By nine-fifteen, the market was bustling. Locals mixed with tourists. Farmers sold produce. Craft vendors displayed handmade goods. Musicians played on the corner. And Dodo's cats conducted the most effective sales campaign Franklin had ever witnessed.

The strategy was simple but brilliant. Sherlock, the orange tabby, would crawl into a Cat Sak—currently "The Midnight Zoomies"—and emerge with perfectly timed cuteness just as potential customers approached. His head would pop out of the opening, eyes wide, expression saying "I'm adorable and also trapped send help or maybe treats."

Customers would melt. "Oh my god, look at the cat in the bag!"

"That's Sherlock," Dodo would explain. "He's demonstrating the Cat Sak's comfort and security features. Notice how he can burrow completely or peek out depending on his mood and paranoia level."

"How much?"

"Forty-five dollars for the standard sleeping bag. Sixty-five for the carrier. Eighty-five for the convertible model." Dodo would pull out another Cat Sak. "All hand-knitted using premium acrylic yarn that's machine washable because cats are disgusting creatures who vomit strategically."

Meanwhile, Pancake —the gray with white paws who somehow looked distinguished despite being a cat—would be demonstrating the carrier model by sitting regally in one, accepting pets from passersby like a monarch receiving tribute.

And Princess —the calico with attitude problems— would wander the market, somehow always returning with customers. She'd lead them back to Dodo's booth with the confidence of a cat who understood sales funnels and customer acquisition.

"Your cat just walked up to me and meowed until I followed her," said a tourist from Atlanta, slightly bewildered.

"That's Princess. She does targeted recruiting." Dodo showed her "The Sunset Special." "She's never wrong about matching cats to their ideal sleeping bags. The colors suit you."

"The colors are for the cat."

"The cat's aesthetic reflects the owner's inner self. Basic psychology." Dodo held up the bag. "See how the orange suggests optimism? The pink indicates nurturing qualities? The purple screams 'I make questionable life choices but own them completely'?"

The tourist from Atlanta bought two Cat Saks.

By ten AM, Dodo had sold six sleeping bags, three carriers, and one convertible model to a woman who described her cat as "extra dramatic and possibly sociopathic." The cats had eaten approximately fourteen treats (offered by customers who couldn't resist), knocked over one display of artisanal jam (Princess's fault), and gathered intelligence from at least seven different vendors.

"The honey lady said Morrison's been asking about art dealers," Sherlock reported via meaningful eye contact.

"I don't speak cat," Dodo reminded him.

Sherlock meowed in exasperation and knocked over "The Drama Queen."

"Art dealers. Got it." Dodo righted the Cat Sak. "Anything else?"

Pancake appeared from the direction of the goat cheese vendor, looking smug.

"The cheese lady says there was a well-dressed man at the market last week asking about local artists," Dodo translated. She had no idea how she knew what Pancake was communicating —she just did. The cats had explained it once using interpretive dance and strategic toy mouse placement. Dodo had understood perfectly. "Expensive suit. European accent.

Bought artisanal cheese like he was collecting rare artifacts."

"Conrad Fischer," Dodo muttered. "Had to be."

A customer approached—middle-aged woman, kind face, carrying reusable shopping bags filled with vegetables. "Are these really for cats?"

"Certified by three professional feline quality control experts," Dodo said, gesturing to her sales team. "Would you like a demonstration?"

"I don't actually have a cat."

"The cats say you're about to adopt one."

"I'm not—"

"Princess is rarely wrong about these things. She's predicted six adoptions this year. All successful. One somewhat chaotic but ultimately heartwarming." Dodo pulled out a lavender-colored Cat Sak she'd labeled "The Beginner's Special." "This one's perfect for first-time cat owners. Forgiving design. Easy cleaning. Comes with a guide on feline manipulation techniques."

"I'm really not—"

Princess wound around the woman's ankles, purring. Sherlock emerged from his sleeping bag looking pathetically cute. Pancake somehow conveyed aristocratic approval of this potential adoption.

"Fine," the woman sighed. "I'll take the lavender one. And maybe I'll stop by the shelter next week. Just to look."

"The cats win again," Dodo announced after the woman left.

Donnie returned from browsing the produce stalls carrying heirloom tomatoes and looking bemused. "Did you just convince someone to adopt a cat they don't have using a sleeping bag as evidence?"

"The cats convinced her. I just facilitated the transaction."

"That's terrifying."

"That's sales."

By eleven, word had spread through the market about Dodo's cats. Vendors were sending customers over "just to see the cats in the bags." The cats, understanding they were celebrities, performed with increasing theatricality. Sherlock's peek-a-boo timing became flawless. Pancake added regal slow-blinks. Princess started doing a routine where she'd burrow into a Cat Sak, pop out suddenly, and frighten unsuspecting customers (who then felt compelled to buy the bag as apology for screaming).

But the cats weren't just selling. They were gathering.

"Mrs. Henderson says the lavender sachets are outselling everything because people are stressed about the murder," Dodo reported to Donnie during a lull.

"The cats told you this?"

"Princess eavesdropped while the lavender lady

was talking to the goat cheese lady. Then she knocked over a sachet display as confirmation signal."

"Of course she did."

"The bread vendor's nephew works at the tobacco warehouse. Says the studio is still crime scene taped. FBI was there yesterday collecting evidence." Dodo accepted a twenty-dollar bill from a customer buying "The Drama Queen" for her supposedly dramatic Siamese. "Pancake obtained this information in exchange for allowing ear scratches."

"The cats are better investigators than most police."

"The cats contain multitudes." Dodo watched Sherlock lead another customer back to the booth. "Also they're mercenary attention seekers who understand that looking cute equals treats. Capitalism at its finest."

The lunch rush brought even more customers. The market hummed with energy—live music from the corner stage, vendors calling out specials, the smell of fresh bread and coffee and the particular scent of outdoor markets in good weather. The cats worked overtime, demonstrating products, recruiting customers, gathering gossip, and occasionally causing minor chaos that somehow always resulted in sales.

By noon, Dodo had sold twenty-two Cat Saks, taken seven custom orders, and collected enough market intelligence to brief the entire Tuesday night mahjong group. The cats had consumed approximately thirty treats (she'd lost count), knocked over three displays (Princess was definitely doing this strategically for attention), and generated what Sarah the bread vendor described as "the most effective guerrilla marketing campaign I've ever witnessed."

"Your cats are terrifying," a craft vendor named Linda said, watching Princess lead yet another customer back to Dodo's booth.

"Your pottery is lovely," Dodo countered. "The cats say the blue vase will sell within the hour to someone driving a Subaru."

"That's oddly specific."

"Cats are oddly specific creatures."

The blue vase sold at twelve-thirty to a woman driving a Subaru.

"I'm not even surprised anymore," Linda admitted.

The market closed at one PM. Vendors packed up, customers dispersed, the musicians finished their last song. Dodo loaded her remaining Cat Saks into Donnie's truck while the cats supervised from their respective carriers (premium models, naturally).

"Good day?" Donnie asked.

"Twenty-two sales. Seven custom orders. Enough market gossip to fuel Tuesday night mahjong for a month. Princess predicted two adoptions, one break-up, and a possible embezzlement scheme at the hardware store." Dodo settled into the passenger seat. "Also Sherlock says you should check the bakery's flour supplier. He heard something about shipment irregularities from the produce vendor's dog."

"He heard this from a dog?"

"Animals communicate across species lines. It's basic ecology."

"It's basic chaos."

"Same thing."

On the drive home, Dodo tallied her sales—almost a thousand dollars from Cat Saks, which would fund yarn purchases for next week's inventory and also a donation to Franklin's animal shelter because the cats had insisted (via strategic meowing near her wallet).

"The cats want me to tell you something," Dodo said as Donnie pulled into her driveway.

"Should I be worried?"

"The goat cheese lady's cousin works at The Slanted Window. She heard Nguyen talking on the phone about paintings. Said he sounded angry. Agitated. Like something had gone wrong." Dodo unbuckled her seatbelt. "This was just days before Fischer was killed."

Donnie went still. "The cats heard this?"

"Princess was under the goat cheese table eating dropped samples. The cousin was restocking inventory. Princess reported back during the noon rush using interpretive tail positions."

"I'm going to call Morrison."

"The cats recommend that course of action." Dodo gathered her things. "Also Pancake would like salmon for dinner as payment for quality intelligence gathering."

"Pancake gets kibble."

"You wound his professional pride."

"Pancake can join a union and negotiate better."

Dodo smiled. Because this was Franklin. Where Saturday farmers market meant fresh produce and handmade crafts and also cats conducting corporate espionage while selling sleeping bags. Where murder investigations involved mahjong groups and bakeries and feline intelligence networks.

Where community meant showing up, selling Cat Saks, gathering gossip, and using every available resource—including three cats with questionable ethics and excellent sales instincts—to help solve crimes.

"Same time next week?" Donnie asked.

"The cats insist. Apparently there's going to be a new honey vendor with information about suspicious art collector behavior. Sherlock is already planning his reconnaissance strategy."

"Of course he is."

Dodo watched Donnie drive away, then looked at her cats. "Good work today, team. Capitalism and justice: the perfect combination."

Princess meowed agreement. Pancake looked smug. Sherlock was already asleep in his carrier, exhausted from a hard day's work selling and spying.

Just another Saturday at the Macon County Farmers Market. Where Cat Saks sold themselves, cats gathered intelligence, and Franklin's most chaotic vendor somehow always knew exactly what was happening in town.

The cats, naturally, took all the credit.

As they should.

Evelyn Cho spent Saturday morning in the deep forensic accounting work that had defined her career at GBI—the kind of meticulous financial investigation that looked boring from the outside but revealed everything from the inside. She sat at Maya's apothecary back room—her unofficial office now—with four laptops running simultaneous database queries, two legal pads covered in notes, and a thermos of Maya's special focus tea (green tea with ginseng and a hint of rosemary). The scent of dried herbs filled the room. Outside, Franklin was having a Saturday morning. Inside, Evelyn was hunting a ghost.

James Park existed. She was certain. But he existed carefully, professionally, with the kind of financial invisibility that suggested training.

She'd started with the obvious: credit card records, bank accounts, property ownership, business registrations. Nothing. No James Park aged 25-35 in the databases she could access. Which meant either he used a different name for financial transactions, or he operated entirely in cash, or he wasn't American.

So she'd shifted strategies. Instead of looking for Park directly, she looked for Nguyen's money. Where did it go? Who did he pay?

Nguyen Fine Arts International had standard business expenses: gallery rent, employee salaries, artist payments, shipping costs, insurance, marketing. All documented. All legal. All boring.

But buried in the accounting was a line item that appeared monthly: "Consulting Services - $15,000."

Fifteen thousand dollars. Every month. For seven years. No vendor name listed, just "Consulting Services."

Evelyn pulled up the payment records. Wire transfers to a shell company called Pacific Consulting LLC. Registered in Delaware. Officers listed as "various." Address: mail forwarding service.

Classic money laundering setup. But also classic payment structure for someone you wanted to keep off the books.

She traced Pacific Consulting backwards. The company received $15,000 monthly from Nguyen. And then? The money moved immediately. To Singapore. To Hong Kong. To accounts that required significant authentication to access.

Dead end. For now.

But Evelyn had spent fifteen years at GBI

learning that dead ends were just places where you needed better tools. She picked up her phone and called AUSA Rebecca Walsh.

"Evelyn. Tell me you have good news."

"I have a lead. Maybe. Nguyen's been paying someone fifteen thousand a month for seven years through a shell company. Payments go to Singapore and Hong Kong. I can't access those accounts without subpoena."

"That's over a million dollars. What's the consulting for?"

"I'm thinking it's payment for James Park. The man who probably killed Fischer."

Walsh was quiet for a moment. "The FBI mentioned him. Maya Lin's witness statements put him in Franklin multiple times before the murder. But we don't have identification yet."

"Because he's careful. Professional. The kind of person who gets paid through shell companies and operates in cash." Evelyn pulled up her notes. "If I can get access to those Singapore and Hong Kong accounts, I can trace where the money goes after that. Find Park's real identity."

"I'll get you a subpoena. But Evelyn, this takes time. International banking records, multiple jurisdictions, careful legal work. We're talking weeks, maybe months."

"Bea doesn't have months. She's in protective custody now. Every day she's separated from Franklin is another day she loses."

"I know. But this is how it works. We build the

case carefully, or we lose in court." Walsh's voice softened. "I'm sorry. I know this is personal. David's case is connected, Bea's your friend. But we have to do this right."

After hanging up, Evelyn sat back and looked at her screens full of financial data. Somewhere in these numbers was James Park's identity. Somewhere in these wire transfers was proof of conspiracy. Somewhere in these shell companies was justice for David and Bea.

But finding it required patience. And Evelyn had never been good at patience when people she loved were suffering.

Her phone buzzed. Text from Donnie: EMERGENCY. MEET AT MY PLACE. NOW. BEA CALLED. SOMETHING HAPPENED.

Evelyn grabbed her laptop and keys and drove to Donnie's house faster than was legal. When she arrived, the whole mahjong group was already there—Donnie, Maya, Mabs, Dodo, Frankie, Eddie. Everyone looking worried.

"What happened?" Evelyn asked.

Donnie held up her phone, on speaker. "Bea, tell them what you told me."

Bea's voice came through, thin and scared. "Someone tried to access my studio last night. The alarm company called me. Someone used my access code to try to get in, but the FBI had changed the code yesterday as security measure. The alarm went off, they fled."

"Did the alarm company get video?"

"Yes. They sent it to FBI. But they also sent it to me because I'm listed as primary account holder." Pause. "It was him. James Park. The man Maya described. I recognized him from Camp Galang."

Everyone went still.

"You knew him," Maya said. "From the refugee camp."

"Yes. He was... younger then, obviously. Teenager. Maybe sixteen. But I remember him. He was with Minh Nguyen. They were together at the camp. Minh looked after him like a younger brother or cousin or something."

Evelyn's mind raced. Nguyen and Park together at Camp Galang in 1978. Which meant their partnership was forty-five years old. Which meant Park wasn't just an employee. He was family. Chosen family, maybe, or actual family.

"Bea, what was Park's name at the camp?" Mabs asked, already pulling out her laptop.

"I don't remember. Maybe I never knew. There were thousands of people. But I remember seeing him with Minh. Minh was kind to the young boys, helped them survive. Park was one of them."

"So Nguyen and Park have a forty-five-year relationship," Donnie said. "That changes everything. Park's not an employee. He's partner, family, something deeper."

"Which means when we arrested Nguyen, Park lost his protection," Evelyn added. "He's desperate. Trying to get evidence from Bea's studio, probably looking for anything that could implicate him."

"Or trying to finish what he started," Maya said quietly. "If Park killed Fischer and framed Bea, and now Bea's testimony is going to expose him, he might try to silence her permanently."

The room went cold.

"FBI has her in protective custody," Donnie said. "She's safe."

"Is she?" Frankie's voice was sharp. "Park tried to access her studio last night. That means he's in Franklin. That means he knows she's testimony. That means he's planning something."

"We need to find him," Evelyn said. "Before he finds Bea."

"FBI is looking," Donnie pointed out.

"FBI is slow. We're fast." Evelyn pulled up her laptop. "I've been tracking Nguyen's payments. Fifteen thousand a month for seven years to a shell company. That's Park. I know it. And if I can trace where that money goes, I can find him."

"How long will that take?"

"With subpoenas and international banking cooperation? Weeks. Without? I need someone who can access Hong Kong financial databases illegally."

Everyone looked at her.

"I'm not suggesting we break the law," Evelyn clarified. "I'm suggesting we find someone who already has."

Mabs cleared her throat. "I may know someone. Former colleague at GBI. Computer crimes division. He's... resourceful."

"Call him."

While Mabs made calls, Evelyn continued working the numbers. Nguyen's payments. Pacific Consulting. Singapore routing. Hong Kong destination. The pattern was there if she could just—

"Got it," Mabs said, hanging up. "My colleague can access Hong Kong databases. He's retired, lives in Asheville, operates a private cyber security consulting firm now. Technically legal. Mostly."

"Can he help?"

"He said if I ask nice and promise to have coffee with him, yes."

"Promise him coffee, dinner, and a kidney if necessary. We need this information."

Two hours later, Mabs's colleague—a man named Robert Wren had hacked his way through three levels of Hong Kong banking security and found where Nguyen's payments ultimately went.

"Here," Robert said via video call, sharing his screen. "Pacific Consulting receives fifteen thousand monthly from Nguyen. Money immediately transfers to Hong Kong Commercial Bank, account number ending in 4892. From there, it transfers to..." He clicked through screens. "Multiple accounts. Small amounts. Designed to obscure the trail. But if you aggregate them all, they end up at one destination. A personal account in Seoul, South Korea."

"Seoul?" Evelyn leaned closer. "Not North Korea?"

"South Korea. But the account holder has North Korean connections. Dual citizenship maybe, or family ties. Hard to tell from financial records alone."

"Account holder name?"

"Park Ji-woo. Age thirty-one. Korean citizen. Residence listed in Seoul but travels extensively. Has accounts in Singapore, Hong Kong, Tokyo, Los Angeles, and..." Robert checked. "Asheville, North Carolina."

"Asheville," Donnie said. "That's forty miles from Franklin."

"He has a residence there?"

"Apartment. Paid annually in advance. Cash." Robert pulled up property records. "875 Haywood Road, Unit 304. Leased under the name James Park—his American alias, probably."

Evelyn wrote down the address. "Robert, can you see when that account last had activity?"

"Yesterday. Withdrawal from ATM in..." Robert's expression changed. "Franklin, North Carolina. Main Street. Four PM."

"He's here," Maya whispered. "He's been here the whole time."

After Robert signed off, the mahjong group sat in Donnie's living room processing what they'd learned. James Park was actually Park Ji-woo, Korean national, age thirty-one, with North

Korean connections, Nguyen's partner for forty-five years, and currently living forty miles away in Asheville.

And yesterday, he'd been on Main Street in Franklin. Walking past Maya's apothecary, past The Country Kitchen, past the bakery. Close enough to touch.

"We tell Morrison," Donnie said. "And FBI. They can pick him up in Asheville."

"What if he's not there?" Frankie asked. "What if he's here, in Franklin, watching?"

"Then we find him first." Donnie stood up, paced. "He tried to access Bea's studio. He's desperate. Desperate people make mistakes. We use that."

"How?" Maya asked.

"We bait him. Make him think Bea's vulnerable. Draw him out." Donnie looked at each of them. "And when he shows up, we're ready."

"That's dangerous," Mabs said.

"Staying passive is more dangerous. Park's a professional killer. He's not going to stop until Bea's silenced or he's caught. I prefer caught."

Evelyn understood the logic. Understood the risk. Understood that sometimes justice required bait and traps and deliberately putting yourself in danger.

She'd done it before, investigating corruption at GBI. Had worn a wire, met with suspects, gathered evidence while knowing one wrong word could get her killed.

And she'd survived. Because the cause mattered

more than the risk.

"I'm in," Evelyn said. "Whatever the plan is, I'm in."

"Me too," Maya agreed.

"And me," Mabs added.

"The cats are very supportive," Dodo said. "Also I'm in."

"Goddamnit, yes," Frankie muttered.

Eddie looked at Donnie. "You know I support you. But please don't get killed. I'm too old to train a new wife."

Donnie smiled despite the tension. "Noted. Now let's plan."

They spent the next two hours developing a strategy. Leak that Bea was returning to her studio to pack belongings. Make it seem like she'd be alone, vulnerable, distracted. Set up surveillance. Wait for Park to make his move. Have FBI backup ready but not obvious.

It was risky. It was possibly illegal. It was definitely against FBI protocols.

But it was also the fastest way to protect Bea and catch a killer.

By evening, the plan was set. Morrison had been reluctantly informed and more reluctantly agreed to coordinate. FBI was furious but acknowledged they didn't have faster options. And Bea, brave and determined despite her fear, had agreed to be bait.

"I didn't survive Vietnam to hide in America," she'd said. "I'll face him."

Evelyn drove home as sunset painted the mountains gold and purple. Beautiful November evening, cold and clear, the kind that made you remember why you loved these mountains despite the danger they held.

She thought about David. About his idealistic belief that justice was worth any cost. About the night he'd died, car forced off a mountain road by someone who decided his investigation was too dangerous to continue.

And she thought about Bea. About refugee trauma and survival and the forty-five years of building a life only to have it threatened again by someone from her past.

The connections were everywhere if you looked. Nguyen and Park, surviving the camps together, building an empire together, exploiting others together. Fischer and his greed. David and his investigation. Bea and her art.

All connected by money, by trauma, by similar pain then the decision some survivors made to steal from others like them and the decision other survivors made to aid others.

And at the center of it all: the Tuesday Night Mahjong Group, choosing each other, choosing justice, choosing to fight back against darkness.

Evelyn pulled into Maya's driveway. Their home now. Shared space, shared life, shared commitment to keep choosing each other despite how hard it was.

Maya was waiting inside, tea already steeping,

dinner in the oven, creating the comfort rituals that made their life together bearable and beautiful.

"Tomorrow, we set the trap," Evelyn said.

"Tomorrow, we catch a killer," Maya corrected.

"Same thing."

They sat together in the kitchen while November darkness fell outside and the mountains settled into night. Somewhere out there, Park was planning. Somewhere in protective custody, Bea was preparing. Somewhere in Los Angeles federal detention, Nguyen was calculating his options.

And here, in Franklin, the mahjong group was ready.

For justice. For family. For the fight.

Because that's what they did. Tuesday night mahjong against international conspiracy. Found family against predators. Community against darkness.

Ridiculous. Impossible. Exactly what they'd do anyway.

Tomorrow would be dangerous. Tomorrow someone might get hurt. Tomorrow the trap might fail.

But tomorrow they'd try. Together. Refusing to let fear win.

Chapter 14

Detective John Morrison had been a cop in Franklin for twenty-two years, and he'd learned that sometimes the best investigations happened despite federal jurisdiction, not because of it.

He sat in his office Sunday morning reviewing the plan Donnie had outlined—the trap for James Park, the bait using Bea, the coordination with FBI that was more "inform them afterward" than "get permission first."

It violated about twelve protocols. It possibly violated a few laws. It definitely violated Agent Katherine Parker's explicit instructions to "let the FBI handle this."

Morrison was going to do it anyway.

Because Bea Tran was a Franklin resident. Because the Tuesday night mahjong group had earned his respect solving Terry Boone's murder.

And because sometimes justice required bending rules until they nearly broke.

He pulled up the surveillance plan on his computer. Bea's studio, three cameras, two inside, one outside. FBI backup positioned a block away—close enough to respond, far enough not to spook Park. Donnie and Frankie on site as "movers helping Bea pack." Maya and Evelyn at the apothecary as "emergency contacts." Mabs coordinating communications. Dodo... doing whatever Dodo did that somehow always proved useful.

His phone rang. Agent Katherine Parker.

"Detective Morrison. I hear you're planning an unauthorized operation."

"I'm planning a protective detail for a witness packing her belongings."

"With civilian involvement, minimal backup, and no federal coordination."

"I informed you yesterday. That's coordination."

"Informing and coordinating are different things." Parker's voice was sharp but not angry. More... resigned. "Morrison, I understand the impulse. Local case, local victim, you want to solve it. But this is federal now. We have procedures."

"Your procedures are slow. Park Ji-woo is in Franklin. He tried to access Bea's studio. He's desperate. We use that desperation to catch him before he hurts someone."

"Or you spook him and he disappears. Or

someone gets hurt. Or you contaminate evidence and we lose the case in court."

Morrison leaned back in his chair, looked out his window at Franklin waking up to Sunday morning. Church bells ringing. People walking to breakfast. Small-town peace that hid complicated darkness.

"Agent Parker, let me be direct. Bea Tran is my responsibility. She lives in my town. This happened in my jurisdiction. I'm not sitting back while you file paperwork and build cases. I'm protecting her. With or without FBI support."

Silence on the line. Then: "We'll provide backup. Two agents, positioned as you outlined. But Morrison, if this goes wrong, it's on you."

"Understood."

"And tell Donnie Carlisle that if she gets herself killed, I'm arresting her ghost for obstruction."

Morrison smiled despite the tension. "I'll pass that along."

After hanging up, he reviewed the timeline. Ten AM, Bea arrives at studio with David Chen. Donnie and Frankie arrive at ten-fifteen as movers. Bea starts packing, visible through windows. FBI backup in position by ten-thirty. And then... they wait.

Wait for Park to make his move. Wait for desperation to outweigh caution. Wait for the moment when a professional killer made an amateur mistake.

Morrison had set traps before. Drug buys gone

bad. Domestic violence calls turned dangerous. Traffic stops that escalated. Every cop knew the feeling—controlled danger, calculated risk, the hope that training and backup would be enough. This felt different. Higher stakes. More variables. Civilians involved who shouldn't be but were anyway because they loved Bea too much to stay safe.

He understood that. Respected it. Hated that it was necessary.

His phone buzzed. Text from his niece, Tammy, who worked at Donnie's bakery: AUDREY WANTS TO COME TO THE STAKEOUT. DONNIE SAYS NO. AUDREY IS JUDGING EVERYONE.

Morrison smiled. Even in serious operations, there was comedy. That was Franklin. That was community. That was what made small-town policing both maddening and meaningful.

He texted back: TELL AUDREY HER JUDGMENT IS NOTED BUT SHE NEEDS TO STAY AT THE BAKERY FOR SAFETY.

Response: SHE SAYS SHE'S NEVER SAFE WITH EDDIE'S BAKING. HE USES TOO MUCH CINNAMON. NEEDS MORE CHICKEN.

Morrison laughed despite himself. Then he gathered his gear—vest, radio, backup weapon, first aid kit—and headed out.

The tobacco warehouse looked quiet when Morrison arrived at nine-thirty. Sunday morning, most artists gone, just Bea's studio and Lin's upstairs. Good. Fewer witnesses if things went wrong.

He positioned himself in an unmarked car across the street, eyes on the entrance. FBI agents Rodriguez and Martinez were a block south in a panel van. Donnie and Frankie were due in thirty minutes.

And Bea was en route with David Chen, protected by federal marshals until she reached the studio, then "on her own" for the operation.

Morrison's radio crackled. Agent Parker's voice: "Surveillance in position. We have eyes on the studio. No sign of target yet."

"Copy that." Morrison settled in to wait.

Waiting was the hardest part of any operation. The time when your mind invented worst-case scenarios. The time when you second-guessed every decision. The time when you wondered if you should have done this differently, called it off, waited for more intel.

But Morrison had learned over decades that sometimes you had to act on incomplete information. Sometimes you had to trust your gut, your team, your community.

And his gut said Park would come. Desperation made people predictable. And Park was desperate —his partner arrested, his operation exposed, his payday threatened. He'd try to salvage something. Try to silence Bea. Try to escape.

And when he did, Morrison would be ready.

Ten AM. Bea arrived in an unmarked federal vehicle. She got out slowly, looking small and scared but determined. David Chen walked with her to the studio door. They went inside.

From Morrison's position, he could see into the studio through the front windows. Bea moving through the space, looking at her paintings, touching her workstation. Chen stood near the door, alert, professional.

Ten-fifteen. Donnie's truck pulled up. She and Frankie got out carrying moving boxes. They waved to Bea through the window—pre-arranged signal that everything was normal. Went inside.

Now Bea had protection. Donnie, former insurance fraud investigator with thirty years experience. Frankie, military veteran with combat training. Both armed, both ready, both committed to protecting Bea.

Morrison felt slightly better. But only slightly.

His radio: "Movement. Asian male, thirty, approaching from south entrance. Matches Park's description."

Morrison's pulse quickened. "Copy. Do not engage yet. Let him commit."

He watched through binoculars. The man moved confidently, professionally. Dressed casually—jeans, jacket, baseball cap pulled low. But the gait was wrong. Too controlled. Too aware of surroundings.

Military or law enforcement training, Morrison thought. Or professional criminal. Same difference, really. All three taught situational awareness and threat assessment.

The man—Park, almost certainly—circled the building. Checking exits. Looking for cameras. Assessing security.

Smart. Careful. Exactly what Morrison would do if he were planning a hit.

"He's casing," Morrison said into his radio. "Setting up approach. Stay alert."

The man disappeared around the back of the building. Morrison shifted position, trying to keep visual. Lost him.

"Anyone have eyes?" he asked.

"Negative. He's in the blind spot between buildings."

Damn. Morrison got out of his car, moving carefully, staying low. He needed visual contact. Needed to know what Park was doing.

A sound. Glass breaking. Fire alarm. Smoke billowing from the back of the building.

"He's creating a diversion!" Morrison ran toward the studio. "All units move in! Now!"

The front door burst open. Bea, Chen, Donnie, and Frankie evacuated fast—exactly as they should in a fire. But Morrison saw Park emerge from the side, moving toward them with purpose.

"FBI! Freeze!" Agent Rodriguez appeared from the van, weapon drawn.

Park pivoted, saw the agent, ran. Not toward his escape route—toward Bea.

Morrison ran faster. Park was twenty feet from

Bea. Fifteen. Ten.

Frankie stepped between them. "Not happening."

Park swung. Frankie blocked. They engaged —fast, professional, two people with combat training fighting for their lives.

Morrison reached them, weapon drawn. "Franklin PD! On the ground!"

Park kicked Frankie's knee, his bad knee, the one injured in the workplace accident. He went down with a cry of pain. Park grabbed Bea's arm.

"Let her go!" Morrison aimed center mass.

Park pulled Bea in front of him, human shield. "Back off or she dies."

"You kill her, you get nothing. You're already facing murder charges. Add another killing and witness murder, you'll never see daylight again."

"I'm already dead." Park's voice was cold, accented, desperate. "Nguyen's arrested. Operation's blown. I'm finished."

"So surrender. Cooperate. Make a deal."

"There's no deal for killing a federal prosecutor." Park smiled bitterly. "David Cho. That was me. I forced his car off the road. Nguyen ordered it, I executed it. You think FBI will deal with me after that?"

Morrison's blood ran cold. Confession. Park had just confessed to David Cho's murder on federal surveillance.

"Then let Bea go. She's not part of this."

"She's everything. Her testimony puts Nguyen away. Without her, maybe he walks. Maybe I walk. Maybe—"

Bea moved. Fast. Desperate. She stomped on Park's instep, jabbed her elbow back into his solar plexus, twisted out of his grip with the efficiency of someone who'd survived worse than this.

Park staggered. Morrison lunged. Agent Rodriguez was there, tackling Park to the ground. Handcuffs snapped on. Rights read. Professional arrest executed in seconds.

And Bea stood there, shaking, held up by Donnie and Maya who'd run from wherever they'd been positioned.

"I didn't survive the South China Sea to die in a parking lot," Bea said. Her voice trembled but her eyes were fierce. "Not happening."

Morrison holstered his weapon and checked on Frankie. His knee was swelling but he was conscious, alert, angry. "That bastard knew exactly where to kick. Professional training for sure."

"Military?" Morrison asked.

"Something. ROK Army maybe. South Korean special forces." Frankie grimaced. "He's good. I'm better. But my knee's gonna hurt for a week."

FBI agents swarmed the scene. Agent Parker arrived, surveyed the situation with professional assessment. "Detective Morrison. Your unauthorized operation just netted us a confession to federal prosecutor murder, attempted witness murder, and enough evidence to lock Park away for life."

"You're welcome."

"Don't do it again."

"Can't promise that."

Agent Parker almost smiled. "I wouldn't expect you to. Good work. All of you. Even the civilians who shouldn't be here but somehow always are."

Donnie, standing with Bea and Maya, gave a small salute.

She watched as FBI processed the scene, arrested Park, collected evidence. The operation had worked. Against odds, despite protocols, through community coordination and civilian courage.

Bea was safe. Park was caught. Justice was advancing.

But Donnie knew this wasn't over. Park and Nguyen were caught, but the larger conspiracy—the money laundering, the sanctions evasion, the deliberate misuse and attacks on refugees—that was bigger than two men.

That would take time. Federal prosecution. International cooperation. Years maybe.

But today, in Franklin, North Carolina, on a Sunday morning in November, justice had won a round.

And sometimes that had to be enough.

Her phone buzzed. Text from Tammy: AUDREY SAYS SHE KNEW IT WOULD WORK. SHE'S VERY PLEASED WITH EVERYONE. ESPECIALLY BEA. LESS PLEASED WITH EDDIE WHO BURNED THE CROISSANTS.

Donnie smiled. Even in danger, even in victory,

life went on. Chickens complained. Poodles judged. Croissants burned.

That was Franklin. That was home. That was what they'd fought to protect.

And they'd won.

Chapter 15

Bea Tran sat in Morrison's conference room three hours after nearly being killed and tried to process forty-five years of survival and betrayal and the moment when she'd finally chosen to fight back instead of flee.

Her hands still trembled. Her adrenaline still spiked. But she was alive. And Park Ji-woo—the boy from Camp Galang, the professional killer, the one who'd tried to silence her—was in federal custody.

The Tuesday night mahjong group surrounded her. Literally. They'd arranged chairs in a circle, Bea at the center, everyone else creating a protective ring. Maya on her right with tea. Donnie on her left with quiet strength. Mabs with her notebook. Evelyn with her laptop. Dodo with cookies. Frankie with an ice pack on his knee and a grim expression.

Even Eddie was there, and Audrey, who'd somehow convinced someone to bring her from the bakery. The poodle sat at Bea's feet in judgment position, but her usual aloofness was softened. She was protecting, in her way.

"Tell us," Donnie said gently. "Everything. About Nguyen, about Park, about what you know that we don't."

Bea looked at each of them. Her found family. The people who'd risked everything to save her. Who'd fought FBI protocols and international conspiracies and professional killers to get her justice.

She owed them the truth. All of it.

"Camp Galang, Indonesia, 1978," Bea began. "I was fifteen years old. I'd been on the boat for seventeen days. My parents died on day six. I arrived with nothing—no family, no belongings except my grandmother's jade bracelet, no plan except survive."

The room was silent except for Bea's voice and the scratch of Mabs's pen taking notes.

"The camp was chaos. Thousands of boat people, all traumatized, all desperate. Some people helped each other. Some people didn't. That's how it is in crisis—you see who people really are."

"Minh Nguyen was there?" Maya asked softly.

"Yes. He was twenty-three. Older, stronger, more established. He'd been in the camp for six months already, waiting for resettlement. He'd set himself up as... facilitator, I guess. If you needed extra food, you went to Minh. If you needed better tent placement, you went to Minh. If you needed documents or bribes or connections, you went to Minh."

"For a price," Donnie said.

"Always for a price. But when you're desperate, you pay." Bea sipped Maya's tea—chamomile with honey, exactly what she needed. "I was alone, fifteen, barely speaking English. Minh noticed me. Offered help. Said he could get me better food, safer housing, faster processing."

"What did he want in return?"

Bea looked at her hands. "Information. Stories. He wanted to know everyone's backgrounds—where they came from, what they'd survived, what made them valuable to American resettlement programs."

"He was collecting intelligence," Evelyn said.

"Yes. Even then, he was thinking ahead. Building databases of people he could take advantage to line his pockets later." Bea paused. "I told him everything. About my parents dying. About my grandmother's jade bracelet. About my dreams of becoming an artist. About my guilt for surviving when they died."

"And he remembered," Maya said. "For forty-five years, he remembered."

"He remembered everything. That his power. Perfect memory for trauma, for vulnerability, for the exact details he could use to manipulate people later."

Bea stood, paced to the window. Outside, Franklin was going about Sunday afternoon business. People walking dogs. Cars driving to Sunday dinner. Normal life that felt impossibly far away.

"Park Ji-woo—he went by different name then, but it was him—he was sixteen. Minh had taken him under his wing, taught him how to survive in the camp. Taught him how to notice things, how to trade, how to profit from other people's desperation. Park learned fast. By the time I left the camp, Park was Minh's lieutenant. His enforcer."

"They came to America together," Mabs said, checking her notes.

"Different years, different programs. But yes. They both made it. And they stayed connected. Built their empire together. Minh the face, Park the muscle. Minh the businessman, Park the soldier."

Bea turned from the window. "I didn't know any of this until three months ago. I'd put them behind me, honestly. Camp Galang was a lifetime ago. I'd built a new life, new name basically, new everything. I thought I was safe."

"What happened three months ago?" Donnie asked.

"Minh showed up at my studio. I didn't recognize him at first—forty-five years changes faces. But he knew me immediately. Called me by my camp name. Mentioned my grandmother's bracelet. Asked if I still painted water."

The room went cold.

"He'd been watching you," Evelyn said. "Tracking you. Waiting for the right moment."

"Yes. He said he'd followed my career for years. Knew about my 'Between Waters' series. Knew those paintings were worth money. And he wanted them." Bea's voice hardened. "He said he'd helped me survive the camp. Said I owed him. Said the paintings were payment for his kindness forty-five years ago."

"Predator," Frankie muttered.

"Complete predator. When I refused, he brought Fischer in. Legitimate art dealer, professional front. I'd sold some works to him a few years back. Fischer would make offers, pressure me, play good cop while Minh stayed in the background playing puppet master."

"And when you still refused?" Maya asked.

"Park showed up. That was two weeks before Fischer's murder. Park came to my studio, said he was a collector. But I recognized him. His eyes. Same cold calculation I'd seen at Camp Galang. Same willingness to do whatever was necessary to survive."

Bea sat back down, suddenly exhausted. "I knew then it wasn't just business. It was personal. Minh and Park wanted my paintings, yes. But they also wanted me silenced. Because I could identify them. Could testify to their camp activities, their extortion, theft and trading documents."

"That's why they killed Fischer and framed you," Donnie said. "Eliminate the business partner who'd become liability, steal the paintings, silence the witness who could expose their past. Three problems, one solution."

"Exactly." Bea looked at each of them. "And I almost let them. Almost fled, disappeared, changed my name again, started over somewhere else."

"What changed?" Maya asked gently.

Bea smiled through tears. "You. All of you. Tuesday night mahjong. Found family. The realization that I'd spent forty-five years running from Camp Galang, and I was tired. Tired of being afraid. Tired of letting predators win."

She stood again, this time with purpose. "Minh Nguyen survived the boat by preying on others. So did Park. They took the worst thing that ever happened to us—Vietnam, the camps, the loss—and decided that meant they had permission to hurt people forever."

"But you made a different choice," Evelyn said.

"I made a different choice. I survived by painting. By healing. By building community. By choosing to help other artists instead of manipulating them." Bea looked around the circle. "And when Minh and Park came after me, I chose to fight instead of flee. Because I have you. Because I'm not alone anymore."

The room was silent except for Dodo crying quietly and Mabs writing notes and Audrey shifting position to lean against Bea's leg in support.

"So what now?" Frankie asked.

"Now I testify. Everything. Camp Galang, Minh's criminal network, Park's violence, the forty-five years of preying on the helpless. I tell it all." Bea's voice was firm. "And maybe—maybe—some of the other refugee artists Minh stole from will find courage to testify too."

"FBI will protect you," Morrison said from the doorway. He'd been listening, respecting the space but present. "Witness protection if necessary. But after today, after Park's confession and arrest, maybe you don't need to disappear. Maybe we can protect you in place."

"Can I stay in Franklin?" Bea asked.

Morrison and Agent Katherine Parker—who'd also been listening—exchanged glances.

"We'll try," Agent Parker said. "No guarantees. But after what you did today, fighting back, surviving, getting Park's confession... you've earned the attempt. We'll petition for in-place protection. Armed detail. Safety measures. But keeping you here."

Bea felt something break in her chest—relief, hope, the beginning of belief that maybe this time survival wouldn't mean losing everything.

"Thank you."

"Don't thank us yet. Thank your mahjong group. They're the ones who made this possible. Solved the case, caught the killer, built the evidence." Agent Parker looked around the room. "You're all insane, you know that? Civilians taking on international money laundering conspiracies."

"Tuesday night mahjong," Dodo said cheerfully. "We're very committed."

"Apparently."

After the agents left, the mahjong group sat in Morrison's conference room processing everything Bea had revealed. The scope of Nguyen's crimes. The depth of Park's violence. The forty-five years of victimization of helpless refugees hidden in plain sight.

"How many others?" Mabs asked. "How many other refugee artists did they steal from?"

"Dozens," Evelyn said, pulling up her financial research. "I found evidence of at least forty artists whose work passed through Nguyen's galleries. Most were paid a fraction of what their art sold for. Most have no idea they were cheated."

"We find them," Donnie decided. "We document every case. We help them testify if they want to. We make sure Nguyen and Park don't just go to prison for murder—they go to prison for all their crimes against refugees."

"That's ambitious," Mabs said.

"That's necessary." Donnie looked at Bea. "You survived to tell this story. Other survivors deserve the chance to tell theirs."

Bea nodded. "I'll help. However I can."

The meeting broke up around dinner time. The group dispersed to their homes, to their lives, to the brief respite before the next phase—federal trial, testimony, justice pursued through proper channels.

But before they left, they did what they always did. They built the walls for mahjong. Stacked tiles two high, created the square that defined their game space.

"For courage," Maya said.

"For justice," Evelyn added.

"For survivors," Bea said.

They stood around the table looking at the tile walls. The ritual that had become more than ritual. The game that represented community, choice, the deliberate creation of family.

"We did good work," Donnie said.

"We did necessary work," Mabs corrected.

"We did impossible work," Frankie added.

"The cats are very proud," Dodo contributed.

They laughed despite the exhaustion, despite the trauma, despite everything. Because that was survival too. Finding joy in small moments. Finding hope in community. Finding strength in choosing each other.

Bea looked at her found family and thought: This is why I survived. For this moment. For these people. For the chance to fight back and win.

She'd spent forty-five years asking why she

survived when her parents died.

Finally, she had her answer.

She survived to be here. To testify. To help others. To prove that survival could mean more than just existence—it could mean justice, community, love.

The mountains outside Morrison's window stood witness, blue-purple in the evening light. Ancient. Patient. Impartial.

They'd seen everything before. They'd see it all again.

But for now, in this moment, they witnessed victory. Small, imperfect, costly. But victory nonetheless.

And that was enough.

Chapter 16

Two weeks after Park's arrest, Donnie Carlisle stood in her kitchen making Cuban coffee at five AM and thinking about how justice was like baking—you followed the recipe, did everything right, and sometimes it still didn't turn out the way you hoped.

The coffee maker hissed and sputtered. November had turned to December overnight, bringing the first real freeze of winter. Outside, frost covered everything in silver. The chickens huddled in their heated coop. The mountains rose in layers of gray and white, beautiful and unforgiving.

Eddie appeared in the doorway, hair wild from sleep. "You're worrying again."

"I'm always worrying."

"More than usual." He poured coffee, settled at the table. "What is it this time?"

Donnie sat across from him. "AUSA Walsh called yesterday. Federal trial is scheduled for April. That's four months away. Four months of Bea in protective custody, separated from community, waiting to testify."

"They couldn't get an earlier date?"

"RICO cases take time. They're building charges against Nguyen and Park for money laundering, sanctions evasion, art trafficking, and now two murders—Fischer and David Cho. That's hundreds of pages of evidence, dozens of witnesses, international banking records. Walsh says April is actually fast."

"But Bea's stuck in limbo."

"Bea's back in a federal safe house in Asheville. She can't come to Franklin. Can't go to her studio. Can't attend Tuesday mahjong except via video call. She's safe but she's not living." Donnie stared into her coffee. "That's what's bothering me. We caught the killers. We exposed the conspiracy. We won. But Bea still lost."

Eddie was quiet for a moment. Then: "Did she lose? Or did she survive again?"

"What's the difference?"

"Surviving isn't the same as losing. Bea's alive. She has community, even if it's via video. She's going to testify, get justice, help other victims. That's surviving with purpose." Eddie reached across the table, took her hand. "You can't solve everything, Donnie. You can't make the world fair. You can only fight for justice and hope it's enough."

Donnie squeezed his hand. Thirty-five years of marriage had taught her that Eddie was usually right about the big stuff. He saw story structure where she saw evidence. He understood narrative arc where she understood investigation. And sometimes story structure was exactly what was needed.

"What's Bea's arc?" Donnie asked.

"Survivor who spent forty-five years running finally stands and fights. Gets justice. Loses her home but gains herself. That's a complete arc. Not happy, but complete."

"I want happy."

"Happy doesn't exist in real life. Only better and worse." Eddie smiled. "But you did give her better. That counts."

Her phone buzzed. Text from Morrison: NEED YOU AT STATION. FBI FOUND SOMETHING.

Donnie drove to Franklin PD through December frost, heater blasting, mountains watching in their ancient silence. The town was just waking —early risers at The Country Kitchen, trucks warming up in driveways, the Sunday morning peace that made small towns bearable despite their complications.

Morrison's office was warm, crowded. Agent Katherine Parker sat at the conference table with Rodriguez and two other FBI agents Donnie didn't recognize. Evelyn was there with her laptop. Mabs with her research binder. And on video call from the Asheville safe house: Bea.

"What's happened?" Donnie asked.

Agent Parker gestured to a chair. "We found the missing paintings in his Asheville condo. We've also been processing Park Ji-woo's electronics. Phone, laptop, encrypted drives. We found communications with thirty-seven other individuals in the trafficking network."

Evelyn pulled up a spreadsheet. "Thirty-seven people. Across twelve countries. All involved in some aspect of the operation—acquiring art from refugee artists, transporting it, selling it, laundering money, evading sanctions."

"It's bigger than we thought," Morrison said.

"Much bigger." Agent Parker pulled up a network diagram on the screen. "Nguyen and Park were regional managers, basically. North America operation. But there are similar operations in Europe, Asia, Australia. All connected through central command in Singapore."

Donnie stared at the diagram. Nguyen and Park were two nodes in a web that stretched across continents. Fischer had been one of dozens of dealers. And refugee artists—the victims—were everywhere.

"How many artists?" Donnie asked.

"We've identified two hundred and forty-three so far," Mabs said, consulting her notes. "Vietnamese, Syrian, Afghan, Somali, Rohingya, Ukrainian, Sudanese. Anyone fleeing crisis, anyone with artistic talent, anyone desperate enough to accept low payment without questioning."

"That's criminality," Evelyn said. "Industrial scale."

"Exactly." Agent Parker stood, paced. "Which means this case just got exponentially more complicated. We're not prosecuting two murderers anymore. We're prosecuting an international trafficking ring. State Department is involved. Interpol. Multiple foreign governments. This is going to take years."

"Years?" Bea's voice came through the video call, small and worried. "How many years?"

"Hard to say. Three to five for full prosecution. Maybe longer." Agent Parker looked at the screen. "Bea, I'm sorry. This means your protective custody extends indefinitely. We can't let you return to Franklin until the network is dismantled."

Silence on the call. Then Bea's voice, carefully controlled: "I understand."

But Donnie heard what Bea didn't say. Three to five years in protective custody. Three to five years separated from Franklin, from her studio, from Tuesday night mahjong. Three to five years in limbo while federal bureaucracy ground toward justice.

"There has to be another option," Donnie said.

"There isn't. The network knows Bea's testimony will expose them. They have resources, reach, motivation to silence her. She's safest in protection."

"Safe isn't the same as alive."

Agent Parker's expression softened. "I know. But it's all I can offer."

After the FBI left, Donnie sat with Evelyn and Mabs processing what they'd learned. The scope was staggering. Two hundred and forty-three artists. Twelve countries. Decades of searching for and seeking those less able to defend themselves.

"We can't fix this," Mabs said quietly. "It's too big."

"We can fix Bea's part," Donnie countered. "Help her testify. Document her story. Make sure Nguyen and Park go to prison for what they did to her specifically."

"And the other two hundred and forty-two artists?"

"We help them too. However we can. One at a time if necessary." Donnie pulled out her phone. "Mabs, can you create a database? Names, locations, how they were exploited. Something we can share with FBI but also use to contact artists directly."

"That's thousands of hours of work."

"Then we work thousands of hours. Tuesday night mahjong isn't just about playing tiles. It's about community action. We'll coordinate, divide research, build the evidence base."

"Why?" Evelyn asked. "FBI is handling it."

"FBI is handling the prosecution. We're handling the human side. Making sure every victim has voice, support, resources. Making sure this isn't just a legal case—it's a movement."

Mabs nodded slowly. "I can do that. Build the database. Document stories. Create victim impact narratives."

"I'll handle financial evidence," Evelyn said. "Track every transaction, every consignment, every dollar stolen. Make the economic case."

"And I'll coordinate," Donnie said. "Keep everyone organized, communicate with FBI, make sure we're supporting the prosecution without interfering."

They worked through Sunday morning, building frameworks for the massive documentation project. By noon, they had a plan. By evening, they'd recruited the whole mahjong group plus volunteers from Franklin's community.

Because that's what small towns did. When one of their own was hurt, they mobilized. When injustice appeared, they fought. When federal cases seemed too big to touch, they found ways to help anyway.

Donnie drove home as December sunset painted the mountains gold and purple. Beautiful evening. Cold enough to see her breath. The kind of night that made you grateful for warm houses and hot food and people you loved.

Eddie had dinner ready—Cuban-style chicken, black beans, rice. Comfort food. Home food. The taste of Miami translated to mountain kitchens.

"How bad?" he asked.

"Three to five years before Bea can come home. Maybe longer. International trafficking network, hundreds of victims, complex prosecution." Donnie sat at their kitchen table, the place where they'd eaten thousands of meals, played countless games of mahjong with the group, lived their retirement life.

"But you're not giving up."

"Of course not. We're documenting every victim. Building evidence base. Supporting the prosecution. Helping Bea however we can."

"That's thousands of hours."

"That's what community does. We show up. We work. We refuse to let darkness win." Donnie looked at him. "You okay with that? With me spending retirement on another massive investigation?"

Eddie smiled. "Donnie, when you retired from Miami-Dade, I knew you weren't really retiring.

You were just changing jurisdiction. And honestly? I prefer you investigating in Franklin with a mahjong group than in Miami with gang members."

"Fair point."

They ate dinner in comfortable silence. Audrey positioned herself strategically for dropped chicken. The house was warm against December cold. Outside, the mountains settled into night.

Donnie's phone buzzed. Text from Bea: THANK YOU. FOR NOT GIVING UP. FOR MAKING THIS MEAN SOMETHING.

She texted back: FAMILY DOESN'T QUIT. WE'LL SEE YOU HOME EVENTUALLY.

Bea's response: I BELIEVE YOU.

Three words. Simple faith that the mahjong group would figure this out, find a way, make it possible for her to return.

Donnie hoped that faith was justified. Hoped three to five years wouldn't destroy what Bea had built. Hoped justice would be worth the cost.

But hope was all she had. Hope and work and the Tuesday night mahjong group's stubborn refusal to accept injustice quietly.

That had to be enough.

Chapter 17

Maya Lin spent the week before Christmas gathering stories from refugee artists, and what she learned broke her heart and strengthened her resolve in equal measure.

She sat in her apothecary back room with her laptop, a list of forty-three artists Mabs had identified through Nguyen's gallery records, and the growing realization that exploitation was a disease that infected every part of the refugee world.

Outside, Franklin was preparing for Christmas. Lights on Main Street. Wreaths on doors. The smell of pine and cinnamon from The Country Kitchen's holiday menu. Community preparing for celebration while Maya documented trauma.

Her phone rang. Artist number twelve: Anh Pham, Vietnamese-American, age fifty-five, living in Seattle.

"Ms. Pham? I'm Maya Lin, calling from Franklin, North Carolina. I'm helping document Minh Nguyen's abuse of refugee artists. Your name appeared in his gallery records from 2017. I'm wondering if you'd be willing to share your experience."

Silence. Then: "How did you get my number?"

"Public records, cross-referenced with gallery sales. I apologize for calling without warning. You don't have to talk to me. But if you want to share your story, I'll listen and document it for the federal case."

More silence. Maya waited, patient. She'd learned from her grandmother that healing took time, that trust had to be earned, that sometimes silence was the only appropriate response to pain.

Finally: "What do you want to know?"

"Whatever you're comfortable sharing. How you met Nguyen. What he promised. What he delivered. How you were treated."

Anh's story poured out. She'd fled Vietnam in 1979, spent three years in refugee camps, arrived in America with nothing. Learned English. Went to art school. Built a career painting watercolors of memory and loss.

Nguyen had contacted her in 2015. Said he specialized in Vietnamese art. Said he could get her work into major galleries, prestigious collections, wealthy buyers. Said he'd make her famous.

She'd sold him fifteen paintings for three thousand dollars each. He'd told her that was fair market value for emerging artists.

Last year, she'd discovered by accident that one of her paintings had sold at auction for forty-five thousand dollars. Nguyen had bought it from her for three thousand, sold it for forty-five thousand, kept the forty-two thousand dollar difference.

"I called him," Anh said. "Asked why he didn't tell me the real value. He said I'd agreed to the price. Said that was business. Said if I complained, he'd make sure I never sold through galleries again."

"Did you complain?"

"No. I was scared. I'm a refugee. I don't understand American legal system. I thought maybe he could really destroy my career." Pause. "And I was ashamed. Ashamed that I'd been cheated. Ashamed that I'd been so desperate for recognition that I didn't ask questions."

Maya wrote it all down. The extortion. The intimidation. The shame that kept victims silent.

"Ms. Pham, you weren't stupid. You were targeted. Nguyen hunted for refugee artists because he knew you were vulnerable. That's not your fault."

"I should have known better."

"How could you? You trusted someone who presented himself as helping Vietnamese artists. That's normal. That's human." Maya's voice was gentle but firm. "What Nguyen did was wrong. What you did was survive. There's no shame in survival."

After hanging up, Maya sat with the weight of Anh's story. Forty-two thousand dollars stolen. Career threatened. Shame internalized. Multiply that by two hundred and forty-three artists across twelve countries, and the scope became incomprehensible.

She called artist number thirteen: Rashid Ahmadi, Afghan refugee, living in Chicago.

Rashid's story was similar but worse. He'd sold

Nguyen twelve paintings for five thousand each in 2018. Later discovered they'd sold for two hundred thousand total. When he'd complained, Nguyen had threatened to report him to immigration for visa violations—violations Rashid hadn't committed but couldn't afford to fight.

"I withdrew my complaint," Rashid said. "What choice did I have? Fight and maybe get deported? Or stay quiet and survive?"

"You chose survival. That's valid."

"But Nguyen won. He always wins."

"Not this time. He's in federal custody. Charged with money laundering, sanctions evasion, and murder. He's not winning anymore."

"Good." Rashid's voice was fierce. "I'll testify. Whatever you need. I'll testify."

Maya added his name to the growing list of artists willing to speak. So far: eight out of thirteen contacted. Better than expected. Worse than justice required.

By Christmas Eve, Maya had contacted twenty-three artists. Fifteen were willing to testify. Eight weren't—too scared, too traumatized, too certain that speaking out would bring retribution.

She understood. Trauma didn't follow logic. Fear didn't respond to reassurance. Some survivors fought back. Others protected themselves through silence. Both were valid.

But Maya couldn't stop thinking about the eight who said no. The artists who'd been so thoroughly broken by Nguyen's breaking of their trust that they couldn't imagine justice.

That night, Tuesday night mahjong gathered at Donnie's house for their Christmas Eve session. It had become tradition—play tiles, share food, celebrate community. This year felt different. Bea joined via video from Asheville. The group was incomplete, wounded, fighting a battle that seemed endless.

But they gathered anyway. Because that's what family did.

Maya brought tea and stories. Evelyn brought financial evidence. Mabs brought her database of victims. Dodo brought cookies and surprising optimism. Frankie brought his military-grade determination. Eddie brought food. Audrey brought judgment and also affection, in her way. And Donnie brought focus. Purpose. The refusal to let this defeat them.

"Fifteen artists willing to testify so far," Maya reported. "Eight declined. Twenty haven't responded yet. But we're building a victim impact narrative that's devastating."

"FBI will use it," Evelyn said. "AUSA Walsh confirmed they want victim testimony for sentencing even if they don't need it for conviction."

"So we keep working," Donnie said. "Keep documenting. Keep reaching out. Keep building the case that shows what Nguyen and Park really did."

They played mahjong with Bea's video call propped on a chair, visible to everyone. She couldn't physically shuffle tiles or draw from the walls, but she could participate, call out moves, be present in spirit.

"I miss the sound," Bea said. "The tiles clicking. The ritual."

Maya pulled out her phone, positioned it so the microphone caught the tiles shuffling. The click-click-click of mahjong tiles mixing, the sound that meant community, family, home.

Bea smiled through the screen. "Thank you."

After mahjong, after food, after the comfortable rituals that held them together, Maya drove home with Evelyn. December night, cold and clear, stars visible above the mountains. Christmas lights on houses. Peace on earth, the decorations promised. Goodwill toward men.

Maya thought about the fifteen artists who'd agreed to testify. The eight who couldn't. The two hundred and twenty who hadn't been contacted yet. The years of work ahead. The long road to justice.

"Do you think we're making a difference?" she asked Evelyn.

"Yes."

"How can you be sure?"

"Because we're here. Because we're trying. Because fifteen artists who thought they had to stay silent found courage to speak." Evelyn took her hand. "That's difference. Maybe not enough.

But something."

At home, Maya made tea—chamomile with honey, the kind that soothed rather than energized. Tomorrow was Christmas. The apothecary would be closed. She'd spend the day with Evelyn, cooking, resting, trying to find peace in the middle of chaos.

But tonight, she sat at her kitchen table and wrote notes to each of the fifteen artists who'd agreed to testify. Thanking them. Acknowledging their courage. Promising that their stories mattered.

Because they did matter. Every story. Every voice. Every act of choosing to speak instead of hide.

That was resistance. That was healing. That was how you fought back against conmen—one story at a time, one artist at a time, one act of courage at a time.

Maya sealed the letters, addressed envelopes, prepared them for mailing. Small gestures. Inadequate gestures. But gestures nonetheless.

Outside, the mountains stood witness, holding Franklin in their ancient embrace. They'd seen everything—pain, healing, justice, injustice, the long arc of human struggle toward better.

And they'd see this through too. Whatever it took. However long it required.

Because that's what mountains did. They endured. They witnessed. They reminded you that time was long and struggle was temporary and eventually morning came.

Maya believed that. Had to believe that. Because the alternative—despair, surrender, the acceptance that Nguyen and people like him would always win—that was unthinkable.

So she chose belief. Chose work. Chose the long fight toward justice.

And tomorrow, Christmas, she'd rest. Gather strength. Prepare for the next phase.

But tonight, she mourned. For the artists who couldn't speak. For Bea in protective custody. For David who'd died trying to expose this. For everyone who'd been hurt by Nguyen's preying on the weak.

And she promised them all: this would matter. This work would count. Justice would come, however long it took.

That had to be enough.

Chapter 18

January brought bitter cold to Franklin and an unexpected development in the federal case.

Donnie sat in Morrison's office on the second Tuesday of the new year, watching AUSA Rebecca Walsh present via video conference, and trying to process what she was hearing.

"Park Ji-woo wants to cooperate," Walsh said. "He's offering full testimony against Nguyen, detailed information about the trafficking network, and documentation of every operation he was involved in for the past fifteen years."

"In exchange for?" Donnie asked, though she already knew.

"Reduced sentence. Life instead of execution for David Cho's murder. Possibility of parole after thirty years instead of never."

Morrison leaned forward. "That's a hell of a deal for someone who killed a federal prosecutor."

"It is. But his cooperation could take down the entire network. Not just Nguyen. All thirty-seven individuals we've identified plus potentially hundreds more." Walsh's expression was carefully neutral. "Prosecution is considering it."

Donnie looked at Evelyn, who sat rigid in her chair. David's widow. The woman who'd spent six months investigating his death, building the case, finally getting answers. And now the man who'd killed him wanted a deal.

"What does Evelyn think?" Donnie asked Walsh.

"I need to hear from Evelyn directly. That's why I'm calling." Walsh looked at the camera. "Evelyn, I know this is hard. But I need your input. Do we take Park's deal?"

Evelyn was quiet for a long moment. Donnie watched her face—the careful control, the grief barely visible, the calculation of someone who'd spent fifteen years making hard decisions in service of justice.

Finally: "Will his cooperation definitively prove Nguyen ordered David's death?"

"Yes. Park has recordings, emails, financial transfers showing Nguyen ordered the hit and Park executed it."

"And will his cooperation help convict the other thirty-seven individuals?"

"Almost certainly. Park was operational lead for North America. He knows everything."

"Then take the deal." Evelyn's voice was steady but her hands trembled. "David died trying to expose this network. If Park's cooperation accomplishes that, David's death means something. That's worth more than revenge."

After Walsh signed off, Donnie sat with Evelyn in Morrison's office, processing the decision. Outside, January snow was starting to fall—rare for Franklin, beautiful and dangerous at once.

"You okay?" Donnie asked.

"No. But I will be." Evelyn looked at her hands. "David would have taken the deal. He always said justice wasn't about punishment—it was about protecting future victims. Park's cooperation protects hundreds of potential future victims."

"That doesn't make it easier."

"No. But it makes it right." Evelyn stood, paced

to the window. Snow falling on Main Street, covering everything in white. Clean. Fresh. Temporary. "Can I tell you something?"

"Always."

"I wanted Park dead. When I found out he killed David, when I realized he'd been the one who forced David's car off that road, I wanted him executed. I wanted revenge." Evelyn's voice was raw. "But that's not who David married. David married someone who believed in justice, in process, in choosing the harder right over the easier wrong. And if I let revenge win, I lose that person. I lose me."

Donnie understood. Understood the tension between what you wanted and who you needed to be. Understood choosing principle over satisfaction. Understood that sometimes justice meant accepting outcomes that hurt.

"David would be proud of you," Donnie said.

"I hope so." Evelyn turned from the window. "Now what? What happens with Park's cooperation?"

"Now Park testifies. FBI builds cases against all thirty-seven individuals. Interpol coordinates international arrests. The network gets dismantled." Donnie pulled out her notebook. "And we keep documenting victim stories. Keep building the human impact case. Keep making sure this isn't just about prosecuting criminals—it's about helping survivors."

They drove back to Maya's apothecary through

falling snow. Franklin was beautiful in winter—the mountains white-capped, the town cozy and small, smoke from chimneys promising warm houses and hot meals.

Maya was waiting with tea and the understanding that sometimes you needed comfort before conversation. They sat in the back room, drinking herbal blends that Maya had carefully mixed for emotional processing, and watched snow accumulate outside.

"Park's cooperating," Evelyn said. "Offering full testimony for reduced sentence."

Maya's expression was complicated—understanding, anger, sadness all at once. "How do you feel?"

"Like I'm betraying David by allowing his killer to live. Like I'm honoring David by prioritizing justice over revenge. Like I don't know what's right anymore."

"Both things can be true," Maya said gently. "Grief and justice aren't mutually exclusive. Neither are anger and principle."

"But which one wins?"

"Whichever one you choose. That's the power and the burden—you get to decide what David's death means. Revenge or change. Punishment or protection. Personal satisfaction or real lasting reform."

Evelyn was quiet. Then: "I choose reform. I choose protection. I choose making David's death count for something bigger than my grief."

"That's brave."

"That's exhausting." Evelyn smiled weakly. "But it's what he would have wanted."

That evening, Tuesday night mahjong gathered despite the snow. Everyone made it—even Frankie, who drove carefully on his motorcycle through dangerous conditions because "the group doesn't quit for weather."

Bea joined via video from Asheville. The strain showed—shadows under her eyes, tension in her shoulders, the careful control of someone living in limbo.

But she smiled when she saw the group. "It's snowing there?"

"First real snow of winter," Donnie said, angling the camera to show the window. "Few inches already."

"I miss Franklin snow. Asheville gets more snow but it's not the same. Not home."

The word hung in the air. Home. The place Bea couldn't return to yet. Maybe wouldn't return to for years.

"How are you?" Maya asked.

"Surviving. Reading. Painting on cheap paper with cheap supplies because FBI won't let me access my studio. Trying to make art feel meaningful when I can't share it." Bea's voice was carefully neutral. "How's the victim documentation going?"

"Thirty-seven artists contacted so far," Maya reported. "Twenty-two willing to testify.

Database is growing. FBI is using our work to build victim impact cases."

"That's good. That matters."

They played mahjong with Bea calling moves via video. It wasn't the same—couldn't replace physical presence, couldn't replicate the sound of tiles clicking, couldn't provide real community. But it was something. Connection across distance. Ritual maintained despite separation.

After the game, after most people had left, Donnie sat with Maya and Evelyn in the warm kitchen while snow fell outside.

"Four months until trial," Donnie said. "Park's cooperation might speed things up or slow them down—hard to tell. But either way, Bea's stuck in protective custody indefinitely."

"We need to find a way to bring her home," Maya said.

"How? Network's not dismantled yet. Threats are real. FBI says she's safer in Asheville."

"Safer isn't the same as living." Maya's voice was fierce. "Bea's withering in protective custody. She needs community. Needs her studio. Needs home."

"What are you suggesting?"

"I'm suggesting we find a way. Maybe not permanent return. Maybe supervised visits. Maybe protection in place instead of relocation. But something. Anything better than isolation."

Donnie thought about it. Thought about protocols and procedures and the federal bureaucracy that moved slowly by design. Thought about Bea's face on the video call—present but not present, connected but isolated, surviving but not thriving.

"I'll talk to Agent Parker," Donnie decided. "Make the case for supervised visits. Franklin's small enough to secure. We have community support. FBI already has presence here. Maybe we can negotiate something."

"FBI won't like it."

"FBI doesn't have to like it. They have to keep Bea safe. If we can prove that's possible in Franklin, they should consider it."

It was optimistic. Maybe naive. Definitely complicated.

But Tuesday night mahjong had accomplished harder things. They'd solved murders, exposed conspiracies, caught international criminals. Surely they could negotiate one refugee artist's supervised return home.

Donnie drove home through snow that was still falling, accumulating on roads and trees and the mountains that surrounded Franklin. Beautiful. Dangerous. Temporary.

Everything was temporary, she thought. Snow melted. Seasons changed. Grief evolved. Justice advanced incrementally.

The trick was staying committed through the temporary parts. Maintaining hope when outcomes were uncertain. Choosing action over despair.

Eddie was waiting when she got home, fire in the fireplace, hot chocolate ready. Thirty-five years of marriage had taught him when she needed silence and when she needed processing. Tonight was processing.

"Park's cooperating for reduced sentence. Evelyn approved it. Prioritizing justice over personal revenge." Donnie sat on their couch, accepted hot chocolate. "I'm proud of her. And sad for her. And angry at everything."

"That's a lot of feelings."

"That's justice work. Too many feelings, never enough resolution."

Eddie was quiet for a moment. Then: "You're going to try to bring Bea home, aren't you?"

"I'm going to try."

"Even though it's probably impossible."

"Especially because it's probably impossible. That's when trying matters most."

He smiled. "That's my Donnie. Never met an impossible task she wouldn't attempt."

"Is that a compliment?"

"That's a fact. Also a compliment. Also a warning that you're going to drive yourself crazy trying to solve the unsolvable."

"Probably." Donnie leaned against him, comfortable in thirty-five years of choosing each other. "But I have to try. Bea deserves that. Community deserves that. The fight deserves that."

Outside, snow continued falling. Inside, they sat by fire and planned impossible things.

Because that's what you did when you loved people. You attempted impossible tasks. You fought unwinnable fights. You chose hope over despair even when despair seemed wiser.

And sometimes—sometimes—impossible things became possible. Not because they were easy. But because enough people refused to accept the alternative.

Tomorrow Donnie would call Agent Parker. Make the case for Bea's supervised return. Start the long process of negotiating with federal bureaucracy.

Tonight, she sat with her husband and drank hot chocolate and watched snow fall on Franklin.

One day at a time. One fight at a time. One impossible task at a time.

That was enough. Had to be enough.

And if it wasn't? Well. They'd try harder.

That's what the Tuesday night mahjong group did. Try, fail, try again, refuse to quit until justice was done or they'd exhausted every option.

And they had plenty of options left.

Chapter 19

By February, the Tuesday night mahjong group had documented eighty-three refugee artists exploited by Nguyen's network, and Mabs was exhausted.

She sat in the Franklin Library's research room —her usual desk, her usual chair, her coffee thermos that had survived forty-three years of librarianship and six months of retirement investigation—reviewing testimony transcripts and thinking about how justice required paperwork.

So much paperwork.

Eighty-three artist statements. Each one documenting their victimization—how they'd met Nguyen or his associates, what they'd been promised, how much they'd been paid versus how much their art actually sold for, what threats they'd received when they questioned the arrangement.

The pattern was consistent. Contact came through what seemed like legitimate channels —gallery referrals, art fair connections, refugee community networks. Promises of ethical representation, fair payment, access to prestigious buyers. Initial sales at reasonable prices. Then gradual revelation that the work was selling for ten, twenty, fifty times what the artist had been paid. Complaints met with threats—legal action, immigration consequences, career destruction.

And always, always, the system worked because the artists were vulnerable. Refugees. Immigrants. People who didn't understand American systems, who feared authority, who'd survived trauma and just wanted to survive this too.

Predators like Nguyen understood vulnerability. They used it ruthlessly. Built empires on other people's desperation.

Mabs's phone rang. Artist number eighty-four: Khadija Osman, Somali refugee, living in Minneapolis.

"Ms. Osman? I'm Mabel Carter, calling from Franklin, North Carolina. I'm documenting Minh Nguyen's abuse of refugee artists. I understand you worked with his associate, James Park, in 2019. Would you be willing to share your story?"

"FBI already talked to me."

"I know. I'm not FBI. I'm a retired librarian helping build the victim impact case. Your story matters beyond just prosecution—it helps other artists understand they weren't alone, that abuse was a system that was developed to target them, that it wasn't their fault."

Silence. Then: "What do you need?"

Khadija's story was heartbreaking. She'd fled Somalia in 2015, spent three years in Kenyan refugee camps, arrived in America with artistic talent and determination. Park had contacted her through a Somali community organization, presented himself as helping African refugee artists.

She'd sold him twenty-four paintings over three years for two thousand dollars each. Forty-eight thousand total. Later discovered the paintings had sold for over six hundred thousand dollars.

"I confronted him," Khadija said. "Asked why he didn't tell me the real value. He said that was the market rate for emerging artists. Said if I complained, he'd report me to immigration for tax violations I didn't commit. Said no one would believe a Somali refugee over an established dealer."

"Did you believe him?"

"Yes. Because I was scared. Because I didn't know my rights. Because I thought maybe American business really worked that way—everyone taking advantage, everyone protecting their profit, refugees at the bottom getting scraps."

Mabs wrote it all down. The theft. The gaslighting. The internalized belief that maybe this was just how it worked.

"Ms. Osman, you weren't wrong to trust Park. He deliberately targeted you because you were vulnerable. That's not your fault. That's his crime."

"But I should have known better."

"How? You came from a war zone to a refugee camp to America. You were trying to survive through art. Park and Nguyen preyed on exactly that desperation. You couldn't have known."

After hanging up, Mabs added Khadija's testimony to the database. Eighty-four artists now. Each with similar stories. Each defrauded. Each believing, somehow, that it was their fault for trusting.

That was the cruelest part. The victims blamed themselves.

Mabs understood. She'd spent forty-three years as a librarian helping people navigate systems—library catalogs, reference databases, research protocols. She knew that complex systems were designed to be confusing. That confusion created power imbalances. That people who understood systems used to steal from people who didn't.

Nguyen had weaponized that knowledge. Used his understanding of American art markets, immigration law, and refugee vulnerability to build a trafficking empire. And his victims blamed themselves for not understanding what he'd deliberately obscured.

That afternoon, Mabs met with the rest of the mahjong group at Donnie's house to present the compiled testimony. Eighty-four artists. Over three million dollars in stolen value. Fifteen years of thievery.

"This is devastating," Maya said, reading through statements.

"This is useful," Evelyn countered, looking at the financial analysis. "FBI can use this for sentencing. Judges need to see victim impact to understand scope."

"How many more?" Frankie asked.

"At least another hundred artists we've identified but haven't contacted yet," Mabs said. "Plus unknown numbers we haven't found. The network operated in twelve countries. We're only scratching the surface."

Dodo had been quiet, reading testimony with her usual combination of chaos and surprising insight. Now she spoke: "The cats think we should publish this. Not just give it to FBI. Publish it publicly so other refugees know what to watch for."

Everyone looked at her.

"That's actually brilliant," Donnie said. "Public database of profiteering patterns. Warning system for refugee artists. Educational resource."

"FBI won't like it," Morrison pointed out. He'd joined the meeting to coordinate law enforcement angles. "Publishing active investigation details could compromise prosecution."

"Then we wait until after prosecution," Mabs said. "But Dodo's right. This information needs to be public. Needs to be accessible. Needs to protect future artists."

"I can build the database," Evelyn offered. "Secure website, searchable by artist name or associate name or gallery name. Cross-referenced with known patterns. Updated as we gather more information."

"And I can create educational materials," Maya added. "Rights education for refugee artists. How to verify gallery contracts. Red flags of warnings . Practical resources."

Mabs felt something settle in her chest. Purpose beyond documentation. Work that would matter beyond just this case. A legacy project that could protect people for years.

"Let's do it," she said. "Document now, prosecute next, publish after. Create lasting resource from temporary tragedy."

That evening, alone in her house with her cat Sherlock (borrowed from Dodo during a previous case and never returned), Mabs thought about legacy. She'd spent forty-three years as a librarian. Her career was over. Her professional identity complete.

But this—this documentation project, this victim advocacy, this exposure of ciminality—this felt like the work she'd been preparing for. Every research skill she'd learned. Every database she'd mastered. Every organizational system she'd developed. All of it useful now for something that mattered.

She pulled up her computer and drafted a

proposal. "The Refugee Artist Protection Project: A Comprehensive Database of Patterns of Theft and Protective Resources."

Goals: Document all known cases of refugee artist misuse. Create searchable database accessible to artists, advocates, and law enforcement. Develop educational materials on rights, contracts, and red flags. Establish ongoing reporting mechanism for new cases.

Scope: Start with Nguyen's network (200+ artists). Expand to other known trafficking operations. Eventually create international resource.

Timeline: Documentation complete by trial (April). Database launch after prosecution (Summer). Educational materials ongoing. Long-term maintenance through volunteer network.

She sent the proposal to the mahjong group. Responses came immediately:

Donnie: YES. THIS IS EXACTLY WHAT WE NEED.

Maya: I'LL DEVELOP THE EDUCATIONAL COMPONENT.

Evelyn: I'LL BUILD THE DATABASE AND HOST IT.

Dodo: THE CATS APPROVE. ALSO I'LL MAKE A LOGO.

Frankie: SECURITY PROTOCOLS NEED WORK BUT I'M IN.

Even Bea, from protective custody in Asheville: THIS IS BEAUTIFUL. MY STORY MATTERS

BEYOND JUST MY CASE. THANK YOU.

Mabs sat back, looked at Sherlock who was judging her from his position on the desk. "We're doing something good here," she told the cat.

Sherlock blinked slowly, which Dodo had explained meant approval or possible nap time. Hard to tell with cats.

But approval or nap, the work continued. Eighty-four artists documented. Hundred more to contact. Database to build. Educational materials to create. Website to launch. Legacy to establish.

All of it overwhelming. All of it necessary. All of it exactly what forty-three years of librarianship had prepared her for.

Mabs opened her laptop and started drafting the database structure. Fields for artist name, country of origin, date of contact with Nguyen/associates, art sold, payment received, actual sale price, difference stolen, threats received, willing to testify, current status.

Simple structure. Devastating content. Powerful tool.

She worked until midnight, building the framework that would hold eighty-four stories and eventually hundreds more. Building the resource that might protect future artists. Building meaning from trauma.

Outside, February cold settled over Franklin. Inside, an elderly librarian built databases and imagined justice.

Because that's what you did when you retired. You didn't stop working. You just worked on things that mattered more than salary.

And this mattered. Every documented story. Every protected artist. Every prevented extortion.

This mattered most of all.

Chapter 20

March arrived with the promise of spring and the reality of approaching trial, and Donnie Carlisle had spent three months negotiating with FBI for Bea's supervised return to Franklin.

She sat in her kitchen on the first Tuesday in March reviewing the agreement she'd finally secured from Agent Katherine Parker, and thinking about how sometimes winning looked different than expected.

The agreement: Bea could return to Franklin for supervised day visits. Once per week. Eight hours maximum. Federal protection escort. No access to her studio (still crime scene pending trial). No public appearances. No contact with anyone outside approved list.

It wasn't much. It wasn't enough. But it was something.

Eddie read the agreement over her shoulder. "You got her home. Conditionally. Temporarily. But home."

"For eight hours per week. With federal agents watching. That's not home. That's supervised visitation."

"That's more than she had yesterday. That's progress." Eddie squeezed her shoulder. "Take the win, Donnie. Even partial wins count."

He was right. Donnie had learned over thirty years of investigation that justice was incremental. Perfect outcomes were rare. You took what you could get, celebrated small victories, kept fighting for better.

But she'd wanted perfect for Bea. Wanted full return, complete restoration, justice without compromise. Wanted the happy ending that Bea deserved after surviving so much.

Instead she'd gotten eight hours per week with restrictions.

Her phone rang. Agent Parker.

"The agreement is approved," Parker said. "Bea can start visits this week. First one scheduled for Thursday. We'll bring her to your house—that's on the approved locations list. She can attend Tuesday mahjong via supervised video call. And pending trial outcome, we'll reassess for expanded access."

"Thank you."

"Don't thank me. Thank yourself. You made the case. Documented every security measure, coordinated with local law enforcement, built the argument that supervised visits were feasible. I just had to approve what you'd already proven."

After hanging up, Donnie texted the group: BEA'S COMING HOME. THURSDAY. 8 HOURS. SUPERVISED. BUT HOME.

Responses exploded:

Maya: CRYING. THIS IS WONDERFUL.

Mabs: EXCELLENT WORK. WHAT TIME THURSDAY?

Evelyn: FINALLY. PROGRESS.

Dodo: THE CATS PREDICTED THIS. THEY'RE VERY PLEASED.

Frankie: ABOUT DAMN TIME.

And from Bea: I DON'T HAVE WORDS. THANK YOU. THANK YOU. THANK YOU.

Thursday arrived cold and bright. March had the confused identity of not-quite-winter, not-quite-spring. Frost in the mornings, warmth in afternoons, everything transitional and temporary.

Donnie prepared her house like Bea was visiting royalty. Eddie made Cuban sandwiches. Maya brought special tea blends. Mabs arrived early with research updates. Evelyn set up the laptop for database demonstration. Dodo brought cookies and remarkable emotional intelligence hidden under chaos. Frankie positioned himself near the door in protective stance.

And Audrey, sensing significance, wore her most

judgmental expression while secretly wagging her tail.

The federal escort arrived at noon. Two agents, professional and alert. And between them, looking smaller than Donnie remembered but smiling through tears: Bea.

"I'm home," Bea said simply.

"You're home," Donnie agreed.

They brought her inside. Bea stood in Donnie's living room—the space where they'd played countless games of mahjong, solved two murders, built found family from friendship—and looked around like memorizing details.

"It's the same," Bea said. "Everything's the same."

"We kept your chair," Maya said, pointing to the spot at the mahjong table where Bea always sat. "No one else sits there. It's yours."

Bea touched the chair back. "I've missed this room more than I can say."

They settled around the table. Federal agents positioned themselves discreetly in corners—close enough to protect, far enough to allow privacy. And the Tuesday night mahjong group gathered around Bea like protective circle, like family, like home.

"Tell us everything," Maya said. "How are you? Really?"

"Surviving. Reading extensively. Painting on inadequate materials. Missing Franklin every single day." Bea looked at each of them. "But learning something important. Home isn't just place. Home is people. And you've been home even through video calls and distance."

"Sentimental and also accurate," Mabs said with her characteristic blend of pragmatism and warmth.

They spent the afternoon sharing updates. Mabs presented the Refugee Artist Protection Project—eighty-nine artists documented now, database structure complete, educational materials in development. Evelyn showed financial evidence that proved Nguyen's network had stolen over fifteen million dollars from refugee artists over twenty years. Maya shared testimony from artists who'd found courage to speak.

And Donnie explained the trial schedule. April 15th. Opening arguments. AUSA Walsh prosecuting with FBI support. Park Ji-woo testifying for the prosecution in exchange for reduced sentence. Estimated six-week trial for full RICO case.

"You'll testify in week two," Donnie told Bea. "About Camp Galang. About Nguyen's modus operandi. About how they targeted you specifically."

"I'm ready. I've been preparing for months." Bea's voice was steady. "This is why I survived. To testify. To help others. To make sure Nguyen never hurts anyone again."

Around four PM, they took a break. Federal agents allowed Bea to walk outside Donnie's property—supervised, within boundaries, but outside nonetheless.

Donnie walked with her through the property. Past the chicken coop where the hens clucked their greetings. Past Eddie's garden where early spring vegetables were just starting to emerge. To the back corner where two Adirondack chairs overlooked the mountains.

"I've missed this view," Bea said, sitting down. "The mountains. The way they hold everything. The ancient patience."

"They've been waiting for you to come back."

"I hope I can. Really come back. Not just visits. Full return." Bea looked at Donnie. "Do you think that's possible? After trial, after testimony, after everything?"

"I think we'll fight like hell to make it possible. And if fighting doesn't work, we'll negotiate. And if negotiation doesn't work, we'll find creative alternatives. That's what family does."

"Thank you. For fighting. For not giving up. For eight hours per week when you wanted full restoration."

"Eight hours is just the start. We'll keep pushing for more."

They sat in comfortable silence, watching the mountains in afternoon light. Cold March air, early spring hints, the transitional season where everything was possible and nothing certain.

"Donnie, can I tell you something?" Bea's voice was quiet.

"Always."

"I'm not the same person who left Franklin three months ago. Protective custody changed me. Isolation changed me. Fighting back changed me." Bea looked at her hands. "I was always quiet. Grateful. Careful not to take up too much space. Typical refugee mentality—be invisible, don't cause trouble, just survive."

"And now?"

"Now I'm angry. At Nguyen for targeting me. At Park for trying to kill me. At the system that made me vulnerable. At myself for being quiet so long." Bea smiled slightly. "Maya would say anger is healthy. Is it?"

"Maya's right. Anger is fuel. Use it for change."

"That's what I'm doing. Testifying. Helping other artists. Building the protection project. Using my survival for purpose." Bea paused. "And painting differently too. Angrier. More direct. Less apologetic."

"I'd like to see that work."

"You will. After trial. When I can access my studio again. When I'm really home."

The eight-hour visit ended too quickly. By eight PM, federal agents were signaling time to leave. The mahjong group gathered for goodbyes—hugs, tears, promises to repeat this weekly, determination that this was just beginning.

"Next Thursday," Agent Parker confirmed. "Same schedule. And we'll coordinate special visit for trial prep the week before Bea testifies."

"Thank you," Bea said. Then, to the group: "I'll see

you Tuesday night. Video call. But I'll be there."

After Bea left, the mahjong group sat in Donnie's living room processing the visit. The joy of having Bea present physically, even briefly. The sadness of her leaving. The determination to keep fighting for permanent return.

"Six weeks until trial," Evelyn said. "Then sentencing. Then reassessment of protection needs. Maybe—maybe—full return possible by summer."

"That's optimistic," Frankie pointed out.

"I prefer optimistic to realistic when realistic is depressing," Dodo said. "The cats agree."

They played mahjong that night—just them, without Bea, but in her honor. Shuffled tiles, built walls, drew hands. The ritual that held them together through everything.

"We're going to win this," Donnie said. "Trial, conviction, Bea's return. All of it."

"How can you be sure?" Mabs asked.

"Because we've won everything else. Because we don't quit. Because found family is stronger than international conspiracies." Donnie looked around the table at her people—Maya and Evelyn with their hard-won relationship, Mabs with her relentless documentation, Dodo with her chaotic wisdom, Frankie with his fierce loyalty, Eddie with his steady support, even Audrey with her judgmental presence. "We're Tuesday night mahjong. We do impossible things. This is just another impossibility."

"Inspiring speech," Frankie muttered. But he was smiling.

They played until midnight. Then dispersed to their homes, to their lives, to the six weeks before trial that would determine everything.

Donnie drove home through March darkness thinking about justice and progress and the long fight toward better. Three months of negotiating for eight hours per week. Six weeks until trial. Unknown timeline for Bea's permanent return.

It was slow. It was frustrating. It was insufficient.

But it was movement. Forward. Toward justice. Toward restoration. Toward the possibility that maybe, eventually, Bea could really come home.

And movement was enough. Had to be enough. Because the alternative—giving up, accepting Bea's permanent exile, letting Nguyen's actions destroy more than they already had—that was unthinkable.

So they'd keep fighting. Keep negotiating. Keep pushing for better.

One day at a time. One visit at a time. One small victory at a time.

Until Bea was fully home. Until justice was completely done. Until the Tuesday night mahjong group could gather physically every week without federal supervision.

That was the goal. That was the promise. That was what thirty years of investigation experience, six months of mahjong group coordination, and stubborn refusal to accept defeat looked like.

They'd get there. Eventually. However long it took.

Because that's what family did. Fight until winning. Rest, then fight again. Refuse to quit until justice was complete.

And they were just getting started.

Chapter 21

April 15th arrived with cherry blossoms and federal court, and Donnie Carlisle stood outside the Charlotte Federal Building watching Bea Tran prepare to face her past.

The building was imposing—glass and steel, modern architecture designed to inspire respect for federal authority. Security checkpoints, metal detectors, marshals everywhere. The machinery of justice in physical form.

Bea stood on the courthouse steps with David Chen, her lawyer, looking small but determined. She wore professional clothes—dark blue suit, white blouse, her grandmother's jade bracelet visible on her wrist. The Tuesday night mahjong group surrounded her in protective formation: Donnie, Maya, Evelyn, Mabs, Dodo, Frankie. Even Eddie had come, and Morrison, representing Franklin PD.

"You ready?" Donnie asked.

"No. But I'm doing it anyway." Bea looked at the building. "Three months of preparation. Months in a safe house prison. A year of FBI documentation. All leading to this."

"You'll be brilliant," Maya said.

"I'll be honest. That's all I can be." Bea took a deep breath. "Let's go."

Inside, the courtroom was formal and intimidating. Judge Sarah Martinez presided—sixty-something, Latina, known for running tight proceedings and tolerating no nonsense. AUSA Rebecca Walsh sat at the prosecution table with two FBI agents. Defense attorneys—expensive ones, multiple—sat with Nguyen and Park at separate tables.

Nguyen looked older than Donnie remembered. Three months in federal detention had aged him. But his eyes were still calculating, still assessing, still looking for advantages.

Park sat separately, in cooperation witness

section. He'd testify for the prosecution in exchange for reduced sentence. His expression was carefully blank, professional, the face of someone who'd decided survival mattered more than loyalty.

The gallery was packed. Press in designated section. Refugee artist advocates. FBI observers. And taking up three full rows: refugee artists Nguyen had abused. Eighty-nine of them had traveled to Charlotte for this trial. Eighty-nine people ready to witness justice.

Donnie sat in the second row with the mahjong group, watching everything, cataloging details the way thirty years of investigation had trained her.

Judge Martinez called court to order. "United States versus Minh Nguyen and Park Ji-woo. Multiple counts of money laundering, racketeering, conspiracy, sanctions evasion, and two counts of murder in the first degree. Counselors, are you ready?"

"Prosecution is ready, Your Honor."

"Defense is ready."

"Then let's begin."

AUSA Walsh's opening statement was precise and devastating. She outlined the conspiracy methodically: Nguyen and Park's forty-five-year partnership beginning in Camp Galang. Their deliberate targeting of refugee artists. The criminal network spanning twelve countries. The money laundering operation processing fifteen million dollars. The sanctions evasion funneling funds to North Korea. The murders of Conrad Fischer and David Cho when they became liabilities.

"The evidence will show," Walsh concluded, "that these defendants built an empire on the suffering of refugees. People who'd survived wars, boat escapes, refugee camps—they survived all that only to be fleeced by two men who understood vulnerability and weaponized it for profit. This is not a case about art. This is a case about acting as predators against the most vulnerable."

Defense opened with the expected strategy: acknowledge some impropriety, deny criminal intent, blame overzealous prosecution. Nguyen's lawyer argued that the art business was complicated, that pricing was subjective, that any misunderstandings were honest mistakes not criminal conspiracy.

Park's lawyer took a different approach: his client was cooperating fully, had acknowledged wrongdoing, would testify truthfully. Park deserved consideration for helping dismantle the network.

Donnie watched the jury—twelve people, diverse backgrounds, carefully selected for impartiality. They listened attentively, took notes, showed no emotion. Professional jury doing professional work.

Day one proceeded with foundation testimony. FBI agents explaining the investigation. Forensic accountants detailing money laundering. Immigration specialists describing refugee vulnerability. Building the framework before bringing victim testimony.

At lunch break, the mahjong group gathered in courthouse cafeteria. Bea picked at her food, nervous energy making eating difficult.

"When do you testify?" Mabs asked.

"Day three. Tomorrow is more foundation. Day three, Walsh brings victim testimony. I'm first." Bea set down her fork. "I've practiced with Walsh dozens of times. I know what to say. But seeing Nguyen in person... it's harder than I expected."

"He's just a man," Frankie said. "Old, defeated, facing life in prison. He can't hurt you anymore."

"I know that intellectually. But

emotionally?" Bea looked at her hands. "He's still the man who helped me survive Camp Galang and then used me. Who waited forty-five years to return and expect to use me again. That's complicated."

"Complicated is okay," Maya said gently. "You don't have to have simple feelings about complex trauma."

Day one ended with technical testimony about banking regulations and sanctions law. Necessary but dry. The courtroom emptied slowly, everyone processing the scope of what they'd heard.

Outside, press surrounded Bea. David Chen ran interference, issuing "no comment" repeatedly. The mahjong group created protective barrier until they reached the car.

Donnie drove Bea back to the federal safe house in Asheville. The route was beautiful—spring emerging in the mountains, dogwoods blooming, everything renewing. But Bea stared out the window seeing nothing.

"Tell me," Donnie said.

"I thought I'd feel powerful. Being there. Watching Nguyen face consequences. But I just feel... sad. For everyone. For the artists he hurt. For the person I was at Camp Galang who trusted him. For the forty-five years of swindling. All of it just makes me sad."

"Sadness is appropriate. What he did was sad. Tragic. Wasteful."

"I know. But I wanted to feel angry. Righteous. Powerful. Instead I feel tired." Bea leaned her head against the window. "Is that wrong?"

"There's no wrong way to feel about trauma. You survived. You're testifying. You're helping others. That's enough. You don't have to perform the right emotions for anyone."

At the safe house, federal agents checked perimeter before allowing them inside. Bea's temporary home was nice enough—furnished apartment, security measures, comfortable but not home. Never home.

"I'll be back tomorrow morning," Donnie said. "Seven AM. We'll go to court together."

"Thank you. For everything. For being here. For fighting to bring me home. For believing this matters."

"It matters because you matter. Tuesday night mahjong doesn't abandon family."

Driving back to Franklin, Donnie thought

about justice and sadness and the complicated reality that winning cases didn't erase trauma. Nguyen would go to prison. Park would serve reduced sentence. The network would be dismantled.

But the artists who'd been swindled would still carry that betrayal. Bea would still have nightmares about Camp Galang. David Cho would still be dead. Evelyn would still be a widow.

Justice didn't fix everything. It just prevented more harm and acknowledged that the harm mattered.

Sometimes that had to be enough.

At home, Eddie had dinner ready—comfort food, wine, the warmth that made coming home bearable after hard days.

"How was it?" he asked.

"Sad. Necessary. The beginning of a very long process." Donnie sat at their kitchen table, the place where they'd eaten thousands of meals, played countless mahjong games, lived their retirement life that had turned into investigation after investigation.

"You okay?"

"I'm tired. Of fighting. Of advocating. Of the endless grind toward justice that takes years and leaves everyone damaged." Donnie looked at him. "But I'm not quitting. I'm just acknowledging that it's hard."

"That's growth. Miami Donnie would have just worked harder without acknowledging feelings."

"Miami Donnie burned out and retired to Franklin."

"Exactly. Franklin Donnie knows when to rest." Eddie poured wine. "So rest tonight. Tomorrow you go back. But tonight, you rest."

They ate dinner in comfortable silence. Audrey positioned herself for dropped food. The chickens settled into their coop for the night. Outside, April evening turned the mountains purple and gold.

Tomorrow would bring more testimony. More trauma narratives. More evidence of corruption.

But tonight, Donnie rested. Gathered strength. Prepared for the next phase.

Because there were still eleven days of trial ahead. Still Bea's testimony tomorrow. Still the verdict to come. Still negotiations for permanent return.

Still work to do. Still fights to fight. Still justice to pursue.

One day at a time. One testimony at a time. One small victory at a time.

That's how you survived long trials and longer fights. You rested when you could. You worked when you must. You refused to quit until justice was done.

And tomorrow, Bea would testify. Would tell her story. Would expose Nguyen's manipulation for the court record and public knowledge.

That mattered. Even if it was sad and filled with pain. Even if it didn't fix everything. Even if justice was complicated and imperfect.

It still mattered.

And that had to be enough.

Chapter 22

Day three of the trial began with Bea Tran taking the witness stand, and the courtroom went absolutely silent.

She wore the same blue suit from opening day, jade bracelet visible. She placed her hand on the Bible, swore to tell the truth, and sat down with the composure of someone who'd survived worse than a federal courtroom.

AUSA Walsh approached the witness stand. "Please state your name for the record."

"Bea Tran. Originally Tran Bao Linh, but I've used Bea Tran since arriving in America."

"Ms. Tran, where were you born?"

"Saigon, Vietnam. 1963."

"And you left Vietnam in what year?"

"1978. I was fifteen years old. I left on a boat with my parents and approximately sixty other people."

Walsh walked Bea through the escape methodically. The boat. The South China Sea. Seventeen days at sea. Bea's parents drowning on day six. Bea arriving at Camp Galang, Indonesia, alone at fifteen with nothing but her grandmother's jade bracelet.

The jury was riveted. This wasn't legal theory. This was something they would never have to go through. This was human survival.

"At Camp Galang, did you meet the defendant Minh Nguyen?"

"Yes. He was twenty-three. He'd been in the camp for six months already. He positioned himself as someone who could help—get extra food, better housing, faster processing."

"Did he help you?"

"Yes. He got me better tent placement, extra rations. He seemed kind at first. Protective." Bea's voice was steady. "That's how he worked. He identified vulnerable people and offered help. Then he collected information about them. Then he used them to get what he wanted from others."

"What kind of information?"

"Stories. Backgrounds. Whet they had done before, who they had worked for, Who they knew. What made each person valuable and what each person might want to stay hidden. He was building a database of background and refugee trauma that he could exploit later."

Nguyen's lawyer objected—"Speculation, Your Honor"—but Walsh had laid foundation through previous testimony. Judge Martinez allowed it.

"Did you tell Mr. Nguyen your story?"

"Yes. Everything. About my parents drowning. About my guilt for surviving. About my dreams of becoming an artist. About the jade bracelet being my only connection to my grandmother." Bea touched the bracelet. "I trusted him completely until he started using me to get him what he wanted. I was a child when Nguyen found me in the refugee camp. I had no parents left—my mother and father drowned in the South China Sea. I had no food, no protection, no voice. Nguyen saw that silence in me and turned it into his leverage.

He told me survival had a price. That my body was the only currency I had. He used me to get what he wanted—information from men who thought a girl's whispers were harmless, favors from officials who would trade compassion for access, money from those who paid for what should never have been for sale.

I did not consent. I did not choose. I was young. He taught me that obedience was survival, that silence was safety. Every time he pushed me forward, I learned that my body was not mine—it was his tool, his bargaining chip.

I survived, but survival is not innocence. Survival is endurance. And endurance leaves scars you cannot see. Nguyen enslaved me, and Park hurt me, and I carried that pain into every breath I took afterward.

You ask me how he used me? He used me the way men use weapons—without care for the damage, only for the power it gave him. And I was the weapon he wielded."

"Did you also meet Park Ji-woo at the camp?"

"Park was not just a man in the camp. He was the shadow that followed every step. Nguyen used words and promises to bind me, but Park used his fists, his presence, his cruelty. He was the enforcer—the one who made sure silence stayed silence.

When Nguyen wanted something, Park made sure I obeyed. When Nguyen traded me for favors, Park was the one who reminded me what happened if I resisted. He didn't need to speak much. His hands, his eyes, the bruises he left, those were his language.

He hurt me because hurting was his power and his joy. He made me understand that my body was not mine, that my voice was not mine, that even my breath belonged to someone else. He was the punishment behind Nguyen's bargains, the violence that kept me compliant.

You ask me about Park's role? He was the cage. He was the threat that turned everything into inevitability. He was the reason I learned to endure without protest, to survive without hope. And every scar he left reminded me that survival was not freedom—it was captivity."

Walsh established timeline: Bea and Nguyen both resettled in America, different years, lost contact for decades. Bea built life as artist in Franklin. Began painting "Between Waters" series about her refugee experience.

"When did you next encounter Minh Nguyen?"

"August 2024. He showed up at my studio. I didn't recognize him at first—forty-five years changes faces. But he knew me immediately. Called me by my camp name. Mentioned my grandmother's bracelet. Asked if I still painted water."

"How did that make you feel?"

"Violated. Like he'd been watching me for years. Waiting for the right moment to use what he knew about my trauma. Like my nightmares would all come back."

Walsh introduced evidence: gallery records showing Nguyen had tracked Bea's career since 2015. Had attended exhibitions using false names. Had documented her "Between Waters" series and calculated its value.

"What did Mr. Nguyen want from you?"

"My paintings. Specifically, the 'Between Waters' series. He said they were worth money. Said I owed him for helping me survive the camp. Said the paintings were payment for his forty-five-year-old kindness."

"What did you say?"

"I refused. Those paintings are my story. My salvation and healing. My parents' deaths. My survival. They're not for sale, especially not to someone who wanted to profit more from what he had already forced me to do. They were part of me. He'd already sold me once. Never again."

Walsh walked Bea through Fischer's harassment, Nguyen's escalating pressure, Park's reconnaissance of her studio. Building toward the murder with documentary precision.

"On November 1st, 2024, Conrad Fischer came to your studio. What happened?"

Bea described the meeting. Fischer's final offer—three hundred thousand for the series. Her refusal. His anger. His retreat to the bathroom. Her decision to make tea, to calm down, to breathe.

"When you returned from the kitchen, what did you find?"

"Conrad Fischer dead on the floor. Four of my paintings missing."

"What did you do?"

"I called 911. I was in shock. I couldn't understand what had happened. I thought maybe heart attack, maybe natural causes. I didn't know about the poison. I didn't know someone had killed him and stolen my work."

"When did you realize you were being framed?"

"When Detective Morrison told me

about the plant-based poison. Asian variety. Something that would implicate me or Maya Lin, the two people in Franklin with botanical knowledge." Bea looked directly at Nguyen. "That's when I knew this wasn't random. This was planned. Personal."

Walsh presented evidence: Lin Nguyen's testimony about hearing footsteps, security footage showing Park in Franklin, financial records proving payment for the poison, the bathroom window escape route.

"Ms. Tran, why do you think the defendants targeted you specifically?"

"Because I could identify them from Camp Galang. Because my story could expose their forty-five years of extorting refugee artists. Because I refused to be silent." Bea's voice was strong now, angry in the healthy way Maya had taught her. "They thought I was alone. Vulnerable. Easy to frame and silence. They were wrong."

Walsh's final question: "Are you afraid of the defendants?"

"No. I was afraid for forty-five years. Afraid of camps. Afraid of drowning. Afraid of losing everything again. But I'm done being afraid. I survived Vietnam. I survived the boat. I survived their conspiracy. I'll survive this too. And I'll help every other artist they victimized find courage to speak."

Cross-examination was brutal. Defense tried to shake Bea's timeline, questioned her memory of Camp Galang, suggested her paintings weren't worth what she claimed, implied she'd fabricated connections between her survival story and Nguyen's business.

But Bea held firm. She'd spent three months preparing. She knew her truth. And nothing defense threw at her could shake testimony built on lived experience.

By afternoon break, prosecution rested Bea's direct testimony. She stepped down from the witness stand exhausted but unbroken.

In the hallway, Maya wrapped her in a hug. "You were perfect."

"I was honest. That's all I could be."

"Honesty is revolutionary when everyone's expecting you to be silent," Evelyn said.

The rest of day three brought corroborating testimony. Lin Nguyen confirmed hearing different footsteps. Security footage showed Park's Toyota at Bea's studio. Poison supplier identified as the cash customer who bought Asian plant alkaloids.

And then, devastating for defense: AUSA Walsh called refugee artists to testify about Nguyen's crimes.

Artist after artist took the stand. Vietnamese, Syrian, Afghan, Somali. Each telling similar stories: initial contact through legitimate-seeming channels, promises of fair representation, sales for far less than actual value, threats when they questioned the arrangement.

Anh Pham from Seattle: "He bought my painting for three thousand, sold it for forty-five thousand, kept the forty-two thousand difference."

Rashid Ahmadi from Chicago: "When I complained, he threatened to report me to immigration for violations I didn't commit."

Khadija Osman from Minneapolis: "He knew I was vulnerable. Somali refugee, didn't understand American laws. He used that knowingly."

By day's end, twelve refugee artists had testified. The pattern was undeniable. The jury looked horrified.

That evening, the mahjong group gathered at their Charlotte hotel. Everyone was staying for the trial—Maya had closed the apothecary, Mabs had suspended library research, Frankie had taken leave from work, Dodo had arranged cat care. They were all in, completely committed.

"How many more victim testimonies?" Mabs asked.

"Walsh has twenty-three artists total," Evelyn said, checking the witness list. "She'll call them over the next three days. Build overwhelming pattern evidence."

"And then?" Bea asked.

"Then Park testifies for prosecution. Confirms Nguyen ordered both murders. Provides documentation of the entire network. And defense has to somehow explain away his continuing cheating plus two murders."

"They can't," Frankie said flatly. "Evidence is overwhelming."

"Don't celebrate yet," Donnie warned. "Defense attorneys are expensive and creative. They'll try something."

But even Donnie felt optimistic. The trial was proceeding exactly as planned. Evidence was devastating. Jury was engaged. Justice was advancing.

They ordered room service and played mahjong in Bea's hotel room—federal agents permitted it as "therapeutic activity." The tiles clicked, familiar and comforting. The ritual held despite everything.

"I did it," Bea said during the game. "I testified. I faced him. I told my truth."

"You did," Maya confirmed. "And you were magnificent."

"I was honest. There's a difference." Bea drew a tile. "But it felt good. Powerful. Like I finally took back what Nguyen stole forty-five years ago—my voice. My agency. My right to tell my own story."

Later, alone in her hotel room, Bea stood at the window looking at Charlotte's lights. Big city, federal court, justice system grinding toward verdict.

She thought about the fifteen-year-old girl who'd arrived at Camp Galang with nothing. Who'd trusted Minh Nguyen because she'd needed help to survive. Who'd carried that betrayal for forty-five years without even knowing it.

That girl had become a woman who

painted trauma into beauty. Who built community in Franklin. Who found family in Tuesday night mahjong. Who chose to fight back when predators came calling.

And tomorrow, that woman would watch as more refugee artists told their stories. As the pattern of misuse became undeniable. As justice moved closer to conviction.

Bea touched her grandmother's jade bracelet—the one constant through Vietnam, the boat, the camps, America, everything. Her grandmother had survived too. Multiple wars, colonization, occupation. Had given Bea this bracelet with simple instruction: Survive.

Well, Bea had survived. And now she was doing more than surviving.

She was fighting. Testifying. Helping others. Changing outcomes.

She was living.

And that was revolutionary.

Chapter 23

Week two of the trial brought Park Ji-woo to the witness stand, and the courtroom learned exactly how professional killers operated.

Park wore orange prison jumpsuit, handcuffed, flanked by marshals. His cooperation deal meant testifying truthfully in exchange for reduced sentence. Life with possibility of parole instead of execution.

AUSA Walsh walked him through his entire relationship with Nguyen. Meeting at Camp Galang when Park was sixteen, orphaned, desperate. Nguyen taking him under protection, teaching him how to survive through using others. Their partnership continuing forty-five years.

"Did you kill Conrad Fischer?" Walsh asked directly.

"Yes. On November 1st, 2024. Minh

ordered it. I executed it."

The courtroom went silent.

Walsh methodically established timeline. Nguyen had decided Fischer was becoming liability—too greedy, too careless, too willing to push Bea Tran in ways that risked exposure. Park was instructed to eliminate Fischer and steal Bea's paintings, making it look like Bea had killed him in dispute over art.

"How did you poison Fischer?"

"Plant-based alkaloid. Purchased from specialty supplier in Asheville. Slow-acting, designed to implicate Bea. I dosed Fischer's coffee during their meeting."

"And the paintings?"

"I was hiding in the studio. Entered before Fischer arrived, concealed in storage area. When Bea went to make tea, I poisoned Fischer, waited for poison to take effect, then took the four paintings and escaped through bathroom window."

"Why those four paintings specifically?"

"Minh had buyer in Singapore waiting. Those four told the marketable parts of Bea's story—escape, survival, arrival. The other two were too painful, too real. Wouldn't sell as well."

Defense tried to discredit Park on cross. But his testimony was supported by documentary evidence: texts with Nguyen discussing "Franklin problem," financial transfers paying for poison, flight records putting Park in North Carolina on murder date.

Most damaging: recordings. Park had secretly recorded conversations with Nguyen starting in 2023, insurance policy in case partnership dissolved. The recordings were devastating.

Nguyen's voice: "Bea Tran won't sell. We need to eliminate Fischer and take the paintings. Make it look like she did it."

Park's voice: "That's risky. She has community support."

Nguyen: "She's a refugee. Alone. Vulnerable. No one will believe her over evidence."

Park: "When?"

Nguyen: "November 1st. I'll be in Los Angeles establishing alibi. You handle Franklin."

The jury heard Nguyen order murder. Heard him dismiss Bea as "alone, vulnerable." Heard forty-five years of predation distilled into cold calculation.

Then Walsh asked the question everyone had been waiting for: "Did you also kill David Cho?"

"Yes. Federal prosecutor. Investigating art trafficking connections to STX Associates case. Minh ordered hit. I forced Cho's car off mountain road in July 2023. Made it look like accident."

Evelyn, sitting in gallery, didn't react visibly. But Donnie saw her hands clench, saw Maya take her hand, saw the controlled grief of someone hearing confirmation of what she'd already known.

Park's testimony continued for two days. He provided documentation of entire network: thirty-seven operatives across twelve countries, two hundred and forty-three artists, fifteen million dollars laundered, connections to North Korean sanctions evasion.

By end of week two, prosecution had built overwhelming case. Murder, conspiracy, racketeering, money laundering. All documented, corroborated, undeniable.

Defense started week three with their case. They challenged timing, questioned motivations, suggested Park was lying to get reduced sentence. But evidence was too strong. Documentary records, financial trails, victim testimony, recordings—all of it supported prosecution's narrative.

Nguyen didn't testify—Fifth Amendment right against self-incrimination. His lawyer argued reasonable doubt existed, that Park was unreliable witness, that refugee art pricing was subjective not criminal.

But jury's expressions suggested they weren't buying it.

Closing arguments came Friday of week three. AUSA Walsh summarized methodically: "Forty-five years of ongoing corruption targeting the most vulnerable. Two murders to protect profits. Hundreds of refugee artists betrayed by someone who claimed to help them. The evidence is overwhelming. Justice requires conviction."

Defense's closing: "Reasonable doubt exists. Park's testimony is self-serving. Art pricing is subjective. Tragic deaths, yes. Criminal conspiracy requiring RICO prosecution? Not proven."

Judge Martinez gave jury instructions—legal standards, burden of proof, how to weigh evidence. Sent them to deliberate Friday afternoon.

The mahjong group waited in courthouse cafeteria. Hours passed. No verdict.

Judge dismissed jury for weekend. Deliberations would resume Monday.

Donnie drove everyone back to Franklin for Sunday respite. They gathered at her house for Tuesday night mahjong despite it being Saturday.

"Do you think they'll convict?" Bea asked.

"Yes," Donnie said. "Evidence is too strong."

"But juries are unpredictable," Mabs added. "I've researched cases where overwhelming evidence still led to acquittal."

"Don't borrow trouble," Eddie said. "The jury heard Nguyen order murders. They heard victim testimony. They saw the pattern. They'll convict."

That night, Bea stayed in Franklin—special

permission granted since trial was paused. She slept in Maya's guest room, surrounded by her found family, home for the first time in four months without federal supervision.

"I miss this," Bea said at breakfast Sunday. "Franklin. Mountains. Community. Mahjong. Everything."

"Soon," Maya promised. "After verdict, after sentencing, we negotiate permanent return. You'll be home for real."

Monday morning, they drove back to Charlotte. Jury deliberations resumed. Hours passed. Lunch break. More deliberation.

At 4 PM, word came: verdict reached.

Everyone rushed to courtroom. Press filled in. Gallery packed. Nguyen and his lawyers stood. Park and his lawyers stood.

Jury filed in. Twelve people who'd spent three weeks hearing about immigrants exploited and were about to decide what justice was.

Judge Martinez: "Has the jury reached a verdict?"

Foreperson: "We have, Your Honor."

"On the charge of racketeering, how do you find?"

"Guilty."

"On the charges of money laundering?"

"Guilty on all counts."

"On the charge of murder in the first degree regarding Conrad Fischer?"

"Guilty."

"On the charge of murder in the first degree regarding David Cho?"

"Guilty."

For Park: guilty on conspiracy charges, money laundering, one count of murder (Fischer). His cooperation meant reduced charges for David Cho's murder—manslaughter instead of murder one.

But for Nguyen: guilty on everything. All counts. No mercy.

The courtroom exhaled collectively. Bea wept quietly. Evelyn sat very still, processing. Maya held both of them.

And Donnie felt something she hadn't felt in months: hope that justice was possible, that fighting mattered, that truth could win against evil.

Judge Martinez set sentencing for May 15th. Remanded both defendants without bail. Dismissed court.

Outside, press swarmed. David Chen issued statement: "Justice was served today for Bea Tran and the two hundred and forty-three refugee artists cheated by this criminal enterprise. This verdict sends clear message: vulnerability is not weakness, and predators will face consequences."

The mahjong group didn't talk to press. They just held each other in the courthouse plaza, crying and laughing and processing three weeks of testimony and four months of investigation and forty-five years of criminality, finally receiving justice.

"We won," Bea said. "We actually won."

"You won," Donnie corrected. "By being brave enough to fight back. By testifying. By refusing to stay silent."

"We all won," Maya said. "All two hundred forty-three artists. All refugee communities. Everyone who was told to be grateful and quiet and accept it. Today we won."

Bea was still unable to fully feel her work as a victory and was still standing in the Charlotte federal courthouse lobby, surrounded by the Tuesday night mahjong group celebrating when the two men in dark suits approached with badges and a folder thick with paperwork.

"Beatrice Tran?" the taller one said, though his tone made it clear this wasn't really a question.

"Yes?" Bea's voice was small. Tired. She'd just spent three days on the witness stand reliving forty-five years of trauma. She'd watched Nguyen receive life without parole. She'd thought it was over.

"I'm Agent Kovacs with Immigration and Customs Enforcement. This is Agent Miller. We need you to come with us."

The celebration stopped. Donnie moved immediately to Bea's side. "On what grounds?"

"Ma'am, this is federal business—"

"I'm asking on what grounds." Donnie's voice had gone deadly calm. Her investigator voice. The one that meant she already knew this was wrong and was building a case in real time.

Agent Kovacs pulled out paperwork. "Ms. Tran's naturalization application from 1982 contained material omissions. She failed to disclose ongoing criminal associations and—"

"That's insane," Maya interrupted. "She was a victim. She testified against—"

"She failed to disclose that she was working with individuals engaged in international trafficking—"

"She was being exploited," Evelyn cut in, her financial forensics brain already seeing the angle they were using. "She was a child refugee who was trafficked. That's not 'criminal association,' that's victimization."

"The determination has been made that Ms. Tran knowingly omitted material facts on her citizenship application." Agent Miller was reading from a script, his voice flat. "Under Section 340 of the Immigration and Nationality Act, citizenship obtained through fraud or misrepresentation can be revoked. She needs to come with us for processing and removal proceedings."

"Removal." Donnie's voice was ice. "You mean deportation."

"Ma'am—"

"She's a United States citizen. Has been for decades. She pays taxes. She votes. She owns property. She just testified in a federal trial that resulted in convictions for international trafficking and two murders." Donnie stepped between Bea and the agents. "You're not taking her anywhere without proper legal representation."

"Federal immigration enforcement doesn't require—"

"Stop." The voice came from behind them. Judge Sarah Martinez, still in her robes, strode into the lobby with the kind of authority that made federal agents pause. "I presided over this trial. I heard three days of testimony about Ms. Tran's victimization. You're not removing anyone from this courthouse."

"Your Honor, with respect, immigration enforcement falls outside judicial—"

"With respect, Agent Kovacs, I'm invoking my authority under 8 USC 1252 to stay removal pending judicial review of the denaturalization proceedings. Ms. Tran has the right to contest this in front of an immigration judge. You will not detain her without proper due process." Judge Martinez pulled out her phone. "I'm calling the Federal Public Defender's office right now. I may even appoint a private attorney to represent her, as is my privilege. One I'm sure might have a few folks sit up and pay notice. And the ACLU. And probably the New York Times, because this is exactly the kind of post-trial retaliation that needs public scrutiny."

Agent Kovacs's jaw tightened. "We have our orders."

"Then your orders just met judicial oversight. Ms. Tran is not leaving this building in your custody. Is that clear?"

The agents exchanged glances. Agent Miller's hand moved toward his hip—not threateningly, but like he was used to compliance through implied force.

"Don't." Frankie O'Hara's voice was quiet but carried military certainty. He'd positioned herself next to Donnie, and his body language said he'd spent twenty years in combat zones and wouldn't hesitate. "We're not letting you take her."

Frankie was quickly joined by two court bailiffs with a nod from Judge Martinez.

"Interfering with federal immigration enforcement is—"

"A fight you don't want to have in front of witnesses, cameras, and a federal judge who just stayed your removal order." Frankie didn't move, but somehow seemed larger. "Back off."

Morrison appeared with more local sheriff's officers. "There a problem here?"

"These agents were just leaving," Judge Martinez said. "After receiving my stay order and being informed that any attempt to detain Ms. Tran will result in immediate contempt charges and a very public lawsuit. Maybe even arrest, if they piss me off enough."

Agent Kovacs stared at Bea. She'd gone absolutely still, her face empty of color, her breathing shallow. Forty-three years of building a life in America, and two men with badges could threaten to erase it all because she'd been trafficked as a child.

"This isn't over," Kovacs said.

"You're absolutely right," Judge Martinez replied. "Because I'm escalating this to the Fourth Circuit and filing a formal complaint about post-trial witness intimidation. You came after her specifically because she testified. That's retaliation. That's illegal. And that's going to be very, very public."

The agents left. But the damage was done.

Bea collapsed into Maya's arms, shaking. "They're going to send me back. To Vietnam. To nothing. Everything I built—"

"No," Donnie said firmly. "No, they're not. We won't let them."

But even as she said it, Donnie knew this was a different kind of fight. Federal immigration enforcement didn't care about logic or justice or years of citizenship. They had power and fear and the weight of bureaucracy behind them.

This was war. Again.

The news hit social media within hours. **ICE ATTEMPTS TO DEPORT TRAFFICKING VICTIM AFTER TESTIFYING AGAINST CRIMINALS**. **FEDERAL WITNESS THREATENED WITH DEPORTATION**. **35-YEAR CITIZEN TARGETED FOR REMOVAL AFTER HELPING FBI**.

By Monday morning, it had gone national.

The Tuesday night mahjong group met at Donnie's house for emergency planning. They'd added some people: a public relations specialist who'd worked on refugee cases, two lawyers from the ACLU, and a clerk representing Arthur Kennedy, the only living retired Supreme Court Justice .

"The legal argument is bullshit," said Rachel Kim, the ACLU attorney. "They're claiming she 'omitted material facts' on her 1982 naturalization application by not disclosing her 'association' with Nguyen. But she was fifteen years old. She was being trafficked. That's not an association, that's victimization."

"Can they actually denaturalize her?" Maya asked, holding Bea's hand.

"Technically, yes. There's precedent for revoking citizenship obtained through fraud. But this isn't fraud—this is a trafficking victim who was too traumatized to disclose abuse on paperwork filled out 35 years ago as an unrepresented minor refugee." Rachel flipped through documents. "The problem is the current administration has been aggressively pursuing denaturalization cases to politically energize a voter base. They've created a special task force specifically to review old citizenship applications, looking for 'discrepancies.'"

"So they're going through records trying to find ways to strip citizenship from naturalized Americans," Evelyn said flatly.

"Essentially, yes."

"That's terrifying," Mabs said quietly.

"That's the point." Rachel looked grim. "Fear. Uncertainty. Making immigrants—even citizens—feel like they're never really secure. Like they can lose everything at any moment."

"What do we do?" Donnie asked.

"We fight. In court, in public opinion, and

politically. I'm filing an emergency motion to dismiss the denaturalization proceedings. Judge Martinez's stay helps, but we need more."

"I can reach out to Governor Cooper," Eddie said, "My family's donated to his campaigns. He's been vocal about protecting immigrant communities."

"And Attorney General Stein," added the PR specialist. "He's filed amicus briefs against federal immigration overreach before."

"What about local officials?" Morrison asked. "Macon County commissioners? Franklin's mayor?"

"Already on it," Eddie interjected. "I just called Mayor Lewis. She's drafting a resolution of support for the town council meeting Thursday."

Bea sat silently through all of this, looking small and exhausted. Finally she spoke. "Maybe I should just go."

Everyone stopped.

"What?" Maya's voice cracked.

"Maybe I should just... leave. Voluntarily. Before they deport me. At least that way I'd have some dignity. I could pack my things. Say goodbye properly." Bea's eyes were dry but devastated. "I don't want to fight anymore. I'm tired."

"No." Maya took both of Bea's hands. "You don't get to give up. Not after everything you survived. Not after you testified and brought down Nguyen and saved hundreds of other artists from his network. You don't get to let them win."

"They already won. They can take away my citizenship. My home. My—"

"They can try," Donnie interrupted. "But they have to go through us first. Through Franklin. Through every person who knows your story and sees this for what it is—retaliation against a witness who had the courage to testify."

"I'm not brave enough for this fight."

"You already were," Evelyn said quietly. "You stood in federal court and told your story to the world. You faced Nguyen across a courtroom. You chose justice over safety. That's the bravest thing anyone could do."

"And look what it cost me."

"It hasn't cost you anything yet," Frankie said. "Because we're not losing this fight."

Governor Roy Cooper issued a statement Tuesday afternoon:

*"*The attempt to denaturalize and deport Beatrice Tran is a cruel injustice that North Carolina will not tolerate. Ms. Tran is a productive*

citizen who helped federal investigators bring down an international trafficking network. She is a victim being punished for coming forward. My office will provide every resource necessary to fight this wrongful deportation, and I call on federal authorities to immediately drop these proceedings."

Attorney General Josh Stein followed with his own statement:

"Federal immigration enforcement has lost sight of basic justice. Denaturalizing a 35-year citizen, an internationally famous artist for failing to disclose childhood trauma experienced in a brutal dictatorship on decades-old paperwork is not law enforcement—it's persecution. North Carolina stands with Beatrice Tran and will fight this abuse of power."

By Wednesday, the Macon County Board of Commissioners passed a unanimous resolution declaring Bea a valued community member and calling on federal authorities to cease deportation proceedings.

Thursday, Franklin's town council held a packed meeting where residents lined up to speak in Bea's defense.

"She teaches art classes at the community center," said a mother of three. "My daughter learned to paint from her. She's part of this town."

"She volunteers at the library," Mabs testified. "She helps kids with literacy programs. She reads to seniors at the care facility. She is Franklin."

"She pays her taxes and mows her lawn and brings cookies to neighborhood meetings," said Bea's neighbor. "She's more American than half the people who voted for this guy in the White House.."

The mayor's voice shook when she read the town's resolution:

*"*The Town of Franklin, North Carolina, stands in solidarity with Beatrice Tran. We recognize her as a valued member of our community, a victim of trafficking who showed extraordinary courage in testifying against her abusers. We call on federal authorities to cease deportation proceedings immediately and to recognize that justice means protecting witnesses, not punishing them."*

The vote was unanimous.

By Friday, the story had reached national news. CNN. MSNBC. Fox News. The New York Times ran an editorial titled "When Citizenship Means Nothing: The Case of Beatrice Tran."

Social media exploded. #StandWithBea trended for three days. Immigration advocacy groups made her case a rallying cry against denaturalization proceedings. Artists' organizations issued statements. Refugee resettlement agencies held vigils.

The pressure mounted.

But federal bureaucracy moved slowly, and ICE didn't back down easily.

March became April. April became May. Bea lived in limbo—technically free pending court proceedings, but knowing that at any moment, a different judge or a policy shift could end everything. Men in battle gear might show up at any time, ignoring the judge's order; they've done it elsewhere.

She couldn't leave protected custody without permission. She had to check in weekly with ICE. She wore an ankle monitor. Her artwork suffered because her hands shook too much to hold brushes steady.

The Tuesday night mahjong group became her anchor. She traveled to play every week, played tiles, shared meals, and reminded Bea that she belonged here in Franklin. That home was more than paperwork.

Maya moved in with her. Not officially —Bea's attorney said cohabitation could "complicate" things—but practically. Maya was there every night, holding Bea through nightmares, making tea, painting beside her when Bea could manage to create.

"I'm sorry," Bea said one night in May, watching Maya work. "I'm sorry you're stuck with this. With me like this."

"I'm not stuck. I'm here. There's a difference." Maya didn't look up from her canvas—she'd started painting again too, alongside Bea. Solidarity in art. "And you're not 'like this.' You're exactly like you've always been. Strong. Surviving. Fighting."

"I don't feel strong."

"Strength isn't feeling brave. It's staying when you want to run. It's getting up every morning even when you don't know if you'll still have a home by nightfall." Maya finally looked at her. "You've been doing that for forty-three years. You're the strongest person I know."

The legal proceedings dragged on.

Rachel Kim filed motion after motion—challenging the denaturalization proceedings, arguing selective prosecution, demonstrating that Bea had been targeted specifically for testifying. The government countered with arcane immigration law and bureaucratic filings ignoring legal precedents.

Judge Martinez stayed actively involved, issuing orders that kept Bea from being detained while the appeals process continued.

Senator Tillis's office issued a statement

calling for review of the case. He wasn't running for re-elction and didn't need a presidential endorsement. Senator Burr remained silent. Congressional representatives split along predictable lines.

But public opinion was overwhelmingly on Bea's side.

By July, over 200,000 people had signed petitions demanding ICE drop the deportation proceedings.

By August, North Carolina's state legislature had sent a formal letter to the Department of Homeland Security questioning the prosecution and threatening a total obstruction of federal immigration enforcement in the state.

By September, the legal costs had reached $75,000. The Tuesday night mahjong group had started a legal defense fund. Dion donated the first $10,000. The town of Franklin raised $15,000 through community fundraisers. Artists from across the country sent contributions.

Bea tried to refuse. "I can't let you all—"

"You're not letting us do anything," Donnie cut her off. "We're choosing this. We're choosing you. That's what community means."

October brought the breakthrough.

Judge David Thompson of the Fourth Circuit Court of Appeals issued a blistering opinion dismissing the denaturalization proceedings:

"The government's attempt to revoke Ms. Tran's citizenship based on alleged 'omissions' from a 1982 application filled out by a teenage trafficking victim is not merely unjust—it is unconscionable. Ms. Tran was fifteen years old, newly arrived from a refugee camp, traumatized by exploitation, and filling out complex legal paperwork in a non-native language. To claim she 'knowingly' omitted information about her trafficker is to fundamentally misunderstand the nature of trauma, the power dynamics of exploitation, and the vulnerability of refugee children."

"Furthermore, the timing of these proceedings—immediately following Ms. Tran's testimony in a federal criminal trial that resulted in significant convictions—strongly suggests retaliation rather than legitimate immigration enforcement. This court will not permit federal agencies to punish witnesses for cooperating with criminal investigations."

"The denaturalization proceedings are dismissed with prejudice. Ms. Tran's citizenship is affirmed. The government is enjoined from pursuing

any further deportation actions based on this or related matters."*

The ruling was unanimous. All three judges.

When Rachel called with the news, Bea was in her studio, trying to paint. Maya answered the phone.

"We won," Rachel said, her voice breaking. "Bea, we won. It's over. You're staying."

Bea dropped her paintbrush. It clattered on the floor, splattering blue paint across tile. She didn't move to pick it up.

"Are you sure?" Her voice was barely audible.

"Dismissed with prejudice. They can't appeal. You're safe. You're home."

Maya wrapped her arms around Bea, and this time when Bea cried, it wasn't from fear.

The Tuesday night mahjong group gathered that evening at The Slanted Window. Dion had closed the tasting room to regular customers—this celebration was private.

They drank local wine and ate charcuterie and didn't play mahjong because Bea couldn't stop shaking.

"I thought I'd lost everything," she said,

holding Maya's hand and a glass of Rosé Saignée. "My home. My community. Everything I'd built in forty-three years. I thought they'd send me back to nothing."

"You never would have had nothing," Mabs said firmly. "We'd have figured something out. Canada, maybe. Mexico. You're famous. Somewhere you could be safe and we could visit."

"But I'd have lost Franklin."

"Franklin wasn't going to lose you." Donnie raised her glass. "To citizenship that can't be taken away. To a country that serves its people. To communities that fight for their own. To Bea Tran, who survived trafficking, testified against monsters, and then survived our government trying to punish her for it."

"To Bea," they all echoed.

"And to justice," Evelyn added. "Even when it takes months and $75,000 in legal fees and a Fourth Circuit opinion to achieve it."

"Was it worth it?" Bea asked suddenly. "All the money. The time. The stress. Was I worth that fight?"

The table went silent. Then Maya spoke.

"You testified knowing they might do this. You knew standing up could cost you your citizenship, your home, your life here. And you testified anyway because 316 other refugee artists deserved justice." Maya's voice was steady. "You were worth fighting for before that. You're certainly worth fighting for after."

"Besides," Dodo added, "the cats were very clear that abandoning you was unacceptable. And we don't ignore the cats."

Everyone laughed—exhausted, relieved laughter that came from surviving something that should never have happened in the first place.

"What do we do now?" Bea asked.

"We live," Donnie said. "We play mahjong. We sell dog treats and Cat Saks and drink local wine. We paint and garden and read and cook. We show up for each other. We build lives worth protecting."

"And if ICE comes back?"

"They won't. But if they do—" Frankie smiled grimly. "—we'll be ready. They don't understand what Americans will fight for."

Outside, darkness settled over Franklin. The mountains held everything in their ancient embrace. Somewhere, Bea's studio waited with unfinished paintings. Maya's apothecary held herbs for healing. Donnie's bakery would open Monday morning to community and dogs. Evelyn's laptop held financial records on six new cases. Mabs's library waited with books and refuge.

Franklin held its own.

And Beatrice Tran, naturalized citizen of the United States for decades, victim of trafficking, survivor of exploitation, artist, community member and friend, was finally, truly, undeniably on her way home.

The government had tried to take that away.

The community had said no.

And this time, the community won

Chapter 24

Presentence investigation and the mandatory appeals completed brought sentencing and the beginning of Bea's permanent return negotiations.

Judge Martinez sentenced Minh Nguyen to life without parole on murder charges, plus fifty years for racketeering and money laundering. Park Ji-woo received life with possibility of parole after thirty years for his cooperation.

"The crimes documented in this case," Judge Martinez said, "represent the worst predation of vulnerable refugee communities

I've ever heard. This court recognizes that the harm extends far beyond financial—you stole stories, weaponized trauma, and betrayed trust in ways that compound original suffering. Maximum sentences are warranted."

Victim impact statements took entire day. Twenty-three artists testified about how Nguyen's had disrupted their careers, their trust, their sense of safety in America.

Bea spoke last. "I survived Vietnam. I survived the boat. I survived refugee camps. I thought surviving meant staying quiet, being grateful, not causing trouble. Minh Nguyen exploited that belief for forty-five years. But I learned something through this trial: survival isn't silence. Survival is fighting back. Testifying. Helping others. That's real survival."

After sentencing, AUSA Walsh met with the mahjong group. "FBI will reassess protection needs. With Nguyen and Park in federal prison, immediate threat is substantially reduced. We're inclined to approve Bea's return to Franklin with monitoring but not protective custody."

"How soon?" Bea asked.

"Two weeks. We need to process paperwork, coordinate with local law enforcement, establish protocols. But yes. You're going home."

Bea cried. Maya held her. The whole group celebrated quietly—this was the goal they'd been fighting for since November.

"What about the other artists?" Mabs asked. "The ones who testified?"

"FBI is offering assistance—relocation if desired, protection if needed, support regardless. We're also coordinating with refugee advocacy organizations to provide long-term resources."

"And the Refugee Artist Protection Project?" Evelyn asked.

"Your database is invaluable. FBI wants to partner with you—official collaboration between federal resources and community knowledge. We'll fund the project, help expand it internationally, make it sustainable."

It was more than they'd hoped for. Not just justice for Bea. Justice for all refugee artists. Resources to prevent it from happening again. Federal partnership to make the work sustainable.

"When do we start?" Mabs asked.

"Immediately."

Two weeks later, on June 1st, Bea returned to Franklin permanently.

The Tuesday night mahjong group met her at the town line—literally standing at the "Welcome to Franklin" sign with balloons and tears and Audrey wearing a bow tie for the occasion.

"Welcome home," Donnie said.

"I'm home," Bea whispered. "Really home."

Her studio had been released from crime scene status. She'd arranged for professional cleaning, new paint, exorcism of the violence that had happened there. When she walked in, it was her space again. Hers to paint in, create in, heal in.

The first thing she did was start a new painting. Seventh piece in the "Between Waters" series. This one titled "The Community That Saved Me."

It showed seven women and one poodle arranged around a mahjong table, mountains visible through the window behind them. Found family. Tuesday night ritual. Home.

She painted for weeks, processing everything. The trial. The testimony. The victory. The return. Each brushstroke therapy, each color choice intentional.

The mahjong group resumed normal schedule—Tuesday nights at the library, tiles clicking, comfortable rituals. Bea in her chair. Maya bringing tea. Evelyn calculating probabilities. Mabs documenting everything. Dodo sharing cat wisdom. Frankie protecting everyone. Donnie coordinating. Eddie observing. Audrey judging.

Life returning to normal. Except nothing was normal anymore. They'd exposed international conspiracy, helped convict murderers, changed federal policy on refugee artist protection.

Normal was different now. Better. More purposeful.

"What's next for you?" Maya asked Bea one Tuesday in July.

"Paint. Testify at other trials—FBI has seventeen more prosecutions coming from the network we exposed. Help other artists through the Protection Project. Live." Bea smiled. "And play mahjong every Tuesday."

"Good priorities," Mabs approved.

That summer, the Refugee Artist Protection Project officially launched. Website went live. Database accessible to artists, advocates, law enforcement. Educational materials in eight languages. Reporting mechanism for new cases. The work Mabs had started in February had become international resource.

Eighty-nine artists had provided testimony for the database. Another hundred and fifty-four had been contacted and were considering participation. The network was growing, healing, becoming something powerful.

Evelyn managed the technical side. Mabs handled documentation. Maya developed educational resources. Donnie coordinated with law enforcement. Dodo made the logo—surprisingly professional despite featuring a subtle cat silhouette. Frankie established security protocols. Eddie helped with grant writing. Even Bea contributed—artwork for the website, victim testimony guidance.

And the Tuesday night mahjong group became known not just for solving murders but for local advocacy. They'd turned local tragedy into international resource. Found family into movement.

"We did good work," Donnie said one evening after mahjong.

"We did necessary work," Mabs corrected.

"We're not done," Evelyn added. "Seventeen more trials. Hundreds more artists to contact. Years of work ahead."

"Good," Frankie said. "I was getting bored anyway."

They laughed. Because that was survival too. Finding humor despite trauma. Finding joy despite fight. Finding each other despite everything.

The mountains watched through Franklin windows, ancient and patient. They'd witnessed this story—crime, investigation, justice, healing. They'd see what came next.

And what came next was more work. More trials. More artists helped. More systems changed.

But also: more mahjong. More tea. More community. More life lived with purpose and people you loved.

That was justice too. Not just convictions. Not just sentences. But the healing that came after. The community that sustained. The choice to keep living, keep fighting, keep hoping.

Bea painted it all. The new series was called "After the Storm." Healing. Community. Mountains. Hope. The life you built when you stopped running and started standing still.

It was her best work yet. And it was all hers. Just art made from survival and community and love.

That was revolutionary.

Chapter 25

September brought Bea's first art show since the trial, and Franklin turned out in force.

The regional museum in Asheville had offered to host "Between Waters: Complete Series"—all seven paintings including the new piece Bea had completed about her mahjong family. The show opened on the first Friday in September, and the turnout was overwhelming.

Refugees from across the region attended. Artists Nguyen had used. Advocates who'd helped with the Protection Project. Press documenting the story. FBI agents including Katherine Parker. Judge Martinez. AUSA Walsh. Morrison and local law enforcement. The whole Tuesday night mahjong group, of course. And hundreds of Franklin residents who'd supported Bea through everything.

The paintings hung in order, telling story

chronologically. The boat. The water. Parents drowning. Arrival in America. Building new life. Survival. And finally: the mahjong table with mountains behind.

Viewers wept. Bea's technique was extraordinary—spare, economical, every brushstroke carrying emotional weight. The water looked alive. The mountains felt ancient. The community radiated warmth.

"This is your legacy," Maya said, standing in front of "The Community That Saved Me." "Not just surviving. Transforming survival into beauty."

"It's our legacy," Bea corrected. "I couldn't have painted this without you. Any of you. The community made this possible."

The museum had printed artist statement for the exhibition. Bea's words explained each painting, contextualized her refugee experience, and ended with: "Art is how I process trauma. But community is how I heal. Thank you to Franklin, to the Tuesday night mahjong group, and to everyone who fought for justice. You saved me. These paintings are my gratitude rendered in watercolor and hope."

Press interviewed Bea extensively. She talked about the trial, about Nguyen's forty-five-year exploitation, about the two hundred forty-three other artists, about the Protection Project.

"Are the paintings for sale?" one reporter asked.

"No. These are mine. My story. Not for profit. Not for collectors. Mine." Bea smiled. "But I'm creating new work that will be for sale, with proceeds supporting the Refugee Artist Protection Project. Art that helps other artists."

The show ran for three months. Thousands attended. Reviews were glowing. Several museums requested to host the exhibition afterward. International interest emerged.

But for Bea, the most meaningful moment came opening night when twenty-three refugee artists who'd testified approached her together.

Anh Pham spoke for the group. "We wanted to thank you. For going first. For being brave. For showing us that testifying was possible. We wouldn't have had courage without your example."

"I had courage because of my community," Bea said. "Find your community. Support each other. That's how we change things—together, not alone."

They stood in a museum gallery, surrounded by paintings of water and survival, twenty-four refugee artists who'd chosen to fight back. Who'd testified against their oppressors. Who'd helped each other heal.

"This is revolution," Dodo whispered to Donnie. "Quiet revolution. But revolution nonetheless."

"The cats knew," Donnie said seriously.

Because after eighteen months of Tuesday night mahjong, she'd learned that sometimes Dodo's chaos contained profound truth.

That evening, after crowds departed, the mahjong group gathered in museum courtyard. They'd brought tiles, set up portable table, were playing under stars with mountains visible in distance.

"This feels right," Evelyn said. "Celebrating Bea's art with our ritual."

"Everything we do together feels right," Maya added.

They played until midnight. Security guards allowed it—"cultural activity," they called it, but really they were just charmed by seven people and a poodle playing a Chinese game under September stars in museum courtyard.

"What's next?" Frankie asked. "We solved two murders, exposed international conspiracy, launched protection project. What do we do now?"

"Live," Bea said simply. "Paint. Play mahjong. Help other artists. Enjoy being home."

"Boring," Frankie muttered. But he was smiling.

"Give it time," Donnie said. "Franklin always has another mystery. Another injustice. Another fight."

"You sound eager," Mabs observed.

"I'm retired. I can be eager about local mysteries without career consequences."

"You were never actually retired," Eddie pointed out. "You've solved two murders since moving here."

"Three if you count the HVAC company fraud case."

"That wasn't murder, that was insurance fraud."

"Still counts."

They laughed. Because that was Tuesday night mahjong. Work and play and family and purpose all mixed together until you couldn't separate them.

The mountains watched from darkness, ancient and knowing. They'd witnessed Bea's journey—from boat escape to refugee camp to Franklin to art show. They'd witnessed the mahjong group's formation, their fights, their victories.

And they'd witness whatever came next. More mysteries, probably. More injustices to fight. More community to build.

But tonight, they just witnessed seven friends and one poodle playing mahjong under stars, celebrating survival and art and found family.

That was enough. That was everything.
That was home.

Chapter 26

October brought the first of seventeen additional trials from Nguyen's network, and the Tuesday night mahjong group found themselves traveling to testify.

Evelyn went to Atlanta to present financial evidence. Mabs flew to Los Angeles with database documentation. Maya provided expert testimony about crimes against immigrants. Even Dodo testified—about community intelligence gathering and how gossip networks had helped identify criminals.

Donnie coordinated everything from Franklin, managing schedules, supporting witnesses, ensuring the refugee artists who testified had resources and protection.

"We've become professional witness coordinators," she told Eddie one evening.

"You've become justice advocates," he corrected. "There's a difference."

The trials proceeded through fall. Four convictions by November. Eight more cases pending. The network was being dismantled piece by piece—operatives arrested, assets seized, victim compensation funds established.

But Bea stayed in Franklin, painting. She'd done her testifying. Now she healed through art.

"You should paint this," Maya suggested one Tuesday night, gesturing to the mahjong table mid-game. "Not just the static image from your exhibition piece. The actual game in motion."

Bea considered. "A series. Multiple paintings showing single game from start to finish. Tiles shuffling, walls building, hands being played. Community in action."

"Perfect."

She started the new series: "Tuesday Nights." Twelve paintings, one for each phase of standard mahjong game. Building walls. Dealing tiles. Drawing. Discarding. Calling mahjong. Scoring. The ritual captured in brushstrokes.

It became her best technical work. Each painting precisely documented real game they'd played, but infused with emotion. You could see friendship in the tile placement. Love in the careful hands. Family in the mountains visible through every window.

"This is your magnum opus," Mabs said, viewing early pieces.

"This is my healing," Bea corrected. "Everything else was about trauma. This is about what comes after—community, ritual, joy despite everything."

Meanwhile, the Refugee Artist Protection Project was expanding internationally. Partnerships established in Canada, UK, Australia, Germany. The model was replicable: document, provide resources, support testimony, prevent future harm.

By December, three hundred and seventeen artists had contributed to the database. FBI estimated at least thousand more were still undocumented victims of various trafficking operations.

"We're just beginning," Evelyn said at year-end mahjong planning session.

"Good," Frankie said. "World needs more Tuesday nights fighting injustice."

They played mahjong that December evening, snow falling outside, fire warming Donnie's living room. One year since Fischer's murder. One year since everything changed.

"We should mark the anniversary," Dodo suggested. "Not celebrate murder. But acknowledge transformation. How crisis became catalyst."

"The cats have thoughts about this?" Frankie asked.

"Always. They suggest ritual burning of something symbolic. Like... bureaucratic paperwork? Or maybe just more cookies."

They laughed. Because Dodo was chaos wrapped in wisdom wrapped in more chaos. But she was family. They were all family. Found through murder, sealed through investigation, maintained through weekly ritual.

"To Bea," Donnie said, raising her wine glass. "Who survived everything and taught us that survival is revolutionary."

"To community," Maya added. "Which makes survival possible."

"To Tuesday nights," Mabs said. "Our anchor in chaos."

They toasted. Played mahjong. Ate Eddie's cooking. Watched Audrey judge everyone equally. Did the things that made them family despite having no blood connection or legal obligation.

Just choice. Weekly choice to show up, play tiles, support each other.

That was enough. That was everything.

January marked one year since Park's arrest and brought unexpected developments.

Frankie O'Hara came to Tuesday night mahjong with news. "I found something. About my wife's death."

Everyone went silent. Frankie's wife had died three years ago in what was ruled workplace accident. But Frankie had always suspected foul play—the evidence didn't quite match accident profile, EPA had been investigating environmental violations at the facility, timing was suspicious.

"What did you find?" Donnie asked.

"EPA investigator contacted me. Said they're reopening the case. Found evidence suggesting the accident might have been staged to prevent testimony about illegal waste disposal." Frankie's voice was tight with controlled emotion. "They want me to review the evidence. Help build the case."

"Do you want help?" Maya asked gently.

"I want Tuesday night mahjong to solve another murder." Frankie smiled grimly. "You're good at this. And I need... I need family for this. Can't do it alone."

"You never have to do anything alone," Bea said. "That's what we've learned. Community makes the impossible possible."

"Then it's settled," Donnie said. "After we finish the refugee artist trials, we investigate Frankie's wife's death. Proper investigation. Justice."

"Book Three," Eddie murmured, novelist brain already structuring narrative.

"This is real life, not a book series," Frankie said.

"Everything's a book series if you pay attention long enough."

They played mahjong that night with new purpose. Another mystery. Another injustice. Another chance to fight back.

Because that's who they'd become. The Tuesday night mahjong murder mystery group. Found family that solved impossible cases. Community that refused to let darkness win.

"I'm scared," Frankie admitted later. "What if we investigate and find nothing? What if she really did die in accident? What if I've been wrong for three years?"

"Then you have an answer," Donnie said. "Truth is better than uncertainty. And we'll help you process whatever we find."

"And if we find murder?"

"Then we catch another killer. We're getting good at that."

February brought resolution to the refugee artist trials. All seventeen cases convicted. Network completely dismantled. Victim compensation totaling forty-three million dollars distributed. The exploitation exposed, prosecuted, ended.

"We did it," Evelyn said, reviewing the final case. "Every person in Nguyen's network—convicted, imprisoned, assets seized."

"Justice," Mabs said simply.

The Refugee Artist Protection Project hosted celebration in March. Three hundred seventeen documented artists. International partnerships. Federal funding secured. Sustainable advocacy established.

Bea gave keynote speech. "One year ago, I was in hiding. Afraid. Isolated. Waiting to testify against people who'd threatened my survival. Today, I'm home. Painting. Living. And helping build system that protects other artists. This transformation happened because of community. Because people showed up, fought back, refused to accept injustice. Thank you to everyone who made this possible. Especially to the Tuesday night mahjong group—my found family who saved me by teaching me that survival isn't silence. It's resistance."

Standing ovation. Tears. The recognition that sometimes individual stories become movements. That one artist's fight could create systemic change.

After the event, the mahjong group gathered at Donnie's house—their usual spot, their comfort space.

"What's next?" Dodo asked. "We solved murders. Changed international policy. Built sustainable advocacy. What do we do now?"

"Frankie's wife," Donnie said. "We investigate. We find truth. We get justice."

"And after that?"

"Whatever Franklin needs. Whatever justice requires. Whatever Tuesday night brings." Donnie looked around the table at her family. "We're not retiring from this. We're in it. Permanently."

"Good," Frankie said. "Because I need you."

"You have us," Maya promised. "Always."

The mountains watched through windows, ancient and patient. One story ending. Another beginning. The cycle continuing.

Because that's what communities did. They persisted. They fought. They transformed tragedy into justice, over and over, as many times as necessary.

Tuesday night mahjong was just getting

started.

Epilogue

Six months later.

Bea Tran stood in front of her completed Tuesday Nights series at Franklin's first annual community art show, and thought about transformation.

Twelve paintings. One complete mahjong game. Community rendered in watercolor and love.

The show was held in the library—the same library where they played every Tuesday. Morrison had helped set up. The whole town had turned out. Even Nguyen's prosecution had brought tourists interested in the "refugee artist justice story."

But Bea wasn't thinking about tourists or press or international attention.

She was thinking about family.

The Tuesday night mahjong group stood together in front of the paintings. Donnie and Eddie, thirty-six years of marriage visible in how they stood. Maya and Evelyn, two years of choosing each other despite trauma. Mabs with her precision and warmth. Dodo with her cats and chaos and surprising wisdom. Frankie preparing to investigate her wife's death with their full support. Even Audrey, judgment position fully engaged.

"It's beautiful," Maya said, looking at the series. "You captured us perfectly."

"I captured truth," Bea corrected. "This is who we are. Community that showed up. Fought back. Chose each other. That's worth painting."

Outside, April evening turned the mountains gold and purple. Spring fully arrived. Dogwoods blooming. Everything renewing.

One year since trial. Eighteen months since Fischer's murder. Two years since Bea had started building life in Franklin.

So much had changed. The refugee artist network dismantled. Protection Project established. International advocacy launched. Justice achieved. Home secured.

And with the seized millions, Franklin had built something lasting: a museum dedicated to Refugee Art, its glass walls catching mountain light, its galleries filled with testimony in color and clay. The museum stood as both sanctuary and archive, a place where survival became creation, where exile became expression.

From that seed grew the annual Festival of Refugee Art. Each May, tens of thousands came to Franklin—pilgrims of justice and beauty—filling streets with music, murals, and stories. The town once known for quiet mountains now carried a new name whispered across continents: Franklin, the refuge of art.

But the most important thing hadn't changed: Tuesday nights.

Every Tuesday, they gathered. Shuffled tiles. Built walls. Played games. Maintained ritual that held them together through everything.

"What's your next series?" a viewer asked Bea.

"I'm painting Frankie's story next. His wife. The EPA investigation. The fight for truth." Bea looked at Frankie. "With permission."

"With gratitude," Frankie corrected. "Someone needs to document what we're about to do."

Another fight for justice. Another chapter.

That evening, after the art show, after the crowds departed, the mahjong group gathered at the library for regular Tuesday night game.

Same table. Same chairs. Same tiles. Same ritual.

Everything transformed. Nothing changed. Both things true simultaneously.

They built the walls. Shuffled tiles. Dealt hands.

"I've been thinking," Bea said during the game. "About what mahjong means. It's strategy game, yes. But it's also about community. About how you can't win alone. About how sometimes you sacrifice your own progress to help others. About how the game matters less than playing together."

"Deep thoughts for a tile game," Frankie said.

"Deep game disguised as tiles," Evelyn corrected.

They played until midnight. Then

dispersed to their homes, their lives, their individual journeys that somehow all converged every Tuesday in Franklin library.

Bea walked home alone—well, not alone. Maya walked with her, as she often did, enjoying spring evening and mountain views and comfortable silence.

"Are you happy?" Maya asked.

"Yes. Scared about Frankie's case. Worried about the protection project's sustainability. Concerned about thousand artists still undocumented. But happy. Home. Painting. Living." Bea smiled. "I spent forty-five years asking why I survived when my parents died. I finally know the answer."

"Why?"

"To be here. To fight back. To help others. To paint. To play Tuesday night mahjong. To build found family with seven people and one judgmental poodle." Bea looked at the mountains, ancient and patient. "I survived so I could create this life. This community. This meaning from trauma."

"That's beautiful."

"That's revolutionary."

They reached Bea's apartment—small, affordable, perfect for her needs. She'd hung her own paintings on the walls, the ones that didn't sell or exhibit. Her private collection. Her journey rendered in watercolor.

"Same time next Tuesday?" Maya asked.

"Always," Bea promised.

Because that was the answer to everything. Tuesday nights. Community. Found family. The ritual that held them together through murder investigations and international conspiracies and personal trauma.

Tuesday nights were their anchor. Their rebellion. Their revolutionary act of choosing each other over and over despite difficulty.

And next Tuesday, they'd gather again. Shuffle tiles. Build walls. Play games.

And if another mystery appeared? If another injustice needed fighting? If another person needed saving?

Well. They'd handle that too.

Because that's what the Tuesday night mahjong murder mystery group did.

They showed up. They fought. They refused to let darkness win.

One game at a time.

One case at a time.

One Tuesday at a time.

THE END

The Mahjong Murder Mysteries continue in Book Three: "THE DRAGONS LIED"

How many people have to die before an accident becomes murder?

THE DRAGONS LIED
A Mahjong Murder Mystery
Book Three of the series

Prologue

November, Present Day

The Little Tennessee River runs cold in November, carrying more than water through the valleys of Macon County. It carries memory. It carries the chemical tang of things that shouldn't be there—industrial effluent, corporate decisions, the peculiar metallic taste of secrets kept too long. Frankie O'Hara stands at the river's edge at dawn, three years and eight months after his wife drowned surrounded in air, and thinks about what rivers remember.

The mountains rise around him, ancient witnesses clothed in bare November trees. They've seen generations of people try to live here—Cherokee who named these waters, settlers who cleared these slopes, families who built lives in the spaces between stone and sky. The mountains have seen it all, and they're patient with grief. They understand that some losses take years to name.

Frankie's boots are wet. He's been standing

here long enough for the cold to seep through leather, for his feet to go numb, for the sunrise to paint the ridges gold and then fade to ordinary daylight. In his hand, he holds Casey's field notebook—the last one, the one the EPA investigation never bothered to read. Water-stained pages. Her handwriting. March entries that end abruptly on a Tuesday because equipment fell and bodies break and sometimes love just stops mid-sentence.

He opens it. The spine cracks like bones.

March, Three Years and Eight Months Earlier

Casey O'Hara woke before dawn on the Tuesday she would die, and for thirty-seven minutes, she was purely happy.

This was notable because happiness, for Casey, was usually complicated—tangled up with data and worry and the constant awareness that the world was breaking faster than she could document its fractures. But on this particular Tuesday morning in March, with Frankie's arm across her waist and the bedroom window showing the first gray hint of approaching light, she was happy in the uncomplicated way of someone who doesn't know they're living their last hours.

She watched him sleep. Twenty years of military service had left Frankie with the ability to wake instantly at threat, but the gift of sleeping deeply when he felt safe. That he felt safe with her—this environmentalist who brought work stress home like pollen on her clothes, who woke him at midnight to explain streamflow dynamics, who cried over dead rivers—this was the miracle Casey never quite believed.

"I can feel you watching me," Frankie said without opening his eyes.

"Creepy or romantic?"

"Both. Schrödinger's observation."

She kissed his shoulder. "I'm going to the facility today. Final documentation on the discharge violations. Everything I need to prove they're dumping untreated waste into the river."

"And then?"

"And then I file the report. And then federal investigation. And then Holcombe Industrial gets what it deserves." Casey sat up, pulled on the flannel shirt Frankie had worn yesterday. It smelled like him—woodsmoke and coffee and the particular scent of a man who split firewood before breakfast. "Derek's going to fight it."

"Let him fight." Frankie opened his eyes, reached for her hand. "You've got truth. That's a better weapon than he has."

Casey believed him. In that moment, in that bedroom with March light just beginning to touch the mountains visible through their window, she believed that truth mattered. That documentation could stop corruption. That rivers could be saved and justice could be served and environmental engineers could fight corporations without dying.

She believed all of this for thirty-seven more minutes.

Then she went to work.

November, Present Day

The notebook is mostly technical—pH levels, flow rates, chemical concentrations that meant something to Casey's trained eye but read like poetry to Frankie now. Numbers as elegy. Data as love letter from someone who cared enough to measure the world's breaking.

But there are personal entries too. Scattered thoughts Casey wrote during lunch breaks, sitting by the river she was trying to save:

March 10: Saw a kingfisher today at the discharge point. How do we tell it the water it's fishing in is poison? How do we explain that the river it depends on is being murdered for profit? Sometimes I think the hardest part of this work is bearing witness. Knowing what's being lost. Knowing who's choosing profit over life. And still getting up the next day to document it anyway.

*March 15: Frankie asked me last night why I do this. Why I care so much about rivers and regulations and corporate compliance when it would be easier to just live our lives and ignore the corruption. I told him: because someone has to remember. Someone has to stand at the river and say "this is wrong" even when no one wants to hear it.

March 18: Derek Holcombe is lying. I can prove it. The question is whether proof matters to people who profit from lies.

March 19 was the last entry. Just three words, written in the margin of a data table:

For the river.

She died at 3:47 PM. The mounting brackets failed. Three hundred pounds of industrial filtration equipment fell. And Casey O'Hara, who'd spent her last weeks documenting corporate crimes and protecting water and believing that truth was weapon enough—

She drowned in air, crushed under metal that had been weakened systematically, deliberately, by people who couldn't afford her truth. Her lungs crushed - unable to absorb air.

The EPA called it an accident.

Frankie closes the notebook. Breathes

mountain air. Watches the river flow past, carrying its burden of chemicals and memory and all the things Casey died trying to prove.

An accident.

He thinks about the word. How it means: no one's fault. How it means: random chance. How it erases deliberation and motive and the careful corporate calculus that murder by equipment failure is cheaper than environmental compliance.

The mountains hold their silence. The river keeps flowing. And Frankie O'Hara, who has spent three years and eight months learning to live with absence, finally understands that some griefs can only be survived by transforming them into purpose.

* * *

March, Three Years and Eight Months Earlier

Casey spent her last morning taking water samples.

She worked methodically, the way she

always did—collecting samples every fifty meters along the discharge point, labeling each vial with coordinates and time stamps, photographing the oily sheen on the water's surface that shouldn't be there, that proved Holcombe Industrial was dumping untreated effluent to save money on chemical treatment.

The river ran cold and fast, spring-swollen with snowmelt from the high peaks. In another month, it would slow and warm and wildflowers would bloom along its banks. Casey wouldn't see that. But she didn't know it yet, so she planned for it anyway—mentally cataloging the species she'd observe, the seasonal patterns she'd document, the long-term monitoring she'd establish to prove the facility's crimes weren't isolated incidents but deliberate corporate policy.

She believed in the long term.

She believed she had time.

At 11:30 AM, she sat on a flat rock beside the river and ate the sandwich Frankie had packed for her—turkey and swiss, his mother's bread recipe, the crusts cut off because even after four years of marriage he remembered she didn't like them. She called him.

"How's the water?" he asked.

"Poisoned. Profitable. Provable." Casey watched a water strider navigate the surface film. "I'll have enough evidence by end of day to shut them down. Federal investigation. Criminal charges. Maybe even jail time for the executives."

"Be careful."

"Always am." Casey took a bite of sandwich, chewed, swallowed. "What are you making for dinner?"

"That chicken thing you like. The one with lemon and rosemary."

"I love that dish."

"I know."

"I love you."

"I know that too." Frankie's voice carried smile and concern in equal measure. "Come home safe, Case."

"Always do."

She hung up. Finished her sandwich. Took three more water samples. And at 2:30 PM, she went back to the facility to file her preliminary report—the one that would trigger federal investigation, the one that would cost Holcombe Industrial millions in fines and lost contracts, the one that made her dangerous.

The equipment fell at 3:47.

But before that, there were seventy-seven minutes when Casey O'Hara was alive and working and believing that documentation mattered. Seventy-seven minutes when she moved through the facility collecting evidence and preparing reports and planning the long-term monitoring studies she'd never complete.

Seventy-seven minutes when she was someone's wife, someone's hope, someone who believed rivers could be saved.

And then she was gone.

A Thousand Thanks

Dear friend,
We are so grateful that you have chosen to

spend time with us in Franklin, NC. While this is a work of fiction, it does take place in a real Smoky Mountain town, Franklin, North Carolina, with real places, real businesses, and most importantly, real beautiful people.

Eric and Norma Hendrix are extremely gifted musicians and friends whose talent graces our community. A Novel Escape Bookstore is my favorite hometown bookstore, and the owner, Liz, truly believes a good book makes a great day —a philosophy that guided the creation of this novel. At The Slanted Window Tasting Room, owned by Dion and his family at SenAmore Vineyard & Farms, I have enjoyed some great local wines in a wonderful setting and eaten too much wonderful food. They are the only vineyard and winery producing local wines in Macon County, and their hospitality is as exceptional as their Sangiovese.

The Smoky Mountain Dog Bakery, while in the neighboring town of Waynesville, has a special place in my heart. My wife and I started the bakery in 2008. We sold it ten years ago to a wonderful, talented woman who has grown the business above my dreams and won a dog bowl full of awards along the way. It is a regional draw for any dog lover, and I remain grateful to be part of its origin story.

The Macon County Farmers Market is a Saturday morning treasure where community gathers, local growers share their harvests, and yes—occasionally—cats might sell hand-knitted sleeping bags. The vendors, volunteers, and organizers who make the market possible deserve our thanks and our patronage.

To the real town of Franklin, North Carolina—thank you for being the kind of place where neighbors help neighbors, where Main Street businesses are run by people who know your name, where newcomers become family, and where community isn't just a word but a daily practice. You are the heart of this story.

To the volunteers, small business owners, farmers market vendors, bookstore staff, librarians, animal shelter workers, and everyday heroes who make small towns work—you inspired every character in this book. Your quiet heroism deserves celebration.

To the refugee and immigrant communities who enrich our nation with your courage, resilience, and contributions—Bea's story is a tribute to your strength. May we always be the country that says "welcome" and means it.

To my readers—thank you for taking a chance on a retired insurance investigator, a dog bakery owner, a poodle with opinions, and a group of friends who solve mysteries over mahjong tiles. I hope you'll return to Franklin for many more Tuesday nights.

And finally, to Mary Susan, my partner in all things, my writing partner and muse, whose decades of mahjong expertise and creative collaboration made the Mahjong Murder Mystery Society possible—this book exists because you believed in these characters and this world. Your wisdom, patience, and willingness to read draft after draft shaped every page. Thank you for the bourbon by the creek, for believing in stories, for building a life in these mountains, and for reminding me that the best mysteries are the ones we solve together. And lest I forget, thank you for rescuing our Audrey and teaching me how to enjoy happy hour with our chickens.

Visit Franklin. Meet wonderful, beautiful people. Sip a glass of wine or a local beer. Explore our bookstore and farmers market. Spoil your dog at the bakery. Watch a sunset in our mountains.

Join us here.

Because Franklin isn't just a setting—it's home. And now, it's yours too.

With gratitude,

Walt

Check Out My Other Books!

Discover More Stories

Hey there, reader! If you enjoyed this book, I wanted to let you know that I have a few more stories you might like. Here's a quick look at some of my other works:

- **Sanctuary** - From wrongful prosecution to federal conspiracy, from traditional healing to modern corruption, *Sanctuary* delivers a gripping exploration of how far people will go to protect what they love—and whether past sins can be redeemed through service to justice.

- **When the Sky Fell on the Mountains** - Inspired by the real devastation of Hurricane Helene in Western North Carolina, this novel honors the resilience of mountain communities while exploring the darkness that can flourish when power goes unchecked.

- **The Ruff Patch** - What happens when an eleven-year-old activist, a collection of traumatized rescue dogs, and a small Ohio town collide with corporate greed and municipal corruption? Democracy gets messy—and hilarious.

- **Dead Man's Tiles** – A gripping mystery that unravels secrets one tile at a time. If you're into suspense and a touch of the unexpected, Dead Man's Tiles should be on your reading list.

I hope you'll check out these books and find something that speaks to you. Thanks for reading, and happy exploring!

Join me on Facebook at "Walter A Cook Author" or online at www.Waltercookauthor.com

I'd love to hear from you with comments or reviews on GoodReads, Amazon or Facebook!

Made in the USA
Coppell, TX
01 February 2026

70253792R00218